C⊕DENAME: SCARLETT

A Novel By

E. S. Brown

CODENAME: SCARLETT Copyright ©2021
Line By Lion Publications
www.pixelandpen.studio
ISBN: 978-1-948807-15-9

Cover Art:Thomas Lamkin Jr.
Editing By:Ian Jedlica

LINE BY LION
PUBLICATIONS

For you, Mom

1

KINSHASA – DEMOCRATIC REPUBLIC OF CONGO

THE dark brown briefcase – with its worn and tattered edges and countless scratches and scrapes – slammed loudly onto the small rickety wooden table. A nearly empty water glass clattered with its last bits of ice as it teetered close to the table's edge. Thick dark hands with deep dry lines pressed on the latches of the briefcase and the locks on either side of the handle popped open.

Maris Correa didn't remove her sunglasses as she coolly watched the man sitting across from her spin the briefcase around. The Congolese man was big and muscular, filling out his gray woven Louis Vuitton suit to near bursting – it looked like it could tear apart any moment at the seams. She found it odd that he was so well-dressed, not that well-dressed men in the city were rare, but considering his cargo, she felt it could bring unwanted attention. She was in stark contrast to him, with her faux-leather short-cut black jacket hanging unzipped over her simple beige blouse that was casually untucked over her brown slacks, which in turn just touched the top of her matching Oxfords. She was much smaller in stature compared to her company, while still being fit and athletic, and her honey-colored hair was pulled back and twisted into a tight bun on the back of her head.

She looked around, taking in the details of her surroundings. The rundown bar, located on the outskirts of Kinshasa, the Democratic Republic of Congo's capitol megacity, was lit only by sunlight shining in from the open glassless windows on the front of the old wooden building. Other than the bartender, there were five other patrons in the bar – all men who appeared to be locals. They sat at their own little tables, lost in their drinks.

"Do not worry about them," the Congolese said when he noticed her gaze, his deep voice dripped with the heavy French accent common to many in the city. "The locals have no interest in our affairs. People here know to keep their noses out of where they do not belong."

He opened the briefcase, revealing its contents to Maris.

The inside of the case was divided into six equally sized red velvet lined compartments that shared a common velvet covered lid. Maris lifted the front edge of the lid and swung it upward on its long golden hinge. She lowered her sunglasses to get a better look, exposing her wistful brown eyes. Reaching into the case, she delicately grabbed one of the items inside and held it up. The sunlight stretching into the bar from the open window behind the man sitting across from her caught the small opaque stone between her thumb and first finger. A dark car, silhouetted by the incoming sunlight, pulled up in front of the bar, momentarily disrupting the light coming through the windows.

Maris took a small magnifying glass from a jacket pocket and examined the stone. She twisted and turned the nugget in the light, inspecting it carefully. She then reached into an inside pocket of her jacket and removed a small device the size of a deck of cards with a small cone shaped tip protruding from one end. A tiny needle stuck out of the apex of the cone. She pressed a button on the device and held the needle to the stone in her hand. After a few seconds the thermal absorption diamond tester let out a short beep. Satisfied with the test, Maris set the stone aside.

"You will find them all to be – what is the word? – legitimate." The man took a cigar out of the breast pocket of his suit then reached into his front right outside pocket. He brought up a gold plated lighter and took a few light puffs off the cigar as he lit it. The smoke hung in the air between them, briefly obscuring his face as it wafted over Maris. Growing up with a Cuban father, Maris was no stranger to cigar smoke.

She spent the next several minutes taking random stones from the hundreds that filled the six compartments and visually inspected and tested each one. Every test yielded the same result as the first.

The man sitting across from her began to grow antsy. He rapped his knuckles against the table top.

"*Hurry up!*" he exclaimed in French before switching back to English. "I don't have all day. My boss is waiting."

Maris completed the inspection of the stone in her hand and set it in the small pile of stones she had made on the table in front of her. She put her tools back into her pockets then scooped up the raw uncut diamonds she had tested and poured them into one of the briefcase compartments. She closed and latched the briefcase.

The Congolese man smiled. "The price is good because they are from the Central African Republic. Labor is, as you say, cheap there."

Maris sat back as she pushed her sunglasses back up fully onto her face. "While the price is appealing I'm not sure my buyers are interested in the blood associated with these." A slight accent dotted the Cuban-American's words, and her voice held a faint perpetual raspiness that sounded like she had just woken from a sound sleep.

The Congolese leaned forward, his large round eyes piercing through the near black of her sunglasses. "Now is not the time to talk about such matters. The price paid by the villagers who mined these will be nothing compared to what you will pay if you do not pay up yourself."

"The blood of innocents is not a business I typically deal in." Maris dropped a hand out of sight under the edge of the table.

"*Shut up!*" the man shouted in French as he smacked a palm on top of the briefcase. "We have a deal! You will pay me now!"

"The problem, *monsieur*, is that not only am I taking the diamonds, but I'm taking you as well."

"What do you mean?"

Maris slowly brought her hand back up, pointing her Glock 19 over the edge of the briefcase and at the man sitting across from her. The sound suppressor made the pistol appear much larger than normal, but would surely help keep the situation more inconspicuous should trouble occur.

"I'm taking you back to the United States for questioning. We know there's more to where the money from these blood diamonds is going. You're going to help us get to the bottom of it."

The Congolese took more puffs off his cigar. He leaned back and sighed heavily. "Americans. What are you? CIA? FBI? You have no authority here. And you will not be taking me anywhere. Now…" The daggers that shot from his eyes would have killed her if they were real. He leaned forward, unaffected by the gun pointing at him. "Give. Me. My. Money."

"CIA." Maris paused. "And you seem to forget –" she nodded at her firearm "– you're on the wrong side of this negotiation."

The sound of car doors slamming shut reverberated through the bar.

The man let out a deep throated chuckle. "You seem to forget…you are not in America." He looked around the bar as he continued to snicker.

Maris followed the man's eyes and glanced at the five other men in the bar. They were all looking at her, each displaying their own weapons to make it known she was surrounded. Four of them had various sized handguns, while the fifth appeared to be brandishing a pistol caliber bullpup rifle. The bartender was nowhere to be seen, having probably ducked out afraid of what was about to come.

"You were supposed to be alone," Maris said dryly. "That was the deal."

"I go nowhere in the country without security," the man countered.

Two men dressed in dark suits entered the bar and stood behind the Congolese. They had their own Glocks and pointed them at the back of the large man sitting in front of them.

"I go nowhere in the country without security," Maris echoed.

The Congolese let out a full outright laugh that lasted several seconds, waiving his cigar in the air as he bellowed. "You misunderstand your position. If I am your prize, pointing guns at me do no good. You obviously want me alive. And," he gestured with his cigar around the bar, "you are outnumbered and outgunned."

Maris exchanged looks through her sunglasses with the other two CIA officers before settling once again on the man seated across from her.

"You're the one who is misunderstanding," she said with a wan smile. "And you underestimate me."

"We shall see."

The other men in the bar stood and pointed their weapons outright at the Americans.

The Congolese man across from Maris stood and was nearly six inches taller than the CIA men standing behind him. He reached across the table and grabbed the briefcase by its handle. Looking intently into Maris' sunglasses, he said, "I shall be going now."

Maris threw her arms up just in time to block the table that the man suddenly flipped up and sent rushing at her face. The table fell to the side and Maris dove onto the floor next to it. She heard two gunshots from her fellow officers. As she looked around the table, she saw the big Congolese smack one of her fellow CIA officers in the head with the briefcase, causing him to lose balance and stumble off sideways. With his open hand he smacked the other officer on the side of the head. The blow from the bigger and stronger man knocked the officer to the floor and he dropped his Glock. The big man grabbed the gun off the floor and rushed out of the bar. Maris thought she saw bloody bullet holes in his back from the CIA gunshots, but the wounds didn't seem to have any affect or slow the man down.

Gunfire erupted from the other men in the bar. The officer who was off balance from being smacked by the briefcase appeared to dance as he was riddled with bullets. The officer who had been knocked to the floor kicked and spasmed as the machine gun toting bar patron zeroed in on him without mercy. The wooden floor in front of Maris' face exploded into splinters. She rolled away as the floorboards underneath her disintegrated. She cowered behind the flipped table that was lying on its side next to her, though she knew it would do little in the way of providing real protection.

Maris reached around to the small of her back and grabbed the fist-sized cylinder strapped there, yanked it away from its Velcro fasteners, and threw it into the middle of the bar. She shrunk behind the overturned table with her eyes squeezed shut as tight as possible behind her sunglasses and fingers pressed tight into her ears, as the flashbang grenade detonated, emitting its seven million candela of light and 170 decibel bang. Although she had the benefit of expecting the blast, and having undergone training being exposed to flashbangs, the tinnitus still hit hard. Her ears barely registered the muffled sounds of gunfire as her opponents fired their weapons blindly through the bar. She ripped off her sunglasses, popped up over the overturned table, and took five shots around the bar with her Glock. Within moments the five men fell, each struck either in the head or chest from Maris' well-aimed shots.

Maris sprang to her feet and ran towards the bar entrance, barely noticing the bullet ridden CIA officers as she stepped over them. She ran out of the bar, her ears still ringing, and looked left and right down the narrow street. The black mid-sized rental sedan driven by her now-dead companions sat in front of her, taking up nearly the entire width of the road. A local on a motorcycle was coming up from her right. She peered past the rider and saw nothing but empty road. Looking again to her left she saw a few people on the opposite side of the street, and a group of a half dozen teenagers on her side walking in her direction.

Looking past the teens she noticed more movement: a man running away in the distance. If he had been smaller, she probably wouldn't have noticed him past the movement of the approaching teenagers. He also probably would have been much quicker and thus much further along. But the hulk of his size slowed him down and made him easier to spot on the other side of the much smaller youths. She swept her hair away from her face – which had become loose and fallen during the melee in the bar – and raised her gun but couldn't get a clear shot through the group of teens, who were oblivious to the situation around them as they chattered and joked amongst themselves, and didn't notice the weapon aimed in their direction.

Lowering her gun, Maris looked at the black rental car in front of her. It was pointed in the opposite direction from her fleeing target. She immediately assessed it would take too much time to get the car turned around on the narrow street. But unexpected salvation cruised towards her in the form of the man on the motorcycle.

She put her gun into the shoulder holster under her jacket and grabbed the unfortunate man off the motorbike as he cruised by, flinging him to the ground as the cycle skid onto its side. Without offering any apologies Maris rushed to the bike. It wasn't light, but she was able to leverage her five foot eight frame and get the vehicle upright. Mounting it, she restarted the old 1970's brown and yellow painted street bike and sped down the road. The group of teens was practically upon her and she didn't have time to swerve into the street, so she drove through them, forcing them to scatter out of her way.

"*Fucking bitch!*" one of the boys shouted at her in French as she drove past.

All Maris could hear beyond the tinnitus ringing in her ears was the high-pitched whine of the motorcycle. Her Congolese target must have suspected she was in pursuit because he looked back over his shoulder. She was nearly upon him when he turned partway and fired several shots in her direction, emptying the Glock he had picked up from her fallen fellow officer before tossing it aside.

Maris swerved left then right to make for a moving target, but a lucky shot glanced off the outside of her left thigh. It was not enough to cause major damage, but it did give her a decent cut and caused her to wince. The bike wobbled as her body instinctively jerked, before spilling her onto the open road. Thankfully she hadn't been travelling too fast and was able to roll away, though she landed hard on her right shoulder, and the hit against the ground knocked much of the wind out of her. She clamored to her feet and took off running in pursuit of the Congolese man, who was still carrying the briefcase. The short ride on the bike was enough to get her much closer to the man, and with his slower gait, she now thought she had a chance of catching him, despite her limping slightly from the wound on her leg. The adrenaline pumping through her helped her ignore her injuries.

Being in a rundown suburb on the outskirts of the megacity, the street didn't have any other vehicle traffic at the time, but more people were milling about than there had been back around the bar. The man ran straight through two intersections while Maris continued her pursuit. The first intersection was clear but at the next a car coming from the cross street on the left came to a screeching halt as it nearly hit the large man. At the next block ahead of her target, just on the other side of a third intersection, Maris could see what appeared to be a busy street market. If she didn't catch him soon, keeping up through the crowd may prove problematic.

Maris pulled her gun, stopped her run, and aimed again. The man was in her sights, but she was hesitant to take the shot. If she missed, the bullet surely would strike an innocent person in the market just steps beyond. She set off running after him again, just as he entered the commotion of the market.

It was easy to keep an eye on the big Congolese despite his being amongst a mass of fellow Congolese due to his towering height over nearly everyone. But he was sure to catch on to her being close behind, and there was a good chance he knew the market streets with such familiarity he'd be able to navigate and use the disorder of the crowd to his advantage. Maris was halfway through the intersection just before the market when she noticed an open bed city police truck speeding in her direction from the cross street on her right. She couldn't hear the sirens – let alone hear much of anything at all – but could see the lights flashing on top of the cruiser.

Maris quickly holstered her weapon so as to not draw any attention to it by the police. Then she pressed into the wall of people frequenting the market. The police car stopped in the intersection behind her and two officers – in their navy-colored police blues and black berets – exited the vehicle and entered the market behind her.

The market was not one for the claustrophobic.

People were pressed against each other in front of a multitude of colorful booths and overhanging canopies that lined the street, their vendors selling a variety of food, art, and other various trinkets. Music blasted from boom boxes in some of the booths – a strange cornucopia of Western pop, songs in French, and traditional local African music. Cigarette smoke drifted through in plentiful wafts. Her tinnitus was slowly beginning to recede and Maris could faintly hear some of the noise of the bustling market.

Her target's head bobbed up and down as the man maneuvered his way through the mass of marketgoers. He paused a few times and looked back to see if he was still being followed. Maris would duck and tried to make herself incognito in the crush of the crowd. The big man never seemed to notice her and would continue to press forward. Maris in turn would scan the masses behind her, and she would occasionally see the black berets weaving in her direction, but never close enough to give her immediate cause for alarm. Maris wasn't even exactly sure if they were after her or her subject, though she suspected they had been called in response to the gunfight at the bar.

The big man, holding the briefcase tight against his body, pressed forward through three crowded blocks before taking a left down a side alleyway that was devoid of vendors and, as such, empty of people. The man ran off again as Maris burst from the crowd, and the two pursuing police officers were not far behind.

Maris pulled out her Glock as she ran and shouted in French. *"Stop!"*

She heard similar commands from the police behind her, rising above the tinnitus that was now rapidly receding, ordering her and her target to stop.

"Stop! Stop! Both of you!"

The alleyway was two blocks long, and the buildings on either side were old single story business and residence combinations, their backdoors facing the deserted lane that the cat and mouse chase traversed. Maris was rapidly catching up to the large, winded man, while she managed to put a little added distance on the police behind her.

Maris was less than twenty feet away from her target when the pursuit abruptly came to a halt as two police cars screamed into view at the far end of the alley, closing it off. Four policemen leapt from the vehicles, their guns drawn and pointed at the big man and Maris. Shouts in French from the officers echoed through the alley. The big man turned to the nearest door in the building next to him, hoping to find safe passage, but the barred metal gate covering the door was locked, extinguishing the man's hopes.

Maris stopped her pursuit, assessing the situation. Police were all around them with their guns drawn. She didn't have another flashbang, and even if she had, she would have had no real desire to use it on local authorities. Best to do as she was told so as to avoid an international incident. She and her target would be taken in by the local authorities where she would allow her people in Langley sort it all out. She was confident she would have her man in the end.

Maris set her gun on the ground slowly and raised her hands. The large Congolese dropped his gun along with the briefcase, allowing them to clatter to the street. He looked back at Maris and the two officers behind her before returning to face the four policemen in front of him. The four officers suddenly seemed panicked, and began rapidly shouting words in French that Maris understood but made no sense.

"His eyes! Look at his eyes!"

"What is he doing?"

"Stop! Whatever it is – stop!"

What she saw and heard next she almost couldn't comprehend. The officers didn't fire a single shot at the man, instead, they stood stiff and almost lifeless while on their feet. What sounded like ice expanding and cracking emitted from each of them, rather, more like from *within* them. All four officers immediately turned ashen in color – and not just their skin, but their clothes and even the guns they held. Within just a few seconds all four officers had turned into stone statues.

Maris blinked. Surely her eyes were playing tricks in the mid-day sun that hung directly overhead. The heat of the summer day, the pursuit, the adrenaline…they must all be playing into the hallucination. Gunfire erupted from behind her and she dropped to the street, unharmed. Looking up she saw the large Congolese turn to face her direction. A bullet tore through his left shoulder and he flinched, but did not stop. A second bullet hit his right thigh and he staggered, but his expression and gaze remained steady.

That was when she noticed his eyes. They were completely white. There were no irises and no pupils. But it wasn't as if his eyes had rolled into the back of his head, it was as if those traits had simply disappeared.

And then the plain white sclerae of his eyes began to glow.

Maris had the wherewithal to realize that whatever happened to the four officers could happen to her if she didn't take steps to prevent it. She buried her face into the street and covered her head with her hands. She heard the sickening cracking internal sounds from the two officers behind her. For a very brief moment it sounded as if one of the men tried to say something, but was abruptly cut short as he and his fellow officer were rendered silent, turned to stone.

Maris Correa had seen plenty of action in her eight years as a CIA officer. She had graduated from the CIA training program and had been officially inducted into the agency at the age of twenty-four, two to three years ahead of most, since she had already acquired her Bachelor's Degree at the age of twenty. Since then she had become highly regarded as one of the agency's top operatives. Her combination of intelligence, street smarts, and cunning allowed her to accomplish missions all over the world. She possessed an earthy beauty and demeanor that played well on an international level with all types, men and women alike. She had seen torture and she had been tortured. She had been in the company of some of the most dangerous people in the world and lived to tell her tales. She had been exposed to voodoo and the occult, but in the end logic and science had always prevailed.

But nothing compared to this.

Heavy footsteps sounded next to her head and she could feel the big Congolese man standing over her. But there was no way she was going to look up at the man. If he could administer whatever crazy magic he possessed while she didn't look, it would be all the better. She wasn't going to give him the satisfaction of seeing the fear in her eyes.

The buzz of a helicopter flying much too low suddenly sounded overhead, and the downdraft from its rotors whipped through her hair. This was almost immediately accompanied by the sound of more feet slamming into the alleyway. She heard voices – *American* voices through electronic transmitters – echo around the alley. The voices were direct and calm and militaristic.

"There he is."

"Target in sight."

"I see him over the woman."

"Weapons ready."

There were more but they all came too quickly for Maris to understand what was happening. The heavy feet next to her shuffled away and they were accompanied by sounds of people scurrying about. She cautiously peeked up to see what was happening.

Nearby were four rappelling ropes hanging loosely from a large black helicopter hovering high enough above the alley so as to not create a lot of downwash airflow. There were four people dressed head to toe in black tactical SWAT-type gear wearing dark visors unlike any that Maris had ever seen. The rifles that each of the tacticians held were also strange to her. Perhaps these weren't Americans after all.

Bolts of what looked like lightning erupted from the rifles, striking the Congolese man. He let out a deep, guttural inhuman scream as his body twisted and turned and danced uncontrollably in the alley. It looked like he was trying to use his strange power against his attackers, as he would try and focus his grimaced gaze one by one at each of his aggressors but to no avail. Within moments he dropped to his knees and then, his resistance finally ending, slumped forward onto the pavement. The electrical streams stopped and his body lay unmoving and smoking. Maris thought she could smell death coming off him. She struggled to keep the shaking that was building inside her from erupting.

"Target is down. We have the briefcase."

"Check the woman."

One of the mysterious assailants stood over Maris. She looked up, helpless, seeing only the barrel of one of the strange rifles pointed at her face.

"Oh, fuck..." She quietly uttered the words as darkness suddenly overcame her.

2

UNDISCLOSED LOCATION

LIGHT filtered in through dazed eyes...slowly at first, setting everything in an unfocused fog. Then, like a film strip fluttering through a projector, the images flashed faster and faster. The light suddenly flooded in full and all her senses came to life.

Maris sat up straight, taking in a deep breath almost as if she had been abruptly revived from nearly drowning – a sensation she had experienced from a near fatal episode in Italy one summer while learning to freedive. Her lungs felt heavy and her head throbbed with one of the worst headaches she had ever experienced, but at least the tinnitus was completely gone. She went to rub her forehead and realized there was a medical sensor attached to each of her temples. As her wits came about her, she noticed her beige blouse was unbuttoned and her slacks and shoes had been removed, though she still wore her undergarments. Another sensor was tucked into the upper area of her sports bra and attached to her chest. Additional sensors were stuck on the inside of each wrist. Thin wires ran from each node to nearby monitors that showed her heart rate, oxygen levels, and temperature. The sensors on her temples showed her brain activity and the wires at her ankles monitored her activity stress levels.

Despite the diagnostic equipment, she was not in a hospital room. Rather, she was on a sheetless twin-size bed in what looked like a windowless studio apartment. The bed was pressed up against a wall on its left. In front of Maris was a doorway that looked like it might lead to a bathroom. To her right was a small sitting area with two chairs, a small coffee table, a credenza, and a closet with a folding door that was open. Across from that area was the kitchen. The entrance to the apartment was also to her right, between the sitting area and the kitchen.

With her senses kicking in, a stab of pain shot through her left thigh. An ace bandage was wrapped around her leg where the bullet had grazed her. She gently rubbed the cloth bandage around the bullet wound to try to temper the sensation. Knowing how the wound had bled, she guessed it had been stitched up underneath the bandage.

She took another look around the apartment. Despite the absence of any visible cameras, she was certain she was being watched. Not caring, Maris began tearing off all the medical sensors. When she reached up with her right arm to remove the sensor from her right temple, the bruises on her right shoulder reminded her of the hard fall from the bike. She winced but was able to follow through with the task of taking off the sensors. The monitoring equipment began to emit a steady unending beep. She reached over and turned the machines off.

Maris sat on the bed unmoving, certain someone was going to come bursting into the room. But no one came. She stood up, slightly unsteady – more from feeling somewhat disoriented than from her injuries (she had experienced worse) – and headed to the kitchen on wobbly legs. She reached the sink and practically fell forward into it as she turned on the water and began drinking straight from the faucet. Her lips were so parched and her throat was so dry that it felt like the more she drank the thirstier she got. When she finally felt quenched, she splashed cool water to refresh her face and help clear the lingering fog in her head. The headache thankfully began to subside. There were no towels to be found so she dried her hands on her open blouse.

She made her way around the kitchen checking all the cupboards and drawers. All empty. Her thigh still hurting, she limped along the few steps needed to move into the living area, buttoning her blouse along the way. Her torn pants were nowhere to be seen, but she noticed a pair of black slacks hanging alongside her faux-leather jacket in the open closet. She put on the slacks and her jacket, then her Oxfords which were sitting on the floor next to the small coffee table. Moving on, she searched the credenza and closet for her shoulder holster and Glock but they were nowhere to be found. She was not surprised.

The sound of locks being undone on the other side of the apartment door caught Maris' attention. With nowhere to go and no weapons to defend herself, she stood apprehensively to see who was going to enter. The door opened and in walked a man in a dark suit, looking similar to her fellow CIA officers. He was taller than her and barrel-chested, with short salt-and-pepper hair and lines in his face each of which looked like they had their own story to tell. She guessed him to be at least a decade older than her. He was flanked by two men in black uniforms that looked like stripped down riot gear, each of whom carried a modified M4 carbine rifle and looked ready to go into action at a moment's notice. The man in the suit extended a hand.

"I'm Special Agent Brian Masse. Miss Correa?"

Maris took the hand hesitantly, but made sure to shake it firmly. She knew when odds were against her, and she was careful to make sure her movements were deliberate and nonthreatening.

"What is this place?" she asked. Her voice was raw but she still came off as unnerved despite her apprehension. "Where am I?"

"I am not at liberty to provide you any answers, but I'm here to take you to those who are."

One of the armed guards stepped back out of the apartment. Masse gestured to the open door. Maris walked out of the room, followed by the special agent and the other two guards. They were in a long hall with plain gray wall panels and a tiled floor. The hall was lined with doors that presumably led to other apartments. The special agent moved in front of Maris.

"Follow us. And, please, no questions."

Masse led the way, with one of the guards right behind. Maris followed and the remaining guard fell into place behind her. The four of them traversed the hall, around two corners, then to a foyer with four elevators. The agent placed his hand on a palm reader on the control panel between the two elevators on their left and one set of elevator doors opened. The group entered the empty elevator. Masse pressed a few of the buttons on the elevator control panel in what appeared to be a distinct order. Maris thought it looked more like a code being entered as opposed to floors being selected. The elevator began to move downward. No one had uttered a word since they left the apartment, and Maris couldn't handle the quiet any longer.

"I'm guessing I'm not a prisoner since you haven't physically restrained me."

Maris waited and wondered if the agent was going to react. Agent Masse, who was standing in front of her next to one of the guards and facing the elevator doors with his back to her, didn't respond.

"We seem to be going down a lot of floors. I doubt we're in an expensive high rise. I'm guessing we're heading underground." Maris allowed a bit of cynicism to creep into her voice.

Yet still no response from anyone in the elevator.

"I assume we're not in the Democratic Republic of Congo any longer." She paused. "And it seems that –"

Masse finally looked at her over his shoulder. "Miss Correa, if you please, I told you no questions."

Maris was feeling particularly snarky. "I didn't realize I was asking any questions. How do you expect –"

The agent held up a hand with a single finger pointed in the air. "I'd rather you not say anything at all. Your concerns will be addressed. We're almost there."

The elevator came to a stop and the doors opened. The four of them stepped onto a dais of what appeared to be a large monitoring station. The walls were made up of dozens of oversized flatscreen video monitors, each showing different parts of the world – city streets, countrysides and landmarks, deserted areas, popular tourist spots – with geographical coordinates, time of day, and current temperatures displayed across the bottom. The images never remained stagnant, changing every so often to display a different place. There was a single large monitor on the wall directly facing the dais with Kinshasa street scenes playing on it.

The dais had a waist-high rail around its edge that was broken in four areas where sets of stairs led down to the workroom floor. The floor of the room itself had three rows of workstations, all manned with agents and officers performing inputs, occasionally referencing the overhead monitors, and talking to persons unknown through wireless headsets. Some spoke in languages other than English. The workers were a mixture of men and women, older and younger, and came from different ethnic backgrounds.

The dais itself had four individual workstations with chairs. While all four were operating in some capacity – as evidenced by each station's triple monitors that were on and displaying various diagnostic readings Maris couldn't make out from where she stood – only one of the chairs was taken, its occupant huddled over the terminal with his back turned. Everyone wore a variation of a dark suit, though some had shed their jackets in favor of more comfort. Despite all the energy and commotion, the sound from all the activity in the room was muted to a dull roar.

A woman standing in the middle of the dais turned to face Maris as she stepped out of the elevator. Nearly eye-to-eye with Maris, the woman was thin and wore a tight fitting dark gray double breasted military suit jacket with matching slacks. She was in her early fifties, with shoulder length brushed on blonde streaked hair that was braided and tucked under itself and pinned near the base of her neck. She held a stoic posture demonstrating the authority she commanded. There was a kindness in her eyes that Maris suspected disguised her true self.

She shook Maris' hand. "I'm Associate Deputy Director Carrie Berglund. Pleased to meet you, Miss Correa."

Maris was cautious. "How do you know who I am?" She looked around some more, taking in all the activity in the vastness of the room. "What is this place?"

"You're in the command control center of the National Paranormal Defense Intelligence Agency, also known as the NPDIA."

Maris still didn't really know what to make of where she was. "Did you say *paranormal*?" She tried to make out the significance of the scenes on the monitors. Nothing of particular importance seemed to be showing on any of them – no civil unrest, war zones, political gatherings or protestors. The scenes just seemed to be terribly…normal. Or about as far from paranormal you could get, Maris mused.

"Paranormal, mythological, you name it, we chase it down and get rid of it." The straightforwardness in the woman's voice astonished Maris.

"You're not serious, right? I mean, there's no way you're for real. I've seen and heard a lot of shit but ghosts and goblins are another matter."

A resigned look came across the Associate Deputy Director's face. "You don't believe it. Then how do you explain what you witnessed in Kinshasa?"

Maris shook her head. "I had been shot and was concussed from a flashbang and a fall. I was seeing things."

"But you weren't, I assure you." The Associate Deputy Director looked at the guards who accompanied the agent. "You can leave us. I don't think Miss Correa is going to be any problem. Thank you for your assistance, Agent Masse."

Masse and the guards left the dais via a set of stairs that led them to the command control center floor and out a side door.

"How is it I've never heard of this place?" Maris asked. "I've been with the CIA for eight years. I hold degrees in political science and international affairs. Why haven't I ever heard of you?"

"We don't exactly run in the public eye. For that matter, we don't even run in the eyes of the United States government. You can say we're more of a…shadow agency."

"A cryptocracy?" Maris laughed. "I'm sorry. I don't believe in Skull and Bones Illuminati bullshit."

The Associate Deputy Director stiffened as if she seemed to take some mild offense. "We are not Illuminati bullshit, you're right about that. But we don't fall under the thumb of any Federal branch or agency, either."

Maris shot her a sideways look. "Care to give me a crash course in exactly what you are, then?"

"Gladly." The Associate Deputy Director marched around the dais as she spoke, occasionally gesturing out towards the monitors or the activity on the room floor. "Government isn't for the sake of the public. It's for the sake of the media, the public eye. But government is limited as it needs to work within the confines of the law, or at least what the public perceives the law to be. The NPDIA is part of a dark government operating beyond those confines, and outside the scope of the media and public eye. This is where the power truly lies, and where the real games are played."

"So your organization exists outside of the law."

"Consider us the government behind the government. When a mission needs to be accomplished that falls under the specialties of our organization, whether on a domestic or international level, we take on the operation. We get in, get the job done, and get out."

"Does the President know about this?" The suspicion in Maris' voice was beginning to subside, though she still had a hefty dose of skepticism in her.

The Associate Deputy Director shook her head. "The White House is only privy to statements and information that *we* release, nothing else. But it's better that way. We operate covertly so as to not create an international incident, and the White House is absolved of any responsibilities from our operations. We have our own budgets, our own accountability."

"And Washington doesn't miss any money directed your way?"

"Miss Correa, do you have an actual concept of how much money is exchanging hands in the world on a regular basis?"

Maris raised an eyebrow.

"Over six trillion dollars exchanges hands daily. *Daily*, Miss Correa. Most people cannot fathom the enormity of that kind of cash. And frankly, neither can the banks. Even better, congressional bookkeepers don't miss, let alone account for, what we funnel off. We have people on the inside that ensure the books don't implicate our agency in any way."

"So this entire agency –" Maris gestured around the room "– is built with funds covertly stolen from the Federal government."

The Associate Deputy Director grew more serious. "The U.S. national published debt is over 24 trillion dollars. But the truth? It's closer to 200 trillion. And growing. Our agency is a blip in that. And believe me when I tell you that without us, without this agency, the U.S. government – I take that back – most of the world's governments would not exist."

"So you're not only making obtuse statements but now you're talking in riddles." Maris looked back at the elevator doors. "Is there a ride up out of here? I'm about done listening to this."

"You're quite the spitfire, Miss Correa," the Associate Deputy Director said. "But I've heard that. In fact, I've heard quite a lot about you."

Maris was growing exasperated. "What do you mean?" She walked up and stood nearly face-to-face with the agency associate. "You never answered my question from earlier. How do you know me?"

The Associate Deputy Director stood firm. "Your father has told me quite a bit about you."

"My father?" Maris was astonished. "That's impossible. My father left me when I was four. I barely remember him. There's no way he knows anything about me."

"On the contrary, he may know you better than you know yourself."

Maris was starting to see red. She was usually one to stay collected when growing agitated, but all this was getting to be too much. And for this woman in front of her to spit lies about a family she knew nothing about was really grinding on her. She took a step closer to the other woman and pointed a finger in her face.

"You better explain yourself," Maris demanded through gritted teeth. "Right now."

"It's because I've been watching you a long time," a new voice entering the conversation said. A man's voice.

Maris looked past the woman to the source of the new voice – the lone man sitting at the workstation on the dais. He turned his chair around and looked at her. His skin was a natural sun-dipped bronze, and he had a full head of thick gray hair and a moustache to match. He wore large rectangular rimmed glasses and his skin was so rough it was hard to distinguish between scars and wrinkles. His ruggedness didn't take away from the authoritative yet soothing tone of his voice. When he stood, he was two inches taller than Maris, and his brown eyes were recognizable to her from years of looking into a mirror.

"Hello, my little Mariposa."

Maris' lips quivered.

"*Dad?*"

3

UNDISCLOSED LOCATION

MARIPOSA.

 The name shot through her nerves and her heart. She had not been called that in twenty-eight years…since the last day she saw her father. The memory was fresh and came back to her in a shockwave that almost knocked her off balance.

■■■ ● ● ● ■■■ .

IT was a warm afternoon in the summer of 1992, just weeks before the signing of the Cuban Democracy Act by then President George H.W. Bush. Tensions between the United States and Cuba were high following the recent collapse of the Soviet Union, but none of this was important to a four-year old Maris Correa. She remembers her father, Carlos Correa, talking quite a bit about it, though, at least when he was home, since he was Cuban. He wasn't home a lot as his work kept him away much of the time. The love he had for his family and friends in his homeland always had him concerned, while feeling powerless to do anything about it.

 She was playing in the small front yard of their home in New Smyrna Beach, Florida, just a few miles from the hospital where she was born. Their house was small and the yard was almost non-existent, but none of that ever mattered to Maris, despite her continuing to live in the same home until she left for college after graduating early from high school at the age of seventeen.

 Robin Olson Correa, Maris' mother, was also born and raised in New Smyrna Beach. Robin was twenty-two and had just finished her Bachelor's Degree in Business Administration and Finance at the University of Central Florida when she had Maris. That was also where she met Carlos (he was a professor at the university). The relationship was hardly scandalous as they had no classes together. Carlos was a highly respected professor of Biomedical Sciences at the university, and he was always being called away to give lectures and speeches and teach not only in other colleges around the U.S., but around the world.

"Maris!" her mother called out. "Your father is going to be home any minute!"

Maris was always ecstatic when her father came home. She was friends with a girl her age in the neighborhood whose father was in the U.S. Army, and the friend always talked about how her own father would be away on duty fighting battles. Maris knew her dad was a college professor and not an Army soldier, but she would pretend that he was off saving the world anyways just like her friend always claimed her father to be doing. So when Carlos was home from his assignments, to Maris, it was like he was coming home from war. She rushed up to her mother who stood in the front doorway.

"Get inside and wash up, sweetie. We'll be having dinner as soon as daddy gets home."

Carlos had been away for two weeks – by far not the longest duration of time he had been gone – but it still felt like an eternity to the four-year old. She ran to the bathroom and washed her hands and face (well, she splashed water on her face and called it "washed") and did her best to brush her hair. She always wanted to look pretty for her daddy. She was an only child, and the attention he doted on her always made her feel special.

"Maris! Your daddy's home!"

Maris dropped the brush onto the bathroom counter and ran into the living room just as Carlos walked in. He always looked handsome in his dark suits. She ran to him with her arms outstretched.

"Daddy! Daddy!"

Carlos scooped her up and held her high as he turned a circle with her head just inches from the ceiling.

"My little Mariposa!" he called out. "Oh how I missed you!"

His little Mariposa. This was a nickname Carlos had adopted for Maris early on. The white mariposa was the national flower of Cuba. In addition to *being considered the most beautiful flower in Cuba, there were other reasons why Carlos chose this name for her. For one, despite being half Cuban, Maris' was more fair-skinned than most Cubans due to Robin's European heritage. Also, the flower had been chosen as the national flower to symbolize purity, rebellion, and independence. Maris was a good child, but at the same time could be fiercely independent and even at the age of four wasn't shy about saying what she meant (and meaning everything she said), and being blunt about the things she wanted. Carlos believed his daughter personified all the qualities of the flower very well.*

Maris threw her arms around Carlos' neck and kissed him square on the lips. She giggled like she always did as his thick dark moustache tickled her face. He smelled of cologne, a slight sweat, and sweet Cuban cigars. He spent the next several minutes laughing with her, teasing her ("You've grown so much in the last two weeks! You can almost touch the ceiling!"), and simply loving her. He eventually shifted his attention to Robin, and the two of them talked about "adult stuff" through dinner. The small round dinner table barely sat the three of them, but Maris gleamed all the while they ate, just happy her daddy was home.

After dinner, Carlos and Robin had Maris spend a few minutes in her bedroom with the door closed. She kept herself busy playing on her bed with her small stuffed animals – a dog named "Rosie" and a hippopotamus named, appropriately, "Hippo" – while her parents talked about more adult stuff. She could hear their voices, though she couldn't pick up specifically what they were saying. But there was something about the tone that was different. Her mommy's voice was a bit louder and higher pitched than usual, at times bordering on shouting. At one point she thought maybe her mom sounded sad, like she was crying.

It was at this moment she set Rosie and Hippo down and went to her bedroom door. She slowly turned the doorknob and gently opened the door a couple inches, peering outside. Her bedroom was off a very short hallway that branched off the living room and she could not see her parents. She heard them make their way back and forth between the living room and kitchen – which she also could not see – and the voices were clearer.

"I don't believe this," her mommy said. "You just got home and you

drop this on me? On us? What are you going to tell Maris?" She was definitely crying.

"I'm sorry, Robin." There was almost a pleading in her daddy's voice. "I don't know what else to say."

"Well, I'm not going to be the one to tell her. You tell her."

Maris heard footsteps coming towards the hallway. She closed the bedroom door as quickly and quietly as possible and jumped back onto her bed. She had just scooped up Rosie when the door opened. Her daddy stood in the doorway, smiling at her.

"Hey, sweetie, can you come to the living room to talk to mommy and daddy?"

Maris nodded and went to her daddy, still clutching Rosie. He kept his arm around her as the two made their way to the living room. She sat on the loveseat alone (the living room was not big enough for a full-sized couch), and her mommy sat on the edge of a big plush chair that was adjacent to her. Her mommy's hair was a mess from having run her fingers through it, and she held her head in her hands. Maris pulled Rosie tight against her chest.

What happened next was a blur. She didn't remember all that her daddy said, but it boiled down to the biggest shock her four-year old self had ever experienced:

"I gotta leave, sweetie. And I don't think I'm ever coming home."

The explanations – the whys – weren't completely clear to the little girl. It had something to do with work. But it was always about work. Maris didn't understand what made this different, though it obviously was. Her mommy was crushed. And the more her daddy tried to explain it, the more heartbroken Maris became. There were some big words thrown around – words like "responsibility," "allocation," and "designation," that only added to the little girl's confusion – that did nothing to make her feel better.

Then came the inevitable question: When?

"I have to leave tonight."

Maris was absolutely crushed. Did her daddy really mean this? He's leaving and never coming home? He's choosing work over being with her, not for just a couple weeks, but forever?

There were more tears from her mommy – and now from her as well – as her daddy packed a suitcase. Not a lot of words were spoken. Time crawled as she held Rosie tight and watched her daddy pack away his clothes and a few belongings. The last thing he placed into the suitcase before closing it was a framed picture of the three of them from a few months earlier. A sunny happy picture of them at the beach. The suitcase closed, and along with it, any chance of happiness with her father ever again.

A taxi came shortly after and there was a knock on the door. The taxi driver, a gruff middle-aged man, took the suitcase out and asked her daddy to be quick.

Her daddy went to hug her mommy one last time, but she pushed him away.

He turned his attention to Maris and she couldn't hug him fast enough, or hard enough, or long enough. He lifted her up and held her tight – tighter than she had ever held Rosie or Hippo – and kissed her. This time, though, the moustache didn't tickle. She was too sad to feel tickled. He set her down and even though she had never seen her dad cry, she swore there was a tear in his eye this one time.

He told her he was sorry and he loved her. And it was then he said something that she never forgot. He put the palm of his hand on her chest over her heart.

"I will always be right here, watching over you."

She felt frantic and grabbed him around his legs.

"Daddy, don't go!" she cried. But she knew it would do no good.

He held on for a few moments but then finally pulled away. He walked out of the house, and got to the end of the short sidewalk to the street where the taxi waited when he turned around and looked at her one last time.

"I love you. I always will, my little Mariposa."

And then he was gone.

■■■ • • • ■■■

CARLOS looked almost the same as the last time she saw him, except his dark hair and moustache were graying to show his sixty-three years. He wasn't as thin as he used to be, but he wasn't large or unfit, either. He looked to be healthy and spry, like he could take the best of anyone in a fight – no different than when she was a child pretending he was off saving the world.

A wealth of emotions flowed through her: hate, love, confusion, anger. Carlos had been in the back of her mind for the last twenty-eight years. There were many moments where she wondered what she would do if she ever came face-to-face with him again. But now that he was here, in the flesh, she didn't know if she wanted to punch him or hug him. No training, no situation in the CIA or in life had prepared her for this. Carlos took a few cautious steps towards her.

"I'm sure you must have a thousand questions," he said, pensively.

Maris felt tears swelling behind her eyes, but she couldn't comprehend the emotions behind them. She fought to prevent them from streaming down her face.

"I don't even know what to say." There was an edge to her voice that warned Carlos to tread lightly.

"I'll start," Carlos said. "This is where I've been all this time, with this agency. There was never anyone else – no one ever replaced you or your mother. The last three decades of my life have been dedicated to the service of the NPDIA."

Maris stared into her father's eyes, while her hands balled into tight fists. "Why? What have you been doing?"

Carlos took another step closer to Maris. She didn't back away.

"There's so much to tell, my Mariposa."

"Don't call me that." Her eyes narrowed. "Your *Mariposa* died when you left twenty-eight years ago."

Carlos' voice lowered. "I can understand that. You must believe me, what I did was for the greater good. I made the choice to not only protect you, but protect nearly every human."

Maris finally broke eye contact, her eyes rolling in disbelief. "You sound crazy. This whole thing is crazy."

"I can't deny that sentiment." There was a soothing matter-of-factness in her father's voice. "But you've already witnessed it. You saw it for yourself in Kinshasa." Carlos gestured at the large central display monitor on the wall facing them. It still flashed scenes of the Congolese capital.

"Like I said, I was seeing things. That wasn't real." Maris looked at the Associate Deputy Director, who silently watched the exchange between her and her father with interest. She shifted her gaze back on her father.

"I used to not believe, just like you're struggling now," Carlos said, trying to sound reassuring. "When I was teaching at the University of Central Florida, my work caught the attention of people in the government, the dark government, specifically within this agency. They had contacts at the university who befriended me and gained my trust."

"Why you? In the nineties Cubans were generally looked down upon. I mean, I know the university respected you, but the U.S. government? That had to be a hard sell."

"Luckily they were the ones doing the selling. The creators of this agency didn't hold to typical American ideals. They still don't. Even in the fifties when the agency was created, they recognized the need to have a diverse workforce to best do their work worldwide."

"This agency has been around for seventy years?"

Carlos nodded. He stood just arms distance from her now. "This agency was created to quell a surge in malevolent international organizations looking to take over the world. But these aren't your typical corrupt establishments. These organizations aren't run by humans; rather, they're run by what you would call paranormal or mythical beings."

Carlos took a moment to let that sink in. Maris' mind raced. The logical thinker within her fought against what she just heard. But then there were the images of what she witnessed in Africa...the men turning to stone...

She shut her eyes tight and shook her head. After a couple moments she looked at her father again. "What did I see in Africa? What was that?"

"That was a Gorgon."

Maris wanted to find the whole conversation laughable, but couldn't. Things were getting real, fast.

"I don't know much about Greek mythology," she said, "but aren't Gorgons women with a head of snakes? Like Medusa?"

Carlos cocked his head sideways. "Originally, that was what was believed, but mythology and reality don't line up. A whole society of Gorgons was discovered based in the Mediterranean back in the fifties. Hence the creation of this agency and a few others like it around the world. The Gorgons operated in secret until a plot was discovered where they sought world domination. They hold a cult-like belief that they are superior over humans and that they alone should hold all financial and military power in the world. Eventually, an underground war between them and the global agencies created to fight them developed. Every time we thought we had won, it wouldn't take long before they would resurface. Then finally, ten years ago, we did away with them for good. Or so we thought."

"So you really were off saving the world," Maris muttered to herself.

"What do you mean?"

"I would pretend you were like my childhood friend Rachel's father who was in the Army. She would tell me these fantastic stories about how he was saving Americans from Communism. I told myself you were doing heroic things, too."

"I'd like to think I was," Carlos said with humility. "It was a coincidence that it wasn't until after I joined, or should I say was recruited, that the enemy was finally believed to be disposed of. I was a field agent fighting on the front lines back then and I saw some truly crazy stuff. What you saw in Africa was nothing by comparison."

Maris remained quiet. Her brain felt like it was on overload. She wasn't even sure what questions to ask, how to inquire about something that up until a few minutes ago was just made up of wild fantastical stories.

Carlos extended a hand and touched Maris' upper left arm. She didn't pull away, but didn't step any closer to him, either.

"Here," he said. "Let me show you something. Maybe it'll help you make better sense of all this."

Carlos made sure the Associate Deputy Director was overseeing the command center before he led Maris off the dais and onto the workroom floor. This path took them opposite of the direction Agent Masse had taken, and led to a separate door that slid open when they approached. Carlos led Maris through several interconnected corridors that were mostly white and barren of any texture, color, or décor. Walking through the compound, Maris had trouble memorizing their way as all the doors and passageways looked the same. All the entries they passed had windowless sliding doors, their only distinguishing characteristic being a seemingly random number designation. She thought it would be very easy to get lost amongst all the sameness surrounding them.

The pain in Maris' thigh and shoulder started to subside, and before long she was barely limping. Carlos held most of the conversation as he recounted to Maris about his time as a field agent for the NPDIA before becoming chief-of-staff; how he finally stopped seeing field action when he became associate deputy director at the age of fifty-three; and subsequently deputy director at the age of fifty-six, a position he, at this point, held for seven years.

"So you run this place then?" Maris asked.

"Everyone has a boss, but yes, I'm the head of this agency."

"Something you haven't told me is where this agency is? Where are we? Are we in Langley?"

Carlos shook his head as his pace came to a stop outside one of the nondescript doors.

"Far from, actually. We're in the middle of the western Nevada desert."

Nevada? Maris thought. That was one of the last places she expected to hear.

"Every bit of this facility is underground," Carlos elaborated, "including the apartment you woke up in."

"An underground agency literally operating underground. Fitting." Maris pondered for a moment. "Speaking of waking up, what did you hit me with? It wasn't a weapon I had ever seen before. And it left me with one helluva headache."

Carlos let out a wry smile. "There's a lot you're going to be exposed to that you've never seen before."

Her father punched a three-digit code into a keypad on the wall and the door slid open. He motioned for her to go through first, and he followed. The door closed behind them.

They were in a shallow atrium that was solely illuminated from light shining through the large wide bank of windows that made up the upper half of the wall in front of them. And her father was right: she was being exposed to something she definitely had not seen before.

The room beyond the windows was wide and rectangular and bright, despite its dark gray walls. There were three scientists in the room, each wearing a long white overcoat and gloves. What was most curious was what they were inspecting: stone statues. And not just any statues, but the police officers that she watched turn to stone in Africa. The frozen expressions on their faces ranged from surprise to horror to pain. For a moment the thought of the terror they each must have felt before meeting their fate flashed through her mind. She was able to quickly shake that sentiment away, though, as she always had when dealing with emotions associated with the job.

One of the scientists was running a handheld scanning device over one of the statues. Maris couldn't hear anything through the glass separating them, but the device flashed various colored lights depending on where along the statue the scanner was held. The scanner flashed all green when it was held up to the statue's left shoulder. One of the other scientists came over holding what looked like a hacksaw but with its blade missing. A press of a button on its handle and the area on the hacksaw that normally held a blade erupted into a strand of popping, crackling, white-blue energy.

The first scientist maintained scanning the statue while the second put the "energy blade" to the statue's shoulder. The third scientist held on to the frozen police officer's arm while the electrical blade sliced through the shoulder. It didn't take long for the arm to be separated from the body. The scientist held up the severed arm while the first scanned it with the device in his hand. As they did this, Maris was able to see the exposed insides of the arm from where it had been cut off. She had expected the insides to be all stone, but they weren't. Rather, except for maybe a quarter-inch stone crust, the inside of the arm was blood and muscle and bone, as if nothing had happened to it.

"The inside is almost perfectly preserved," Maris muttered, unable to keep from stating the obvious. "What are they going to do with that?"

"Keep watching," Carlos said.

The scientist with the saw set it down on a nearby stainless steel table. He then picked up a chrome-plated device about the size and shape of half a basketball. Wires ran from the rounded end of the odd machine and up into the ceiling. The scientist placed the flat end of the object against the bloody open shoulder stump. Maris watched in awe as the entire statue began to shake.

Then something most unexpected happened.

The stony police uniform began to crack and flake away, revealing the skin of the man underneath. In areas where there had been open skin, however, like the officer's face and remaining hand, raw human parts were exposed as a rocky outer skin layer fell off in pieces. Maris shuddered as the police officer – his face a bloody pulp of its normal self – let out a horrific scream before collapsing to the floor in a bleeding, fleshy mass. The scientist with the scanner looked through the window at Carlos, who just shook his head. Carlos pressed a small button on one of the various control panels built into the wall in front of him

"Try another," Carlos said into an unseen mic.

The semi-spherical device was removed from the dead man's shoulder and placed onto the steel table. The three scientists moved to the next statue, rolling the table with them.

Maris shook her head. "Was that man…still alive underneath the stone?"

Her father shot her a knowing look. She immediately understood.

"Are they all like this? Essentially frozen in a suspended animation?"

"Not all," Carlos replied. "Most are stone through and through. However, once in a while we find a specimen like this and so we conduct our test."

"Test? You're not just…killing them?"

"Not at all. On the contrary, we're trying to bring them back to life, to save them. Unfortunately, with the technology we currently use, the machine invented to remove the stone exterior can only be used when attached to a large and flat unaffected part of the body. We've tried various methods but the shoulder and back areas always seems to work the best. There are thousands of tiny probes that come out of the flat side of the machine and inject themselves into the victim. As you can see, though, there's a side effect of the device also removing all of the skin. In every test we've done the victim has gone into shock and immediately fell over dead."

"I don't know what's worse," said Maris, sickened by it all, "being turned into stone or having your body essentially torn apart."

"These are casualties of war. That's all. We'll eventually figure out how to save them. At least we hope." Carlos gestured to Maris to move down to the far left end of the atrium. "Come this way. There's something else."

At the far end was another sliding door. This one opened on its own as they approached. Beyond was another viewing area with a similar layout of windows overlooking a large room. This room was stark white and brightly lit. Evenly spaced in the room, facing the bay of windows, were three upright gurneys. Each vertical table had a person secured to it with half a dozen thick metal bands that limited nearly all their movement. Strapped to the tables on the left and right were women that Maris did not know. The table in the middle, however, had a very familiar figure.

The large Congolese man from Kinshasa.

Like the women on either side of him, a bulky headset covered the man's ears and, unsurprisingly, his eyes. The big man, along with each of the women, struggled and shifted within the confines of the metal straps that kept them bound to their tables. All three of them let out horrifying hissing and screaming sounds that pierced through the thick viewing glass. Spit flew from their mouths as they bellowed and howled.

"He's alive," Maris said, curious. "Your people didn't kill him."

"No. We need them alive to extract information, and to try and learn more about them. These breeds seem different than the ones from twenty-five to thirty years ago. They're stronger and tend to be a bit more feral."

Maris couldn't tell if the three prisoners were in pain or not. "What are you doing to them?"

"A bit of a sensory torture at the moment. It's part of the interrogation process. The earpieces are emitting constantly changing high pitched tones and the eye coverings are shooting a rapid strobe light brighter than even what your flashbang emitted. They are helpless to not see that light. And the sounds are excruciating."

"That's not much of an interrogation," said Maris.

"Inhuman prisoners require inhuman methods. The torture is intermittent. After several minutes of this our people will come to them in the chamber, turn off the devices, and ask questions to see if they can extract any new information."

Maris watched the spectacle for several long moments. She was processing everything she had just been exposed to – the statues in the other room and now the creatures, the *Gorgons*, in front of her. During that time, Carlos said nothing while he stole occasional glances of his daughter.

"So why are you showing me all this?" Maris said, finally. "I'm a CIA agent. Why would you break agency silence and expose all of this to me?"

Carlos pressed a button on a console in front of him that cancelled the animalistic audio from the other room. The silence was almost as discomforting to Maris as she shifted uneasily, waiting for her father to respond. She wasn't sure she was prepared to hear his answer.

"I want to offer you a job."

4

NEVADA

CARLOS had moved their conversation from the observation rooms to his office on a higher floor of the NPDIA underground headquarters. He sat behind his high-backed leather chair in his deputy director's office. The wall behind him was filled with shelves of books, most for research, but some were casual reading for when he wanted a break from the stresses of the job. He was a voracious reader, and had read most of the over 400 books behind him more than once. There were some breaks among the rows of books, spaces filled with a mixture of artwork, small plants, and various awards he had acquired over the course of his professional career.

Reds and browns filled the room, from his large mahogany desk and the teak wood flooring to the burgundy drapes. Ironically, the drapes framed a large video monitor that showed ever-changing images of outdoor nature scenes and not an actual window, due to the office being underground. There was a large rug on the floor decorated with the National Paranormal Defense Intelligence Agency crest. Maris sat across from him in one of the two wide leather chairs available to guests.

"The position is not to be taken lightly. This is a lifetime commitment. There would be no going back to your life as you currently know it."

Maris looked confounded. "You mean I'd have to disappear. Like you."

Carlos let out a heavy sigh. He knew this wasn't going to be easy for her. "What we do here is of the utmost importance. We're not fighting al Qaeda or Isis, or Communist regimes, or terrorists like you know them. This is so much larger than all of those. And it's an opportunity not extended to many. You wouldn't believe the extreme amount of vetting one goes through to be offered a position here, and that's just for the data analysts like the ones you saw in the command control center, where you first saw me."

Maris looked deflated. "I went from working a case for the CIA in Africa to here in Nevada literally overnight." She looked around, the confusion and disorientation of it all swirling around her head. "At least I think it was overnight. I honestly don't even know how long I was out or how long I've been here."

Carlos settled back in his chair. "It's been two days since Africa."

Maris didn't look reassured. "So why me? Why now?"

"Like I said in the command control center, I've been watching you for a long time. Our systems are ghosted in with CIA servers. No one in Intelligence knows any better. But we see everything everyone there sees. We're also tied in with servers at major colleges and universities – that's how I was recruited back home in Florida."

The memory of the last time he saw his daughter flashed through his mind…

He told her he was sorry and he loved her. And then he put the palm of his hand over her heart…

Maris suddenly spoke up. The same memory had triggered within her as well. "Before you left mom and me, you told me, 'I will always be right here, watching over you.' You literally meant that."

Carlos nodded. "Yes. Yes, I did."

An edge crept into his daughter's voice. "So you knew I was in Africa, in Kinshasa."

Carlos stiffened. "We knew there was a potential situation in Kinshasa involving Gorgons. Then when you were assigned to the case, I personally got involved. I decided that was the best time to extract you."

"Extract me? So none of it was coincidence." She looked gutted.

"No, Maris." It felt strange calling her by her real name, but at the same time, this was beyond family. This was business. "There was no coincidence. *You* were the mission."

Maris' eyes widened. "*I* was the mission? You were after me the whole time?"

"We had our local contact with eyes on the Gorgon, but we also had eyes on you. We were watching you from the moment your plane landed in Kinshasa. My people tracked you to the bar and were surveilling you via a drone through the streets, until we finally dropped on you in that alley. You were never in any real danger."

Maris shook her head. "You let two CIA officers die in that bar."

"We could not jeopardize the primary mission, which was securing you. The Gorgon was a secondary target. We needed to get you both. The Intelligence officers' deaths could not be helped. I'm sorry." He knew his tone was disingenuous. But again, this was business.

Maris stood and paced around behind the chairs. "I don't know. This is all so much, so sudden."

"Unfortunately, time is not on our side. I have to send an agent to the Mediterranean this week. We've been tracking sales of blood diamonds from the Central African Republic and the Democratic Republic of Congo to what we believe are Gorgon representatives in Italy." He reached into one of his desk drawers and pulled out a thick file folder. "There's an underground buyers' summit happening there next Thursday under the guise of a legitimate conference. High security, invitation only. We obtained an invite and our agent needs to be there. We believe that will be the key to infiltrating their network and connecting with the Gorgon leadership. This is an opportunity we can't dismiss."

He paused, ready to let loose the ultimate reason for bringing her here.

"I'd like for you to be that agent."

Maris stopped pacing and stood in front of his desk. He dropped the file folder in front of her. The words "Eyes Only" were printed and repeated on the tape that sealed the folder.

"This folder contains everything to prepare you for the summit. It's being held in a building owned and operated by the tech giant

Hexatetron Corporation. Its owner, Alexei Volkov, will personally be there."

"I've heard of him. Russian billionaire socialite. Big money, fast cars, constantly surrounded by beautiful people. Not only superrich but very intelligent. And not exactly shy about flaunting his wealth."

"And he's a Gorgon."

Maris was taken aback. "What? How can someone so high profile be one of them?"

"We've been onto him for some time. Despite his popular persona, he is difficult to get alone to apprehend or kill. I thought I killed him about a decade ago, but he resurfaced not very long after that. The Gorgon society is super-secret. As you now know, this fight has waged on for decades and the public is none the wiser. There is an immense amount of damage and public relations control whenever an incident involving the Gorgons occurs. It's not easy fighting a war and keeping it under wraps, but we've managed. And, thankfully, the Gorgons themselves don't appear to be ready to make their existence known to the public *en masse*, either. At least not yet."

Maris placed a hand on the folder but did not pick it up.

"So obviously Hexatetron has a hand in all this," Carlos continued, "but we don't really know to what extent. We believe this summit may be the start of something big, piggybacking on the black diamond trade. This is what we need our agent to determine."

Carlos looked at the folder. Maris' hand had not moved off of it.

"There's a plane ticket and a credential for admission to the summit," Carlos continued. "Everything you need and need to know is in there."

His daughter still hesitated.

"Maris, I'm sorry about everything that's happened." His tone changed from stoic and professional to more warm and personal. "If there was a way it could have been done differently, believe me, I would have done it. But this agency needs the best people to battle this threat. That's why I was tapped, because they knew from my work at the university what I had to offer. There was no one better in the world in the field of biological sciences and international affairs. The agency knew that when they approached me. And you know what? I knew it, too. The agency didn't just need someone *like* me, they needed *me*." He paused as he looked intently into his daughter's eyes. "And now we need the best agent available to take part in these missions. We need *you*."

Maris looked up and away. Carlos couldn't tell if she was becoming more contemplative.

"Look," he said, getting more direct again. "It's not like you have a lot to lose. You don't have many personal ties. You don't have a circle of friends that you spend time with. You spend most of your free time either working out, reading, or journaling. You have no social media presence to speak of." He paused. "And there's no boyfriend or girlfriend taking up your time."

That last statement especially caught Maris' attention. She shot him a sharp look. "You really do know a lot about me."

Carlos knew he didn't have to acknowledge that statement.

Maris picked up the folder. She walked around the room again, tapping the unopened file against the palm of her hand. She stopped, her back to him as she faced the door.

Then Carlos heard her break the seal on the file.

Maris turned around with a look in her eyes that were a combination of pain and excitement.

"I'm in," she said.

Carlos smiled at her, a genuine warm smile he had not been able to show her in nearly thirty years.

"Thank you, Maris. We are thrilled to have you. You won't regret it."

"I better not," she said sternly.

Carlos stood and walked over to his daughter.

"Keep in mind, in the agency, I'm your boss, not your father. There needs to be a clear separation between who we are and what we do. It's the job first and always."

"There won't be any problems with that, Director." Her tone was professional, if not a bit cold.

"You'll need to have all your affairs in order within the next seventy-two hours. That includes any final good-byes. The CIA will be alerted that you are being transferred under secrecy. They will not know where you've transferred to and will not be privy to any of this. We'll send people to collect your personal affairs from your apartment in Langley. I can't stress enough that you cannot tell anyone who you are now working for, let alone anything about us. You need to just…disappear."

Maris sighed heavily. "There's one person I do need to say good-bye to personally."

Carlos' eyes dropped slightly. He knew who she was talking about.

"I want transport to Florida. I can be there and back within the seventy-two hours."

Carlos nodded. "I can have one of our jets take you there."

"Thank you," Maris said with a solemn tone in her voice.

"There's one more thing."

"I don't know, Director. What else could there be?"

"All NPDIA agents are given codenames for field use. Standard procedure."

"That's fine. I'm used to having aliases in the field. So what's my codename?"

"Scarlett."

Maris snickered. "Scarlett? Not sure I fit the ideal image of a 'Scarlett.' I mean, the last thing you'd think of is a Cuban-American woman with light brown hair."

"Even better. They'll never see you coming."

Carlos extended his hand to his daughter and was grateful when she shook it. Satisfied, he returned to his desk. He continued talking as he flipped up the hinged top of an ornate rectangular box and took out one of his signature Montecristo No. 2 cigars. He used a cigar cutter from the box to snip the pointed head of the Montecristo and then lit it.

"I'll have someone show you back to the apartment you woke up in. Those will be your accommodations, at least for now. Be sure to read through the dossier and contact me and me alone with any questions. Remember, just seventy-two hours to be ready to go. That'll include a further briefing with our people before you fly out."

"Got it." Maris opened the door to leave the office.

"Thank you, Agent Scarlett."

"Thank *you*, Deputy Director."

Maris left the office, closing the door behind her.

Carlos slumped into the chair behind his desk. He opened a drawer and pulled out an eight by ten framed photo and set it onto an open space on his desk. It was a picture of his wife, Maris, and him from when they visited a Florida beach on a sunny day back when Maris was just four-years old.

It was the picture he had taken with him the last night he saw his family twenty-eight years earlier.

5

FLORIDA AIRSPACE

THE four hour and fifteen minute direct flight to Orlando from Nevada was on a small and otherwise ordinary private jet owned and operated by the NPDIA. Maris was the only passenger on board, save for a single flight attendant, so she had plenty of undistracted time to review the dossier and to contemplate the choice she made.

She opened the "Eyes Only" folder and sorted through its contents. She set aside the plane tickets and inspected the laminated credential. Printed on one side was the word "Summit" along with the applicable date, designed to ensure secrecy for the event; while the other side was emblazoned with the Hexatetron logo: a hexagon with five circles interlaced inside. The credential was clearly designed to make its sponsorship of the event obvious. She found the contrast between the two sides intriguing.

Maris studied the mission itinerary. Everything looked to be meticulously timed, leaving little room for error. Flights were scheduled to take her from McCarran International Airport in Las Vegas, Nevada, to the city of Palermo on the island of Sicily, Italy. There she would be met by a local contact who would drive her to the coastal city of Trapani on the northwestern part of the island.

In Trapani, she was to meet with Alexei Volkov, the Russian owner of Hexatetron, who had a reputation of personally greeting his guests at his many well-known lavish affairs. Apparently, even though this event was shrouded in some secrecy, he didn't intend to forego that practice. She read on and realized she would not be the only one meeting in Trapani. Representatives of some of the top diamond producing countries in the world would also be meeting with Volkov at that time. They were to all be transported by boat to the exotic isle of Pantelleria and finally to their hotel destination. In all it was nearly two full days of travel.

In addition to the itinerary, there was an article on Hexatetron Corporation, its origins and interests, including an exposition of its owner, Alexei Volkov, along with overviews of his past run-ins with the NPDIA. Further documents delivered a crash course on the diamond trade – including a detail of where the bulk of raw diamonds were mined, both legally and illegally – along with an education on the four C's of diamonds: carat, cut, color, and clarity. Maris had a decent knowledge of the industry, including black market trades, from her work with the CIA, but these papers provided a deeper understanding of the dangerous underworld…including suspected links between the underground markets and the Gorgons. She spent a predominance of the flight not only studying the information provided, but completing additional research on her smartphone. She wanted to know everything there was to know about diamonds, Hexatetron, its owner, and Gorgons, and used her time wisely to consume all she could from whatever she could find online.

After reviewing the mission and related materials, her thoughts settled on her choice to leave the CIA. Her father was right about everything he said: she was at the top of her game as a CIA officer; she had few personal ties; and it would be easy for her to disappear. The more she thought about it, though, the more the prospect of disappearing saddened her. She had never taken a step back and looked at her life in the way her father's words forced her to. She remembered hearing once that "your legacy lasts as long as someone remembers you." While she hoped that the good she did for the CIA – the bad people she helped take down and the successful campaigns she had been part of – extended that legacy, ultimately she realized none of it was about her, but rather, about the impact she made on the well-being of the American people. She took solace in knowing her new position at the NPDIA was an even greater responsibility as it affected the people of the entire world for possibly generations to come.

It was near the end of her flight when her thoughts drifted to the people and faces in the CIA she would miss seeing on a regular basis. There were several, though when it came down to it, they were all acquaintances as opposed to actual friends. The job itself didn't lend to making friends since her work was typically classified and she spent a lot of time traveling. There was one person who had made an indelible impression upon her, though, and she knew she had to reach out to that person one last time before she was cut off from the CIA for good.

Maris took out her phone and made a video call. She held her breath while she waited for the person to answer. There was so much she wanted to say…yet at the same time there was so much she couldn't say. The video screen came to life and Maris felt both relieved and anxious.

The African-American woman who answered looked like she could have passed for half of her fifty years. Her medium-brown eyes lit up when she saw who was on the other end of the call.

"Mari!" No one else called her Mari other than this woman. It was a nickname that had come about when they were on a mission together during one of Maris' first years as a field operative. There was no one else in the world Maris would have dared let call her Mari (she never liked the name as she always felt it didn't represent *her*) – at the same time, there was no one else whom Maris could have loved more for calling her that. It was a special name that brought many fond memories when it came to the woman who uttered it.

"Hey, Toni!"

Toni Trent-Eberhardt was like Maris' mentor, magistrate, and a second mother all in one. She guided Maris first hand during nearly all her eight years with the CIA, keeping her in check and routinely judging her field performance. Toni knew the ropes well, as she had been with the agency for nearly thirty years. She was currently the CIA's Chief Information Officer, and she wore a suit and tie, like most of her male CIA headquarters counterparts, despite being a woman. Her flowing brown and blonde hair draped casually onto her shoulders.

"What the hell is going on with you?" Toni asked, concern taking over her excitement. "I was told you were leaving the agency with no explanation. And rumor has it your apartment has been cleaned out." – *Wow, that was fast,* Maris thought – "Is everything alright, Mari?"

"I'm fine, Toni," Maris tried to come across as happy and excited, though inside she felt uneasy with having to lie to the person she was closest to in the CIA. "But, yeah, I'm leaving."

"Girl, why? You know you can tell me what's going on."

Maris felt defeated. "I really can't, Toni, I'm so sorry." She let out a heavy sigh. "I can't believe I'm not there to say good-bye to you in person."

"What?" Toni was shocked. "Don't tell me this is a 'good-bye' call?"

Maris' shoulders dropped. "I wish it was a 'see ya later' call, but I can't say it is."

Toni pulled what Maris always referred to as her "mom voice" as she said, "You better promise me that everything is okay with you. And you know I can tell when you're lying."

Maris forced a smile. "Everything is okay. You have to trust me on that."

Toni looked skeptical but resigned. "Okay."

"Toni…" For a moment words escaped her. "I just had to say good-bye to you. You know I'm not very close to anyone in the agency. You're about as close to family besides my mom that I've ever had."

"I know, dear. I've thought of you as my daughter more than a few times. I wish I could protect you wherever you're going."

"I'll be fine, Toni." *I hope.* "How about you?" She attempted to change the subject. "I know you had an oncology appointment the other day. How'd that go?"

"You remembered about that? I'm doing great! The doctor pointed out I've been cancer free now for over a year!"

"That's amazing, Toni! You're one of the strongest women I've ever known. Not everyone fights off breast cancer like you did. I'm so happy for you!"

"Thank you, Mari! HER2-positive is no joke. But not even cancer can keep a good agent down! You were there for me through it all. You were as supportive as my actual family."

"What do you mean? I *am* your family!"

"Yes, Mari, you're right!"

"And you know that hair is on point!"

Toni fanned herself to mock cool down how hot she was. They both laughed.

The moment of levity was fleeting. The reality of what Maris was going through never escaped her. She gave Toni a look of contentment.

"I know what you're about to say, Mari. You don't need to."

A tone sounded throughout the cabin and the voice of the plane's captain crackled through the overhead speakers. Maris looked away from her phone as she listened to his announcement.

"We're making our final approach to Orlando, Miss Correa."

Maris looked again at the only friend in the CIA she ever knew.

"I wish things were different," Maris said, solemnly. "But please realize that everything I was in the CIA was because of you."

"That means a lot to me, Mari. I've always been so very proud of your accomplishments. I know we never saw each other outside of work. You never did take me up on my offers of after work drinks. Eight years of putting me off and here we are at the final moments without drinks in our hands."

Maris let out a quiet laugh. "I'm sorry. You know me. I can be social for the job, but never off the job. And times like these are exactly why. I hate saying good-bye."

"It's okay. I totally understand. You're one of the best, Mari. I'm sure wherever you're going is for the best."

"I'm sure it is." *It better be!* "But, hey, I gotta go. We're about to land."

"Okay, Mari. You take care of yourself. And don't ever look back."

"Thank you again for everything, Toni. You're the best."

Toni gave a big *Muah!* into the phone. "Good bye, Mari."

"Good bye, Toni."

Maris ended the call. She looked out the window of the plane, steeling herself against any tears that wanted to fall.

6

NEW SMYRNA BEACH – FLORIDA

THE house was just like she remembered it, though she had not visited since leaving for the CIA eight years earlier. It was a small and unexceptional single story abode with a slanted roof, peeling white paint on the outside, and a yellow door. It had a tiny green lawn along with a single-car carport. She was able to visit at least a few times a year while she was in college, but then work tore her away. She hated the reality of work taking precedent over family. And now work was going to drastically change her life forever.

Maris Correa smiled at the memories that were conjured up as she walked from her rental car parked curbside to the front door. With a deep breath she knocked on the door, then took a step back while she waited for someone to answer.

"Coming!" came a woman's voice from inside.

When the door opened, for Maris, it was the reunion of a lifetime. It was certainly better than the one she had with her father. She hugged her mother tight, almost smothering the slightly smaller woman. So many emotions flowed through her. She was excited to be seeing her mother for the first time in so many years, yet she was sad because of the circumstances surrounding the reunion. Her mother was the first to pull away after several long, warm moments.

Robin chuckled a bit while wiping a wistful tear from her eye. "Wow, honey, I've missed you, too. I wasn't sure I was going to ever see you again."

Tears welled in Maris' eyes – from both missing her mother and from knowing the bad news she would be delivering soon. "I'm sorry, Mom, I'm sorry." She still held on to her mother's hands.

"You look a bit of a mess, sweetheart," Robin said. "Are you okay?"

Maris nodded. "Can we go inside? Sit down and talk?"

"Of course!" Robin said as she ushered her daughter in and closed the door behind them.

The inside of the house was still the same: the same loveseat she sat on when her dad said he was leaving. The same plush chair that her mother loved and spent so much time on reading, sewing, watching television – all, of course, in-between preparing meals, doing laundry, vacuuming, and cleaning other parts of the house…the list could go on. There was one item that was different, or rather, more out of place really.

"Rosie!" Maris rushed to the loveseat and scooped up the stuffed dog from where it was propped up in a corner. The toy had roughed up and ragged fur exactly like she remembered it. Maris held the animal high in the air, pretending it was a real puppy. Her injuries were better and she was able to hold the animal up without any overwhelming pain in her shoulder.

"Have you had her out all this time I've been gone?"

Robin looked at Maris like she was looking at the happy-go-lucky four-year old from so long ago, before the sad days had taken over. "I have! She makes her way around the house, kind of like an elf-on-a-shelf. Sometimes she'd sit in the window, wondering when you'd be coming home. I can't believe today is that day! I wish you would've called ahead. I would've tidied up the place and made something for you to eat."

"That's okay. I wouldn't want you to go through any trouble." Maris moved to stand in front of the loveseat. "Can we talk?"

Her mother's expression dropped when she saw the seriousness that fell across Maris' face. Maris wondered if her mother knew what was about to come, having gone through it once before.

Robin sat on the plush chair while Maris got comfortable on one side of the loveseat. She held Rosie on her lap, looking down at the pup for what seemed like a lifetime. Finally, she looked up, the strength within her renewed and ready.

"I'm going away, Mom. And...I'm never coming back."

Her mother sighed as an expression of resignation and understanding came over her. Sadness never quite surfaced, and Maris was actually thankful of that.

"I know," Robin said, softly. "I knew the moment I saw you in the doorway."

Now tears fell openly down Maris' face. She never cried for anyone or anything...except her parents. Her upbringing hadn't been particularly hard, but she was a hard, strong person inside. It was a quality that served her well in the CIA. But when it came to her parents, the emotions ran deep and could cut her like nothing else. She knew this very well about herself, which made the need to disappear from her mother's life forever more important than ever. Disappearing wasn't so much to protect herself, but to protect her loved ones.

"I don't know what to say, Mom. My work, it's –"

Robin shook her head and held up a hand to stop Maris midsentence. "I understand. I do, I really do. When you signed up for the CIA –"

Now it was Maris' turn to interrupt. "It's not the CIA. I'm leaving the CIA, but that's all I can say."

Robin looked worried. "Are you in some sort of trouble? Are you going into hiding?"

"No, it's not anything like that. It's work, it's just not the CIA any longer, and..." Her words drifted off for a moment. The image of her father filled her head. She wanted so badly to tell her mom she had seen him and would be working with him. She wanted to let her mom know he was safe. After all these years...he was safe.

But she couldn't.

"...that's all I can say."

Robin nodded. "Then don't say anything else." The words were spoken with a reassurance that Maris needed. "You know I support you. And love you. I knew when you joined the CIA that you were special and were going to be the best at what you do. I'm sure that's what's led to you doing whatever you're doing now. Whatever happens, I'm so very proud of you."

Maris wiped the tears away with her fingers and dried them as she squeezed Rosie. She smiled while her mother beamed at her with pride. They stood simultaneously, their emotions in sync, and hugged again.

A knock at the door interrupted them.

"Are you expecting company?" asked Maris.

"Not that I know of," Robin replied as she went to the door.

Maris, always on alert, drew back. She quickly set Rosie on the loveseat and put her fingers on the handle of the gun holstered under her jacket in the small of her back. She still carried a Glock 19, though that was originally CIA issue. She had grown fond of the weapon and made sure to have one issued by the NPDIA before leaving Nevada.

Robin opened the door and Maris' knees felt week when she saw who was standing there.

"Rachel!" Maris exclaimed.

Maris and Rachel squealed in delight as they rushed to each other, hugged, screamed some more, and hugged again.

"I can't believe it's you!" Maris exclaimed.

"Ohmigod! Ohmigod!" Rachel repeated over and over. "How have you been? I haven't seen you since you left for college!"

"I know!" They couldn't stop hugging and screeching. "I came home when I could but you were never around!"

"Our timing was horrible," said Rachel. "Work, husband, kids...everything gets in the way!"

"Come in! Sit down! Let's get caught up!"

Robin closed the door and headed to the kitchen as the two women giggled like schoolgirls together. "You two be comfortable. Can I get either of you anything? Coffee? Water? Anything at all?"

"Just water for me, Mom."

"No thank you, Robin," said Rachel.

"Robin?" Maris copied. "First name basis with my mom, huh?"

"We actually see each other quite a bit. We worked together at Resource Consulting Group for a number of years."

"We stayed in touch after I retired from there two years ago," Robin said from the kitchen. "But she stops by and checks on me every once in a while. It was just coincidence that she stopped by just now."

"We've actually become good friends," Rachel added.

Robin brought Maris her water, and over the next hour, the three of them reflected on the girls growing up together in the neighborhood and where their lives took them after. Rachel Roland was Maris' best friend all the way up through high school. The girls lost touch once Maris left for college and never reconnected despite the popularity of social media since Maris never maintained any sort of online presence. Maris shared what she could about her adventures in the CIA, which wasn't much. While Maris had attended college at Georgetown University in Washington, D.C. then moved to Langley, Rachel stayed local and earned a degree in finance. She ended up with a career as a financial advisor with Resource Consulting Group in Orlando, a high-end firm managing nearly $2 billion dollars in assets annually. Rachel's clients held a minimum of a million dollars, which made Rachel a wealthy woman. She had gotten married and had two young children with her husband. Maris loved hearing all about what her best childhood friend had done with her life.

Maris turned her attention to her mother. "You must be doing pretty well, having worked at that firm. Why do you still live here?" She gestured around the room. "I would've figured you'd find someplace better after all these years."

"Simple." Robin smiled. "This is where my only child grew up. There are so many beautiful memories here. And it's a nice place. I know the area. I never saw any point in starting over."

Maris was about to respond when an alarm chimed on her phone. She reached into her jacket pocket and turned it off. She knew what it meant. So did her mother.

The good-byes weren't easy. Maris explained to Rachel, the best she could, how her new job was taking her away from everyone she knew for good. But she was so thankful for having had this last opportunity to spend time with the two people she loved most when she was growing up.

There were more tears, this time from all three of them. Then Maris left the house and went to her rental car out front. She gave one last look at her mother, who was holding onto Rosie, and best friend, and the three of them waved to each other. Then she got in the car and drove away.

She never looked back.

7

NEVADA

UPON her return to NPDIA headquarters, Maris was ordered to meet Associate Deputy Director Carrie Berglund in an area called Level 7, another of the many hidden facilities tucked far below the desert sands of Nevada. This section was separate from the command control center where she had first met the Associate Deputy Director and was reunited with her father. Maris stepped out of an elevator and into a small closed off vestibule. The only way to go was through a set of sliding glass doors. She was immediately impressed by the large room on the other side.

With its walls and floor of exposed rock, the expansive room did nothing to hide the fact that they were underground. There were lockers and cabinets lining one wall, along with two sets of solid doors that led to who knows where. Rolling tables with various items on them – some with video monitoring equipment, others with various weapons including rifles and guns – stood in the middle of the room. Two large freestanding desks each with three computer screens and stacks of books and paperwork were pushed together facing each other on one side, one of which was occupied by an Asian woman wearing glasses and a white lab coat who was engrossed in her work. One of the walls had a large empty area in front of it. Another wall had targets lined up in front – a combination of thick bullseyes, and rubber and plastic mannequins. The Associate Deputy Director greeted Maris from near the center of the room with an outstretched hand. Maris walked up to her and shook it without hesitation.

"It's good to see you, Agent Scarlett."

Maris paused, knowing it was going to take a little bit to get used to that name. "You, too, Ms. Berglund."

"Please, call me Carrie."

Maris provided her a nod in acknowledgement. While the woman still stood straight and proper, Maris was glad that the edge that was in her voice when they first met was gone. She followed Carrie as she headed back towards the desks.

"This is our covert weapons facility. It's not just state-of-the-art, you could say it's more 'ahead-of-the-art.' Here we build and test weapons for use in the war against the mythics."

"*Mythics?*"

"That's the name given to the class of inhumans we are fighting against." Carrie stopped at the desks and turned to look Maris squarely in the eyes. "They aren't all Gorgons, Agent Scarlett. There's a whole world out there that very few of us know a lot about. For now, though," she gestured to the woman seated at the nearest desk, "I'd like to introduce you to Dr. Eun-ha Choi."

The Asian woman didn't acknowledge the introduction, instead remaining focused on the computer monitors in front of her. She paused briefly to adjust her glasses and tuck a piece of her short black hair behind an ear, then continued typing feverishly on the keyboard in front of her. The tapping on the keys was the only sound in the room for over a minute as Maris and Carrie waited for the other woman to pull herself away from her work. At one point she stopped, took a deep sigh and sat back in her chair. Carrie started to say something when the clacking of the keystrokes started again. Carrie looked at Maris apologetically then looked back down at the doctor.

"Dr. Choi…"

The woman put a finger up, silencing her, then completed whatever processing or inputs that had consumed her. Finally finished, the petite woman smiled as she stood and shook Maris' hand.

"The one and only Maris Correa. I've heard a lot about you."

Maris gave Carrie a cursory look. "It seems a lot of people around here have."

The computer at the doctor's desk beeped causing her to break away and do a few more quick inputs. She turned her attention back to Maris, who had a questioning expression on her face.

"I'll save you the trouble of the third degree questions. Yes, I'm young. Twenty-four years old just last week. I'm Korean and came to the United States with my parents when I was two years old. Like my mother, my father was full Korean but an American citizen and in the U.S. Army. My parents met when my father was stationed in Korea. I've always been on an accelerated track of learning by my own choice. I graduated from high school and had an Associate's Degree by the age of twelve. I attended MIT and graduated with a PhD in Materials Science and Engineering. I was just eighteen years old. I've been with the NPDIA ever since. And you can call me either Dr. Choi or by my codename Galaxy, whichever you prefer."

After a brief moment, Maris said, "That sounded rather rehearsed." She did little to hide her candidness.

"Saves a lot of trouble. A lot of people don't believe a little young Asian woman like me should be doing the job I do. My speech takes away most of the questions." She tilted her head as she looked at Maris. "Anything else you'd like to know?"

"I think you've about covered it," Maris answered perfunctorily.

"So 'Scarlett,' huh? You don't really look like a Scarlett."

"Have you known many Scarletts?"

"Honestly can't say I have. You're just not what comes to mind."

"Codenames in many ways are arbitrary," Carrie interjected. "Not necessarily meant to evoke a particular image or response. It's been like that ever since the agency's inception in '53."

Maris gave Carrie a quizzical look. "Do you have a codename?"

"My codename is Ursa. I almost feel like it's been retired, though, since I haven't seen action in the field ever since I got the Associate Deputy Director position."

Maris looked at the doctor. "So you get out in the field? Since you have a codename?"

The doctor shook her head. "I don't do field work. But I am an agent by designation so I was given a codename. I don't care for the 'agent' moniker, though. My name Eun-ha literally translates to 'galaxy,' so the agency thought it was fitting."

"I see."

"Anything else, Agent Scarlett?" Galaxy asked.

"What's your role when it comes to me?"

"My role when it comes to you is to give you the tools you need to be successful on your mission. In short, my job is to help keep you alive."

"Got it." Maris couldn't tell if the small woman was more arrogant or proud.

"So if there's nothing else, Agent Scarlett?"

Maris briskly shook her head.

"Good. Follow me. I'll show you a bit of what we do around here."

"Lead the way, Galaxy."

As Galaxy escorted Maris and Carrie to a nearby table, she said, "It's not always this quiet in here. We aren't used to having visitors so late. During the day there can be up to a dozen scientists and technical experts working on various projects. I practically live here, though. My work is my life, my life is my work."

The doctor picked up what looked like a small, blue jewelry box and held it up for Maris to see.

"We've got our standard issue items," Galaxy said. "But these are non-standard issue."

She opened the box. Inside was a pair of small, gold hoop earrings with gold half-inch long Roman-style columns dangling from them. She showed the open box to Maris.

"Earrings, Galaxy? But we've only just met."

Galaxy didn't play into the joke. "Business, Scarlett. Do you like them?"

"They're fine." Maris' general disinterest was evident.

Galaxy looked at the jewelry almost like a parent looks proudly upon their child. Even under the artificial light the earrings had a striking sheen. She pointed at the left piece.

"This hoop is a micro transmitter speaker. The post that goes through your ear sends an audio signal directly through your earlobe to where your eardrum picks up on the sound. Takes away from the worry of having a potentially visible earpiece lodged into your ear, and it's much more secure as the clasp is reinforced. This other hoop is a finely-tuned microphone."

"Really?" asked Maris. "Seems to me the wearer's voice would get lost in all the noise around it."

Galaxy let out a sigh, coming off as somewhat annoyed. "The micro-receptor is finely tuned and primarily designed to pick up on the wearer's voice clearly above all other sounds. However, it can be tuned remotely either by a control on your agency smartphone or remotely by us here. Zeroing in on the proper voice is not a problem."

While Maris was impressed with the explanations, she still came off as skeptical. "So why the gold columns, then? If all the tech is in the hoops, what are the columns for?"

The look the young doctor gave Maris was serious, even for her. "Who said all the tech was in the hoops?" She held the box up closer to Maris' face. "These columns are tracking devices that easily detach from their hoops. Once pulled away, the column immediately sends a signal to an agency approved device, such as your phone, for example. Your phone already has a securely encoded app designed to pick up on the signal. The device also sends a signal to a satellite array that pings us back here at headquarters."

"We didn't have tech this cool when I was in the field," said Carrie.

"You didn't have me designing the tech then, Agent Ursa," Galaxy retorted as she gave the Associate Deputy Director a pointed look. She closed the jewelry box and handed it to Maris.

"So these are for you. Your ears *are* pierced I hope, Agent Scarlett?"

Maris took the box. "Double-pierced, actually."

"So savage." Galaxy looked like she was about to roll her eyes but stopped short.

"A question. The microphone in the right hoop, who am I talking to?"

"The person on the other end will be me. Half a world away."

"Or me," Carrie added. "Or whoever else here who wants to listen in."

"Including my father?" Maris asked her.

"Including your father," Carrie told her crisply.

Maris looked back at Galaxy who just shrugged and headed towards another table. "This way. There's something else."

The three women stopped at a table near where the mannequin targets were lined against a wall. Galaxy reached down to a lower shelf then pulled up a shiny black box. She set the box on the table and turned it to face Maris before opening the lid.

"I know about your fondness for the Glock 19," said Galaxy. "So I created a modified NPDIA issue version. Just for you."

The box had three items in separate compartments molded specifically to fit them – there was the Glock itself, a loaded clip, and a shoulder holster. Maris picked up the weapon. Instead of the standard flat black color, the gun was a shiny black-chrome. And while its profile was nearly identical to the basic Glock 19, this modified version had a second, much thinner barrel beneath the primary barrel. She held the weapon flat on her palm, testing its weight. It didn't feel too different from the weapon she knew and loved. Galaxy dove into her explanations.

"You obviously notice the secondary barrel. This is for use against mythics. It is a much smaller version of the ECE that you witnessed in Africa."

"ECE?" Maris asked, puzzled.

"Electrical charge eruptors," Carrie explained. She paused before continuing. "Mythics are much stronger and more resilient to typical weaponry. They aren't indestructible, but it takes a helluva lot of steel to take one of them down. We've used ECE's for about a decade with varying degrees of success. But we believe R and D has finally perfected the ECE weaponry. You're going to need this out in the field."

Galaxy took the weapon out of Maris' hand while she continued providing details.

"The weapon has the standard three safeties but there's a fourth here," Galaxy said while she pointed to a tiny button on the gun's handle near the trigger, "in the way of a switch located just behind the secondary barrel. You'll want to take note that this ECE safety is tied in with the trigger safety."

She handed the gun back to Maris.

"With the ECE engaged, the regular trigger gets locked and no bullets will fire. The switch is easily reached by your right thumb – you *are* right handed, aren't you?"

"Yes, I am." Maris was growing weary of Galaxy's sarcasm.

"Good. You can easily reach the safety with your thumb without losing your grip. You can switch back and forth between the two weapons with just the touch of a tiny button."

Maris quickly adjusted her stance, dropping a bit lower as she spun and pointed the weapon at one of the mannequins and fired. A sizzling red electric stream shot out of the secondary barrel attached to the gun and struck her target, blowing the dummy apart into thousands of pieces. Maris was dumbfounded – she had never seen a weapon like this before.

"Instant kill, I suppose," said Maris as she exchanged brief looks with the Associate Deputy Director and the doctor.

"Depends on the target," said Galaxy. "But usually, yes."

"The rifles I saw your people use in Africa shot blue. What's the difference?"

"The ECE rifles in Africa had the capability to switch between blue stun beams and red destruction beams. When we want the target alive we use the blue stun beams."

"Can this one switch between types of beams?" Maris asked as she took the loaded bullet clip out of the case on the table and locked it into the gun. She aimed the weapon at another mannequin against the far wall.

"Your weapon does not switch," said Galaxy.

"Fine by me," said Maris before sending off a dozen standard rounds interspersed with nearly as many electric beams as she quickly switched the ECE safety off and on. Many of the mannequins disintegrated and blew away between the barrage of bullets and red streams.

"Feels good," said Maris.

"Not so much for them," said Carrie, surveying what was left of the destroyed mannequins.

"You have just as many energy shots as you do bullets – fifteen rounds," informed Galaxy. "Use them wisely."

"Is there any way to recharge the ECE?"

"Not in the field. The entire component needs to be replaced, so your Glock would need to be serviced here. It's something we're working on improving."

"Got it," said Maris as she took the holster out of the case.

Galaxy did not seem amused by their verbal banter.

"Good luck, Agent Scarlett." The little Korean woman headed back to her desk, alone. "I have a feeling you're gonna need it."

"Are you sure you're ready for this?" Carrie asked.

Maris looked at Carrie while holding up her new pistol. "As ready as I'll ever be."

8

MOSCOW

FOOTSTEPS echoed through the corridor as the man walked briskly through the arched hallway. The long, straight passage, no wider than a supermarket aisle, was made up of large, taupe bricks. Lighting was crude, coming only from occasional lightbulbs dangling loose from the ceiling by thin electrical wires. Dust and dirt kicked up into small puffs as the man moved down the hall. At the end of the hall was a thick steel door with an electronic keypad in the wall next to it.

Always the consummate dresser, Alexei Volkov buttoned the single button of his near-black, white-polka dotted Dolce & Gabbana suit as he stood in front of the door. The tall, thin man straightened himself and adjusted the sleeves of his suit jacket. He took a handkerchief from an inside jacket pocket and brushed the dust off the cuffs of his pants and his black Versace shoes. He replaced the handkerchief with a palm-sized mirror from another pocket that he used to inspect his closely shorn black hair, thin moustache, and shadow of a beard. His skin was smooth and perfect save for a long horizontal scar on his left cheek. The face looked to be just thirty years old, but the eyes reflected over a century of struggle and pain. He slipped the small mirror back into his pants pocket and adjusted his silver bow tie. He then entered a 5-digit code into the keypad on the wall.

Alexei stood straight with his hands clasped in front of him for nearly three minutes before a loud clanking of heavy steel latches sliding in the door sounded through the hall. He sighed heavily as he watched the door finally move sideways, disappearing into the brick wall. He moved through the opening and the thick door slid back into place behind him, the heavy lock clanging into place.

Unlike the hallway leading up to it, the room was dust free, well maintained, and immaculate. A hearty fire in a large stone fireplace crackled and flickered as it provided the only light to what looked like a large, windowless study. Rows upon rows of books lined the walls to the left and to the right of the fireplace. The room was heavy in deep red tones, from the Brazilian cherry wood floor, walls, and tapestries, to the evenly spaced area rugs and furniture. There was a long wooden table, a desk, and a high-backed velvet chair spaced out on the floor whose shadows added to the gloomy and sullen atmosphere. Much of the room was cast in darkness, out of reach of the glow of the fireplace, creating mysterious areas that could conjure nightmares to those with fear of the unknown.

Alexei spoke in Russian, seemingly to no one, *"You know I don't like waiting."*

"You know I don't like being rushed," came the woman's reply, also in Russian, from one of the dark corners.

Alexei bit his tongue. He could only push his luck so far and didn't want to say anything to anger his host. *"What is it you wanted to see me about?"*

The woman's voice was sedate and fluid. *"Word has it an American has secured an invitation to the summit."*

Alexei's eyes thinned. *"An American?"*

"Yessss." The word was drawn out and dripping with malevolence. *"I'm sure the failure of the Congolese contact did nothing but further alert the Americans to our ongoing existence."*

"He was a damn fool. I told you we should not have sent him. I had much better operatives who would have ensured that the mission didn't get all fucked up."

There were several long moments of silence before the woman responded.

"I disagree. I don't believe it would have mattered who we sent," she said, finally.

"That's quite an assumption. What makes you believe that?"

"Because the person he was set to meet was a woman. An American woman." The words trailed off as if there was more.

"And?"

"Not just any woman. But the daughter of someone you know very well."

Alexei shifted uneasily. He wasn't sure he liked where this was going. *"Who?"*

"An American named Carlossss Correa. But you know him better by his codename... 'Aresss'."

Alexei gritted his teeth as he reached up and touched the scar on his cheek. *"Ares? Are you sure?"*

"My intelligence on this is positive. We must be cautious."

Alexei stammered as he paced in a small circle. He whispered curses to himself in Russian before once again addressing the unseen woman in the dark.

"I will never forgive him for what he took from me."

"And you never should." The woman's voice remained calm. *"But maybe you can finally get some revenge."*

Alexei stopped pacing, his interest piqued. *Revenge.* The thought had been on his mind for ten years. For a full decade Alexei's wrath had been building. Now maybe, just maybe, he would have an outlet to release his fury.

"What do you mean?" Alexei asked, his voice low and growling.

"The American that is attending the summit is Carlos' daughter, Marisss Correa. But she goes by the codename Ssscarlett."

Alexei felt like he had gone blind. The flames blazing in the fireplace paled in comparison to the white rage in his eyes. All the hate within him swelled, fueled by the memories of what Carlos had done, momentarily cancelling out the world around him.

"His daughter is attending the conference," Alexei said quietly to himself as he looked down at the floor, his mind racing.

"Yes...yes!" A hint of compulsion was in the woman's voice. *"Do you see what can happen? What opportunities may arise? She will be half a*

world away from her home. But do not underestimate her or those she works for. Act smart and with your head, not with your emotions."

"She'll be completely within my grasp." Alexei said more to himself than his company. "She will be completely within my control."

The phone in Alexei's pocket buzzed. He took it out and looked at the image that was just sent to him. The woman in the photo with the shoulder length honey hair had eyes that were indisputably the same as those of his mortal enemy. He looked up towards the shadows where the woman waited.

"Revenge shall be yours, yes," the woman said, her tone mindful. *"But you must be careful. She is well-trained and extremely dangerous. Remember what her father did to you."* She paused. *"And to Dimitri! Remember what happened to him! But do not allow that to cloud your judgement and make rash decisions. You have a penchant for allowing your emotions to take control. That would be your undoing."*

Alexei shook his head as if to be clearing a fog from his brain. *"You are correct. I will remain levelheaded. I will wait like I have for the last ten years. Like a crouching tiger, I will be patient and lay in waiting."*

"Have patience, Alexei, and the greatest rewards shall be yours."

He looked at the fireplace and the flames reflected in his amber colored eyes. When he spoke, his voice was strong, his manner assertive. *"Finally…I will finally have my revenge."*

"And that will be the first step in our people taking our rightful place as the true rulers of this world."

Alexei looked back at the shadows and towards the woman he had known for nearly his entire life.

"Our time has come, Alexei. When we first emerged from the shadows all those decades ago, we thought we could win. But our leaders before us underestimated the human resolve and we learned a terrible lesson. Our foolish leaders tried again and we suffered innumerable casualties, including your beloved Dimitri. But now I am in charge. And I will not make the mistakes our forefathers made."

"I have known you for over a hundred years," Alexei said to the shadows. *"I am stronger than ever, and I will serve you better than ever. I am ready for this war."*

The darkness in the corner of the room was pierced by the white glow of two eyes that suddenly appeared and stared back at him. The hiss of snakes as if they were slowly waking from a slumber filled his ears.

"This war will be won," the woman said. *"We are ready."*

9

SICILY

MARIS Correa stepped out of Palermo International Airport and into the heat of the mid-July Mediterranean summer day. The nineteen hour flight from Las Vegas with its irksome layovers made for a long, tiring trip. She was fortunate to travel without any substantial luggage. Her contact in Sicily would have a packed bag for her comprised of local purchases of clothing and some essential items she had provided in a list to the NPDIA travel coordinator prior to her departure. In her modest wicker carry-on bag was the jewelry box with the earrings Galaxy had given her, along with a few cosmetics and toiletries and her phone. Her hair draped over her shoulders, flowing onto a solid, sleeveless, casual forest green dress that split for most of the length of her legs, making it look from a distance like she had on a pair of flowy wide-bottomed slacks. The dress had a matching belt attached at the midsection that looked more like it was there for show than practicality. Her black-and-white patterned flats completed her casual look. She peered over the top of her sunglasses at the man dressed in simple black slacks and white dress shirt waiting curbside in the passenger loading section. She instantly recognized him but did not call him out by his formal name.

"So you're Agent Vector," she remarked. "When I was given the codename of my contact here I didn't expect it to be you. I thought I was meeting up with someone local."

"I'm here, so I'm local."

"I can't argue with that."

Brian Masse, codenamed Vector, opened the front passenger door to the four-door, newer model Alfa Romeo behind him. The car was clean and shiny silver, with wide, low profile tires on black rims, and a black spoiler that stuck up in the rear nearly as high as the top of the car itself. Maris entered the vehicle and he closed the door for her. He then settled into the driver's seat and wasted no time peeling away from the airport. Maris took in the combination of leather and "new car" smell and marveled at the sleek, modern dash with its flatscreen monitor and modern Italian design. Masse pressed a button on the monitor and a GPS map appeared, taking up one-half of the screen. They were over an hour out from their destination in Trapani.

"Nice car," she said. "The rentals I would be stuck with in the CIA weren't ever this nice."

"It's an Alfa Romeo Giulia GTA. It's a company car." Masse responded dryly without taking his eyes off the road. He was his usual warm self.

"Are you a car enthusiast?" Maris asked. There was no response. She looked around the car again before settling her eyes outside the passenger window. "Well, it's definitely state-of-the-art."

"Ahead-of-the-art," Masse corrected.

Maris looked around the interior of the cabin. Although the car was a 4-door sedan it looked far from standard. The all-black interior was sleek and curved with few if any hard corners. The seats were a form-fitting racing style with dual shoulder straps in addition to the standard lap belt.

"I recognize that term. What makes this so special?"

The engine revved and Masse hit the curve of a roundabout quicker than Maris would have liked, the inertia forcing her to hold herself steady.

"This car is completely bulletproof. NPDIA standard. Secure agency-coded Wi-Fi so we never lose a signal as long as you're within a mile of the vehicle. Your agency phone and all its apps will have already automatically networked in."

Maris took out her phone. A notification showed it was connected to a local NPDIA network.

"And those earrings Galaxy gave you back in headquarters, they have also already automatically connected. If you're tracking someone, their location will pull up on the car's GPS. This may all seem trivial, but they're all important features."

They drove on without Masse adding any further details.

After a few moments, Maris said, "That doesn't all seem so very 'ahead-of-the-art' as you stated."

The other agent glanced at her. "It's enough for you to know. I'm the one assigned to the vehicle, not you." There was a touch of disdain in his voice.

She couldn't tell if he was being purposely elusive or just being an ass. Their few interactions had barely been cordial.

"Look, Agent Masse –"

He cut her off. "I need to insist we maintain the practice of keeping to codenames when on assignment, Agent Scarlett."

Maris took a deep breath, choosing to say nothing rather than something that would potentially exacerbate a contentious discussion. She paused to think through the situation with this person she had barely met and didn't remotely know. Over the years she had been forced to interact and deal with all sorts of people, and obviously not everyone was friendly – even the ones that she expected should be. Every person had their own story, their own experiences, that made them the person they were. She knew it was never personal. And Brian Masse – Agent Vector – had a kindness in his eyes that betrayed his gruff exterior.

A number of scenarios ran through her mind. Maybe he was like this towards everyone and not just her. Or perhaps he thought he should have been given the assignment, being the more experienced NPDIA agent. Maybe he felt as though he had been relegated to a role of just being "her driver" and took offense.

Or, maybe he's just an ass, Maris thought, smiling to herself.

Maris settled in and decided to just enjoy the ride. She took solace in knowing she would not be on a plane again for the next few days at least, and she looked forward to checking into the hotel and getting some good rest before the summit the next day. The views of the island were breathtaking for a woman from a small town in Florida. She had been to Italy before, having spent one summer break from college in Trieste, where she visited castles, caves, and churches, and it was on this trip when she spent time in the water learning how to freedive. She had not been to Sicily, though, and her globetrotting with the CIA never afforded leisure time to truly enjoy the foreign lands to which she had traveled for work. It was also nice to have someone else do the driving, as many times she was left to her own devices. While the company could have been better, she still appreciated the lucidity as she took in the postcard perfect views as they made their way to Trapani. The countryside and hills that bordered their route were beyond beautiful. And the occasional views of the sparkling Tyrrhenian Sea on the north side of the island were amazing and beyond picturesque.

The private marina on the fringes of Trapani harbor where Maris was to meet her host was not immediately accessible by car. As such, Agent Vector had to stop over a mile away on a less traveled road than the ones in the heart of the town. Maris let herself out and met Vector at the back of the Alfa Romeo. He opened the trunk and pulled out a small black suitcase, setting it in front of her. He then handed her a small key from his pocket.

"For the luggage," he said.

She took the key from him and placed it in her handbag.

"Follow this path all the way down," Vector told her. "At the bottom you'll see the docks. There's just the one private mooring so you can't miss it."

Maris extended the handle on the rolling luggage and tipped it onto its two wheels. She was going to offer Vector a hand to shake but then thought twice about it.

"Thank you, Agent Vector, for your hospitality."

The man said nothing in return, instead giving her a slight nod before walking back to the driver's side of the car.

"I'll text you my number so you can reach me if you need anything," he said. "If nothing else, message me when you are headed back here so I'll know when to meet you." He got into the car and shut the door.

Maris said nothing in return, instead giving him a slight nod in return before walking away from the car with the luggage in tow. A few moments later her smartphone buzzed. She took it out of her wicker handbag and, not recognizing the number, turned back and looked at the car. Vector was looking at her through the passenger window from the driver's seat holding up his cell phone. She silenced her phone then held it up for him to see.

As Maris started down the narrow path she added the other agent as a contact into her phone under the name "Vector." The walk under the late afternoon sun lasted nearly thirty minutes and wound slightly downward past several tiny, old Sicilian shops and homes until it reached the docks. As the walkway opened up past the buildings and the unadulterated breeze from the sea flowed over her, Maris couldn't decide which blue was prettier: the clear cloudless sky or the pristine azure of the water beyond the docks.

The private dock was easy to spot just as Vector had indicated, but not so much because there was just the one. Sunlight glistened off the one hundred and forty foot long silver-white trimaran moored to the pier. The impressive sleek superyacht looked like it would be as comfortable drifting through outer space as it did floating in the water.

Security was surprisingly light, save for a man in a buttoned-up navy-colored double-breasted pea coat and white pants standing at the start of the wooden dock. Maris wasn't sure how he wasn't sweltering under the heat as she produced her credential for the summit. The man waved her through without incident. She continued on to a narrow boardwalk that ran alongside the mirror-like vessel. *Almaznyy Glaz* – which she translated from Russian meaning "Diamond Eye" – was emblazoned near the wedge-like bow. The walkway took her past the front of the boat and under the wide arched beam that stretched overhead and connected the nearest outrigger. A man stepped off the boarding deck at the rear of the superyacht to greet her. The tall, slim man with the short, dark hair was impeccably dressed, and had a drink in his hand and his arms out wide as he walked up to her.

"*Ciao!*" he said loudly. "*Benvenuto nella mia umile barca!*" *Welcome to my humble boat!*

Although his Italian wasn't perfect, there was a definite arrogance about him despite his choice of words.

"*Ciao!*" Maris called out in return.

"*Mi chiamo* Alexei Volkov. *Come ti chiami?*" *My name is Alexei Volkov. What is your name?*

The Russian. The mission was on.

"My name is Scarlett," she said in English then paused, ever so briefly. The NPDIA had provided her a full name when registering for the summit, including a surname, and she said it out loud as if she had said it a thousand times. "Scarlett Caso."

"American!" Alexei exclaimed, almost gleefully. He took hold of her right hand and kissed the top of it. "It's a pleasure to meet you."

"Pleased to meet you as well," Maris said with a cordial smile.

"Come, let me take you aboard. Leave your luggage. I will have it taken care of." Alexei kept hold of her hand as he escorted her onto the boarding deck. He nodded towards a deckhand who stood aside at attention, seemingly doing nothing but awaiting orders. The deckhand acknowledged the unspoken order in Russian then rushed to the waiting baggage and brought it onto the boat.

"This way, please," Alexei said. His charming smile carried through to his eyes, though Maris wasn't sure if they held a look of trust or some veil of deceit. It was just a few steps to a short set of stairs that led them to the upper deck. "Allow me to get you a drink. It's a two hour trip to the island from here. You should relax."

They walked past an empty open seating area and through a glass door that led to an enclosed cabin with additional seating and a bar. There were very few sharp corners, with the interior architecture full of fluid curves and arches. Even the seating and tables evoked surfs and waves in a sea of upscale tranquility. Windows and skylights spilled natural light from outside to brighten the white walls and ceiling, while the wood floor, cabinets, and counters conjured images of beach wood against an island paradise. A nearly inconspicuous staircase in one area of the cabin led down to the lower deck.

There were three other guests in the cabin, all men, along with a bartender. The men sat near each other on one of the curved couches, talking amongst themselves in English, but each with very different accents. They glanced at Maris as she walked by but otherwise didn't pay her much attention.

"Gentlemen," Alexei said as he chaperoned Maris towards the bar. "I will introduce you in a moment. But first, I shall get my esteemed guest a drink."

They reached the bar and the bartender, a young Italian woman with raven hair and a deep Mediterranean tan, smiled at Maris.

"What will you be drinking today?" Alexei asked.

Maris looked at the bartender. "My drink of choice is Four Roses, Small Batch, over two cubes, please."

"A bourbon lover!" Alexei exclaimed, impressed. "That's quite a taste. Most women I know prefer a more…tropical taste."

"It's a taste I acquired from my father. He used to love bourbon when I was a child."

Carlos Correa. The image of the man flooded Alexei's brain, and a fresh injection of hate burned through his veins. He looked away from her, doing his best to hide his detestation.

Maris leaned in a bit. "Is everything okay, Mr. Volkov?"

The Russian flashed a smile that made Maris think of the Cheshire Cat from Alice In Wonderland, and the kindness in his eyes – no matter how fake it may have been – returned.

"Of course!" he exclaimed, not quite convincing. "And I insist you call me Alexei." He turned his attention to the bartender. "What do we have, dear, for our guest?"

"I don't believe we have Small Batch," the bartender replied with a thick Italian accent. "Let me see what we do have." The bartender went to a nearby cabinet and returned with a bottle filled with a dark mahogany liquid. She set the bottle on the counter in front of Maris. "Looks like we have a 2012 Four Roses Limited Edition Single Barrel."

"That'll do," Maris said. Outwardly she remained her cool despite knowing that the bourbon sitting in front of her, at well over a thousand dollars a bottle, was about as good as it could get. And definitely the best she had ever been given. This mission had certainly placed her in a league unlike she had ever been before.

The bartender put the drink together in no time and handed Maris her glass. Alexei held his glass – half-filled with a bright yellow and red concoction – up in a toast.

"*Za vashe zdorov'ye,*" he said. "To your health, as they say."

Maris didn't need the translation as she possessed a decent grasp of the language. "*Za vashe zdorov'ye,*" Maris repeated. Her Russian accent was normally very good, but she made a point of putting an Anglo-twist on it to not let on how well she could speak the language.

They clinked glasses and each took a drink. It was definitely the best tasting and smoothest bourbon Maris had ever had the pleasure of drinking. Maris held onto her glass, and continued to nurse the drink as they spoke.

"I've heard a lot about you," she said to her host. It was nice to not be the one on the receiving end of that statement for once.

"Really?" Alexei laughed. "You don't say. Please, indulge me."

"You built your mini-Empire as creator and owner of Hexatetron, a global leader of financial and anti-virus software, database and file management systems, and several firmware programs. Your financial status is well documented and well-known. You own several homes and commercial properties worldwide."

Alexei raised an eyebrow while remaining quiet.

"And though most of your products are used in Asian and European countries, you have maintained a respectable global reputation, despite many Western countries' general distrust of Russian industries."

Alexei chuckled. "You have certainly done your homework."

Maris nodded. *You know what they say about keeping your friends close,* she thought.

"You on the other hand," Alexei continued, eyeing her up and down. "I don't know much about the great and beautiful Scarlett Caso out of the United States, other than you being a high end black market diamond buyer and seller."

The NPDIA had conjured a fake profile to attach to her name when registering her for the summit. She had prepared for her "role" as a diamond trader during her trip to Italy.

"Maybe there is more to you than meets the eye," Alexei concluded. His gaze continued to wander over her before settling on her eyes.

"Maybe there is," Maris said coyly.

Alexei broke his eye contact. "Here, let me introduce you to my other guests."

They moved over to the three men sitting on the nearby couches. Alexei used the drink in his hand to gesture to each of the men. "These gentlemen are representatives from some of the top diamond producing countries in the world." He motioned toward the men one at a time, starting with the man on the furthest left. They each nodded in acknowledgement as they were introduced. "This is Embry Beaulieu from Canada. And then Lerato Pretorius from South Africa. Finally this is Adashe Hatendi from Zimbabwe. Gentlemen, this is Scarlett Caso from the United States."

"United States?" asked Beaulieu, with a hint of French inflection in his voice. "I appreciate the idea of my neighbor from the south joining us, but I didn't realize the U.S. was invited to this summit."

"My sponsors have their ways, Mr. Beaulieu," Maris explained. "I'm sure you can understand that I'm not at liberty to say any more. Suffice it to know that I possess the proper credentials."

Pretorius stood and clinked drinks with Maris. "I for one am thrilled to have someone of your beauty joining the conference," he said with a thick accent. "Much better to look at than these ugly faces." He waived his drink at the men on the couch. Everyone laughed.

"You four are the final guests to arrive," Alexei said. "Everyone else is already checked into the hotel on the island."

The voice of the superyacht's captain made an announcement in Russian through an overhead speaker.

"We are leaving port," Alexei loosely translated. "Our journey to Pantelleria will be a little over two hours."

Maris finished her drink. "If you gentlemen will excuse me, I'm going to go freshen up. I had a long flight today."

"Absolutely," Alexei said to her as he took her empty glass. He motioned to the staircase adjacent to the bar. "I have a cabin for you just down those stairs and to the right. There's a washroom down there as well. I will have a deckhand bring you your luggage."

Maris gave her company a polite nod then headed towards the stairs. Alexei smiled as he turned his back to the other men, staring at her as she left. His eyes shot imaginary daggers into her back as she walked away.

The opening to the stairway was partially hidden behind a black latticework that looked much like a piece of art itself as it did part of the boat. Maris made her way down the narrow wooden stairs. At the bottom, a turn to the left would have put her in a small bathroom barely big enough for the sink and toilet that occupied the space, whereas a turn to the right opened into the sleeping quarters. Despite there not being any doors, the area felt very private due to the almost hidden placement of the stairs.

The head of a queen-sized bed rested against the far wood-paneled wall, sitting on a low-profile frame and topped with a thick off-white plush comforter that reached almost to the floor. Half a dozen yellow and white striped pillows were lined up on top of the bed against the wall. Smooth, white walls curved up and away from either side of the bed and were broken up near their tops by rounded rectangular windows opening to the blue sky.

There was a glossy wooden desk with a wicker chair against a wall not far from the foot of the bed. Maris set her handbag on the desk. The only other item on the desktop was a thin vase with a single flower inside. Maris did a double-take of the three-petal white lily, initially mistaking it for a mariposa. It took a lot to catch her off-guard, and the mistaken identity of this flower certainly came close. She brushed the thought out of her mind as a voice called down to her from the top of the stairs.

"I have your luggage, ma'am." The Italian-accented deckhand called out from the top of the stairs.

"You can bring it down."

Maris met the deckhand at the bottom of the stairs and the young man set the hard-cased baggage on the floor. She thanked the deckhand and he quickly retreated back up the staircase. Once he was out of view and the sound of his unseen footsteps took him away from her cabin, Maris picked up the bag and set it on the foot of the bed.

Moving quietly, Maris knew she had to remain alert to anyone who may decide to come downstairs unannounced. She retrieved the key Agent Vector gave her earlier out of her wicker bag, then unlocked and opened the luggage.

Maris removed the clothes – two different style jackets and a few outfits ranging from casual to formal, along with undergarments – and set them aside. The luggage at this point looked empty…though it wasn't. Next she pulled away a false bottom that was also not what it seemed as it was actually a lightweight black briefcase. She set this case next to the now empty baggage and opened it.

There was a handwritten note inside on white paper.

Standard issue. – G.

Maris set the note aside and feasted her eyes on the case's contents. She expected to see her trusty Glock but she actually discovered so much more. Hard black foam core board with custom cut out areas presented her with a bevy of necessities straight out of a secret agent handbook: two gold-plated folding pocket knives; a pair of black leather gloves; a black battery-powered analog watch; a folded scarf with a flower print; a lighter; and a pair of black-framed sunglasses. And, of course, there was her black-chrome modified Glock 19, locked and loaded, its spare fully-loaded clip, and a few different style holsters for various uses.

Thank you, Galaxy! she thought.

Maris removed the gun and the shoulder holster, then shut the briefcase and placed it securely back into the bottom of the luggage. She replaced all the clothing save for a light jacket that loosely matched her current attire, then closed and locked the rolling case. Putting on the holster, along with the gun inside, made her feel more at home. The customized holster ensured that her modified gun didn't look or feel any more bulky than normal, which was reassuring. She put on the jacket and slipped the luggage key into a jacket pocket. She then picked up the note from Galaxy, folded it in half, and placed it into the same pocket.

Finally, she did what she told her host she was coming downstairs to do, which was to freshen up. She took her wicker handbag to the bathroom where she first made use of the facilities, then spent a few minutes touching up her makeup and hair. There were slight bags under her eyes and she more than ever couldn't wait to get some solid rest at the hotel. Figuring she wasn't going to get any more presentable at the moment, she headed back to the upper deck.

The other representatives were gone, most likely having retreated to their own cabins. Alexei was also nowhere to be seen. Maris smiled at the bartender who was biding her time wiping down glasses individually.

"Would you like another drink?" the bartender asked.

"No, thank you. I'm fine."

Maris went through a set of glass doors near the bow of the yacht and out onto its long triangle-shaped forward deck. The sun was blazing but the wind brought on by the movement of the boat felt good against her skin. Her hair whipped back in the breeze as she stood against the silver railing, taking in the beauty of the seas and skies around her. The further out she looked, the more the color of the clear sky and the color of the water looked the same, to where it was nearly impossible to tell where the two met as she tried to distinguish the far away horizon.

After a couple minutes she reached into her jacket pocket and discretely pulled out the note from Galaxy, crumpling it in the palm of her hand as she did. She shook her hair in the breeze as she checked her surroundings, doing her best to make sure no one was watching, and discreetly dropped the note overboard. It quickly disappeared into the breaking water below.

"A beautiful sight to behold!"

The sudden sound of Alexei's voice caught her off guard. She looked back at the Russian quickly, her hair getting in the way as it flipped about in the draft. She pulled it back with a hand to hold it in place while being careful to make sure her jacket did not flutter open and reveal her weapon.

"The water and the sky, I mean," Alexei said, his arms gesticulating in the air around them as he attempted to clarify himself. She noticed he still had a drink – or actually a new one as this one was almost full – in one hand. He moved to the other side of Maris so she could turn back and release her hair, allowing it to fly freely on its own once again away from her face.

"Yes," she said, gazing out and away from her host. "It certainly is."

Alexei took a sip from the glass. "I must say, I am thrilled to have an American be part of our conference. I am not personally privy to disbursement of the invitations, but I can only imagine what your people went through to get one."

"We have our ways, Alexei."

"Ahhh, Scarlett," he paused, tilting his head slightly as he interrupted himself. "Is it okay that I call you Scarlett?"

"Please do. I insist."

"Scarlett, Scarlett..." His voice faded away slightly. "The name epitomizes courage, passion, and joy. All attributes I am sure that you possess."

Maris couldn't tell if he was hitting on her or just being flamboyant. She was no stranger to playing the flirtation game on missions – it was amazing to her what she could get sometimes with just a smile and tone of voice – but she was hoping this wasn't one of those situations.

"In my case I don't think it means anything at all. My parents merely loved the name."

"Your parents are very lucky to have a daughter as breathtaking as you."

Maris looked at the Russian with deadpan eyes. "I'm sorry, Alexei, but I'm here simply on business. I'm not here to make friends. Or to be more than friends." She returned to leaning on the rail, looking out once again at the sea.

Alexei laughed a loud, boisterous laugh.

"I am sorry you misunderstand me!" He took another drink. "My boyfriend would never let me down if he thought I was making advances towards a woman."

Maris felt some relief. "My apologies. And I can understand that sentiment. I'm sure he wouldn't." She let out a small laugh to make it look like she shared in the levity of the moment.

Alexei did his best to lay the charm back on. "Allow me to change the subject. How do you like my boat? She is nice, *da?*"

Maris looked around, marveling at the boat's architecture. "It's quite beautiful. Can't say I've ever been on a yacht quite like this."

"The *Almaznyy Glaz*" Alexei said proudly. "There is nothing quite like her in the world."

"The 'Diamond Eye," Maris translated out loud. "What made you choose that for its name?"

"I don't think it means anything at all," his tone sounded partially mocking as he repeated her response from earlier. "I merely loved the name."

"She is quite spectacular."

"What can I say? I am a proud parent."

Maris attempted to keep the conversation more professional and focused. "I'm honored that you have accepted me as your guest and allowed me to travel with you."

"But of course! I am lucky to have you on board, as your parents were lucky to have you. Your father especially." Again, with the weird, off-putting tone. He took another drink, several gulps this time. "Tell me, Scarlett," he drew himself close to her. "Are you daddy's little girl? His favorite? Always making daddy proud?"

Maris felt uneasy as Alexei went from seemingly flirtatious to creepy in a matter of seconds. She wasn't scared, though. There wasn't much that truly frightened her, least of all creepy men.

She kept her stare focused on the horizon. "As I said, Alexei, I'm not here to make friends. If it's all the same, I'd rather keep my personal life personal."

He smiled and his swagger instantly returned. "You are my guest, and I will respectfully treat you accordingly."

Maris decided she had had enough. She wanted to save her energy for the summit and whatever surprises that was sure to bring. And, for the time being, get as far away from Alexei as possible. She also wanted to do some refresher reading on Hexatetron along with its owner himself. That would be much more productive than wasting time on small talk above deck.

"If you don't mind," she said, "I think I'm going to retreat to my cabin. Get some rest."

"I don't mind it at all. You may do as you please. If you need anything, alert the bartender. She will get you anything you need."

Maris suddenly wondered if she was purposely placed in the cabin that she was assigned so that the bartender could keep easy watch over the staircase that led to her quarters. It didn't matter, though. She wasn't going to be looking for any trouble on this tour.

"Thank you, Alexei. I'll be in my cabin, then."

Alexei smiled, gave a nod, and took another sip of his drink.

Maris turned away and retreated back inside the yacht.

■■■■■ ● ● ● ■■■■■

ALEXEI quickly chugged down the rest of his drink. His heart was beating a hundred miles an hour from the surge of adrenaline coursing through him, brought on by his genuine hatred for the woman who was just in front of him. He stood stone-faced on the bow of his superyacht, defying the pitch of the boat as it cruised at its maximum 22 knots top speed on its way to the island of Pantelleria in the middle of the Mediterranean Sea.

After several moments stewing alone, he threw his empty glass as far out into the sea as he could, his face contorted into a mask of anger and hate, as he recalled the last meeting he had with Scarlett's father, the man he knew as Ares, in Monte Carlo many years ago…

10

MONTE CARLO

TEN YEARS AGO

PULSING lights. Throbbing beats. An intimate dance floor packed with writhing bodies. Some men in tuxedos while others danced in high-end designer T-shirts. Women in the latest creations from the most popular fashionistas in the world. Records spun by the DJ on stage while flanked by hired dancers clad in leather camisoles and little else. A waitress made her way across the floor with a tray of champagne bottles spraying fountains of fiery sparkles into the air. The party had begun, like it did every night, when the doors opened just minutes before midnight. By the stroke of twelve, it was already in full swing.

Jimmy'z was an exclusive nightclub in the Monte Carlo Sporting Complex, and not only was it one of the most prestigious clubs on the Riviera, but also the entire world. The hotspot was routinely frequented by local and international celebrities, the rich, and the powerful – and every one of them was beautiful. Only the elite of the elite routinely were allowed entry into the famous nightspot.

Alexei Volkov was one of those elite. He sat in the middle of his usual wide, curved booth watching the partygoers dance and drink the early morning hours away. Sitting next to him was his boyfriend of seven years, Dmitri Federova. While many Russians didn't support homosexuality, at least not openly, Alexei's position as one of the richest men in the world placed him well above scrutiny. The rest of the booth was filled with acquaintances of Alexei's, local people who called him a "friend" whenever he was around, but whom he actually barely knew.

This night's festivities were a private affair, filled to capacity by personal invitation only. The party's host, a personal friend of Alexei's, was a tall woman with flowing chestnut brown hair, hazel eyes, and glasses. She stood in front of his booth with her lemon drop martini held high to gather everyone's attention.

Very few people had the clout to throw such an extravagant affair, but not everyone was Janet Ponther, global fashion extraordinaire. The likes of Versace and Fendi had their followers, but it was the Ponther line that reigned supreme for nearly a decade. Janet had started off many years ago as an American runway model and one of the original "supermodels" along with the likes of Cindy Crawford, Naomi Campbell, and Linda Evangelista. Her career soared since then, though, as she went from modelling for the world's greatest designers to becoming one of their peers.

The music was loud, so conversations had to be louder to be heard. Even partiers right next to each other had to practically shout to be heard. All eyes in the booth were on Janet as she did her best to shout over the rhythm of the club.

"A quick toast!" Janet said as she looked at Alexei. "Thank you for coming out tonight, Alexei. Your friendship and support means so much! So to you," she held her drink in his direction, "I say, to your health! *Na zdorovie!*"

Her Russian pronunciation of the toast wasn't great, but it got her point across as Alexei and Dmitri beamed. They held their glasses up in return and repeated the phrase in unison.

"*Na zdorovie!*"

Everyone clinked glasses with the people next to them and drank.

"I trust you are enjoying yourself?" Janet asked her special Russian guest.

"Very much so!" Alexei flashed his smile, full of the usual charm, and gave the woman a wink.

Alexei had always thought that if he wasn't gay, Janet Ponther would have been the perfect woman for his taste. She was tall, beautiful, and highly successful, three attributes he very much admired. And there was something about her that he had always found intriguing. Perhaps it was her knack for being one of the most popular designers in the world, while being able to maintain a very private life. Although they were friends, much of their interaction was professional as opposed to personal. The less he knew about her, the more he wanted to know her better.

But pursuit of the one-time supermodel was not what he was about. After the toast he turned and gave Dmitri a kiss that lasted so long it elicited cheers from the people around them, including Janet herself.

"If you need anything," Janet said, "call me if you can't find me. I'll be here all night!"

"Thank you, my dear!" Alexei called out in return.

Janet left to go greet and interact with other partygoers, leaving Alexei and Dmitri with their guests.

"The fashion show today was amazing," Dmitri shouted above the music in his native Russian. *"We were fortunate to have been invited."*

"It's nice having friends in high places," Alexei responded in Russian.

"Thank you so much for inviting us," said the woman sitting on the opposite side of Dmitri from Alexei. Her English was heavily accented by her native French.

"I love this song! Let's dance!" exclaimed another seated on the bench.

Everyone on either side of Alexei and Dmitri quickly cleared out and headed to the dance floor. Dmitri made no moves to leave.

"Don't you want to go dance?" Alexei asked. *"Let's go, it'll be fun. We need to let loose!"*

Dmitri leaned in close to his boyfriend, speaking directly into his ear. *"I think we need to be careful, Lover,"* Dmitri cautioned. *"The war still goes on and we are being hunted by the Americans. I'm worried about all the high profile appearances you've been making."*

Alexei laughed. *"The Americans are not a concern tonight. The war has quieted and is far from here. And their commander Ares is a fool. He is no more of a danger to us than a mosquito buzzing about. He's just a nuisance, not a real threat."*

"I wish you took this more seriously. Traipsing about Monte Carlo and fraternizing publicly with fashion designers and the elite…it's not a good look right now."

Alexei gulped down the rest of his multicolored drink and slammed the empty glass onto the table.

"Tonight is a celebration," he said sternly. *"We are here to have fun and be free from the fight. Tonight we have this party and in a few days the Monaco Grand Prix. I didn't bring an F1 team all the way here to not watch them race. So let's dance and be free and save our troubles for later. Come on, let's go."*

"I just think it would be better to be safe than sorry. We can't be too careful. I would hate for something to happen to you."

Ignoring his boyfriend's pleas, Alexei worked himself out of the booth and made his way to the dance floor with Dmitri following behind begrudgingly. The night continued on and the party raged. Drinks were plentiful. Over the next few hours, Alexei and Dmitri alternated between dancing, visiting the bar, and relaxing in their booth. Janet occasionally joined them on the dance floor. Various people – many of whom Alexei did not know at all but apparently knew who he was – stopped him intermittently for small talk, more than likely to make themselves feel important moreso than for his benefit. Often over the thumping beats Alexei couldn't even make out what they said, instead smiling or laughing along and blindly agreeing with whatever sentiment they expressed.

It was about 3AM when the music stopped and Janet garnered the attention of the partygoers from a place on stage next to the DJ platform. Lights came up throughout the establishment to allow everyone to see each other better. The brightest lights accentuated Janet on the stage. Alexei and Dmitri were about to sit back down in their booth when Janet began an announcement. They remained standing as she spoke.

"I want to thank you all so much for attending the release of my new fall line tonight! With the support of so many, including all of you, this line is sure to be my most popular yet!"

Applause came from the crowd. One voice called out, "We love you, Janet!" which elicited more cheers.

"I love you, too! Thank you!" The cheering subsided and Janet continued. "All of you are so amazing and hold a special place in my heart. I would not be where I am today if not for you. But there is one person here in particular that I want to publicly thank. I have known this man for many years, ever since the start of my fashion business. He was a primary backer then, and has continued to support me behind the scenes in the years since. And even better, not only did he attend the show this evening, but he is with us here right now!"

Janet picked up another of her favorite lemon drops that was waiting for her on the nearby DJ table.

"Many of you know of this man," she continued. "He is the creator and owner of Hexatetron Corporation, a true innovator and global personality, my friend, and an all-around good guy. So, a resounding 'thank you' to Alexei Volkov. Your public endorsement of my new line has raised it to heights greater than I could have ever imagined!"

A spotlight shined on Alexei standing in front of his booth as a round of applause erupted throughout the nightclub in his honor. He gave a proud wave to all the eyes that were on him. His boyfriend smiled broadly and wrapped an arm around him. As the cheers continued, several waitstaff assimilated themselves among dancers on the floor and around the periphery of the club near several of the booths. Some held mini confetti cannons, while others readied unopened bottles of champagne with corks ready to pop.

Janet held her martini high as she made her next announcement.

"And to all of you, thank you so much! This toast is for you!" She took a sip of her drink.

A round of cheers in various languages – French, English, and Russian, among others – resonated through the club, while simultaneously, the pops of two dozen champagne corks shot off like gunshots while the confetti cannons blasted golden flakes into the air.

Alexei turned to give his boyfriend a hug when he saw that he was stumbling.

"Dmitri, what's wrong? Too much to drink tonight?" He laughed as he reached out to his lover.

Dmitri staggered back against the booth table, clutching at his side. Blood was spreading on his custom tailored dress shirt. Alexei grabbed him.

"What happened? Are you okay?"

Dmitri coughed then took a pained breath. *"I...I think I've been shot."*

No one paid attention to the two men as the music thumped once again and the lights dimmed as the party recommenced. Alexei moved his boyfriend to the side and laid him back in the booth. He ripped open his lover's shirt. Blood oozed from a gunshot wound on the left side of his stomach.

"I'm...I should be fine. We are strong, Alexei."

The pop of a second gunshot sounded from across the nightclub and a portion of the table next to Alexei splintered. Partygoers, dismissing the gunshot sounds for popping corks, remained oblivious to the violence as they raved on.

Alexei pulled his boyfriend onto the floor as more shots rang out. *POP! – POP! – POP! – POP! – POP!*

The realization of what was happening abruptly spread through the club. Mayhem struck, mostly on the dance floor below, as people screamed and ran towards the exits in a panic. Alexei, still cowering, looked around frantically, scanning the dark nightspot as best he could for the source of the gunfire. Because the booth area was elevated above the dance floor, he was able to clearly see across the tops of the heads of those scrambling on the floor.

And there he was, on the far side of the club, pointing a rifle in his direction that must have been smuggled in under the long designer coat he was wearing:

Ares.

The NPDIA agent had been a thorn in Alexei's side during encounters in London and Greece months ago. But much of the chatter his people had heard about American movement had quieted down greatly in recent weeks. He definitely did not anticipate being tracked to Monaco, and certainly did not expect such a brazen public attack as that typically was not the Americans' M.O. It had always been the understanding that the Americans wanted to keep the existence of the war underground and quiet. Apparently, Ares had other ideas.

"It's Ares," Alexei said. *"You were right, he's on to us."*

"Ares is here? How did he get in?"

"Probably bribed the doorman. We need to get out of here."

More pops and the table above him continued to disintegrate. Alexei kept his body over his boyfriend in an attempt to shield him.

"Can you move?"

"I think so," Dmitri said. *"Yes."*

Alexei helped Dmitri get on his hands and knees and then led as the two of them crawled in the direction of the front exit. Bullets sprayed around them, a surreal experience as the music still pumped and the lights still rotated and flashed as if the party hadn't stopped. The floor in front of Alexei suddenly exploded into fragments, and he laid down flat onto his stomach. A voice pierced the mayhem, shouting at them from his left.

"This way!" Janet called out. She was crouched behind a side employees-only door and waving to them frantically.

The two Russians scrambled quickly towards the woman when a new source of gunshots rang out. Alexei looked in the direction of the gunfire and saw another man shooting at them from the area of the bar, which was much closer than where Ares had stationed himself across the club. He stopped and motioned Dmitri forward.

"*Go, go!*" he yelled out.

Getting haphazardly to his feet Dmitri, was able to rush on, still holding his side.

Alexei stood fully and glared at the nearby gunner as his eyes glowed white. The agent, not wearing any eye protection most likely due to the ever-changing flashing lights of the club, didn't look away in time. He started to bring his rifle up towards Alexei, but the movement was slow. The man's skin and clothes turned gray and his entire body turned to stone.

A bullet flew past Alexei's head from behind him and struck the statue, causing pieces of stone to shatter away from the frozen agent. Alexei looked back, his eyes no longer white, and saw Ares and another agent approaching rapidly with guns blazing. The two agents looked down and away while continuing to fire their weapons blindly in Alexei's direction.

Alexei ran through the employee door and into a short hallway with private offices branching off of it. The end of the hallway had an EXIT sign mounted to it written in French with an arrow pointing to an opening on the left. He could see Janet leading a limping Dmitri into the opening.

Alexei rushed to catch up and was just at the turn when the employee door slammed open behind him. He expected to have more bullets spray around him but something very different happened. A red electrical beam, erratic like lightning, splattered against the wall at the end of the corridor. The EXIT sign exploded into a shower of sparks. This was something he wasn't familiar with. The Americans had a new weapon in their fight.

The hallway ahead lasted only about ten feet and Janet and Dmitri were pushing through a door that led outside. Alexei ran full speed and pressed through, now just behind his boyfriend and the woman who was trying to save them.

They were on a well-lit city block street, illuminated by street lamps and the surrounding buildings. The complex was just off the nearby marina and the smell of the water hung in the air. Even though it was in the very early morning hours, there were quite a few people walking up and down the street enjoying the cool and cloudless May dawn. The passersby ignored the trio, no one noticing Dmitri's bloodstained shirt.

Janet was close to hyperventilating. She had one hand on her chest and put her other hand on the outside wall of the club to hold herself up.

"Oh my god, oh my god, oh my god!" she blurted quickly. "What happened to that man back there? It looked like he turned into stone!"

"I don't know," Alexei lied. "But we've got to keep moving."

Alexei put an arm around Dmitri, who was beginning to do better, his Gorgon physique allowing him to heal more quickly than a human would have if shot in the stomach. Regardless, he still limped and was fortunate to have Alexei there to provide the additional support. Alexei had just begun to usher the three of them along when Ares and the other agent entered the street with weapons drawn.

"Stop!" Ares commanded. "All of you, hands up!"

Bystanders in the area cleared out quickly as shock and panic spread through the boulevard. Janet stood just a little more than arm's length away from the Americans with her back to them and her arms were raised high. She looked at Alexei and Dmitri as tears caused by a combination of adrenaline and fear streamed down her face. Alexei felt a genuine sadness for her, sorry that she had gotten caught up in this, especially on such a special night. He was close enough to reach up and wipe her tears away, but he restrained himself from doing so.

"You! Miss!" Ares shouted out. "Step aside slowly."

Janet shook her head, not in defiance, but to try and clear some of the confusion of what was happening out of her head. Alexei looked into her eyes, also shaking his head slightly.

And then his eyes turned white.

Janet's mouth opened as she started to say something, but within seconds her entire body had turned to stone.

"I'm so sorry," Alexei whispered in Russian.

Alexei moved fast, giving the statue of the fashion mogul a hefty side kick, forcing it to fall backwards. Ares jumped back, but the tipping statue clipped his rifle, causing it to drop to the ground. Caught off-guard, the two Americans nearly bumped into each other to avoid the falling stone figure. The rocky incarnation of Janet Ponther smashed to the ground into pieces.

Alexei took the opportunity to flee with his boyfriend. In just moments bullets were again raining upon them. They moved as fast as they could across the street towards an unassuming structure with rollup garage doors. Alexei moved quickly, half dragging Dmitri towards the building.

Then Dmitri cried out as a bullet hit him in the middle of his back. And then another in his shoulder. Dmitri fell to the street. Alexei yelled out, but he couldn't hear himself as his brain filled with a fog of panic and anger and despair. He knew Dmitri would be okay as long as he got him to safety and could be allowed to properly heal. His boyfriend was dead weight as he tried to drag him on. A bullet slammed into Alexei's left shoulder and the pain weakened his grasp, causing him to stumble backwards and Dmitri to collapse face down.

Alexei caught his balance and screamed out in a rage, his eyes white as he tried to make eye contact with Ares and the other attacking agent. But the Americans, now sporting eye protection since they were out of the confines of the dizzying lights of the nightclub, were unfazed by his Gorgon powers. He watched in horror as Ares raised his rifle and red lightning shot forth and struck Dmitri as he lay helpless in the street.

Dmitri's voice was weak as he called out to Alexei in Russian. *"Go, Lover, go. Save yourself."*

Alexei's eyes, no longer white, filled with tears. He knew he had to go.

He scampered backwards, still watching Dmitri as his boyfriend, his lover, his life, turned into a blackened and charred version of his former self right before his eyes. While Ares shot the deadly rays, the other American continued to pump bullets into Dmitri's body, ensuring his demise.

Having reached the garage, Alexei smashed his good shoulder into a door and practically fell inside from his momentum. The place was completely dark, and being so early in the morning no one else was around. His Gorgon eyesight helped him see better as he quickly moved through the familiar structure, into the main garage, and to his objective.

His Haas Ferrari VF-20 Formula One racing car.

The sounds of voices and footsteps from the building entrance caught his attention.

"Be sure your night vision is on. He can't have gone far." It was the unmistakable voice of Ares.

Alexei slammed a fist against a button on the wall that initiated the electric garage door opener. The noisy stainless steel door began to move up slowly, sure to garner the attention of his pursuers. He leaped into the open cockpit of the sleek black and white car and hastily punched the ignition switches. The rumble of the engine sounded louder than ever through the intake vent over his head since he was not wearing a helmet. He wasn't a professional driver, but owning the team had afforded him several opportunities to drive the car on private tracks. He knew enough to use the car for his getaway.

He didn't have to wait for the garage door to rise very high before he released the manually operated clutch paddles on the steering wheel and pressed on the gas. Starting the car so quickly wasn't ideal, but he didn't have time to perform the usual warm-up steps. The wheels screeched and smoked and the car seemed to be stuck in time as for a few moments it actually didn't move forward.

Just as the Americans came running into the smoke-filled garage, Alexei shot the car forward and out to make his escape. He made an immediate right turn and the backend of the racer nearly fishtailed over the top of the still smoldering blackened corpse of Dmitri in the middle of the road. Gunshots penetrated the high-pitched whir of the engine and bullets streaked out of the hazy garage. Most missed the low-profile vehicle, though a couple did glance off the rear wing without doing any major damage.

Alexei drove down the empty street and had traveled several blocks in a matter of moments as the 800 horsepower engine did its work. Before long the street was no longer as devoid of patrons as it was near the club, as he was now several blocks away and those around him weren't aware of the mayhem that had occurred. He was breathing heavily and he fought tears as his adrenaline began to subside and the reality of the loss of his boyfriend filled his thoughts. He finally slowed the car as he became aware that he was creating quite a stir among the people on the street.

The car slowed to a stop in the middle of an intersection. People were pointing and taking pictures of the car – and of him. It wasn't everyday people got to see a Formula One racing car up close, on a regular street, let alone driven by one of the richest men in the world. He ignored them, his only thoughts being on his lost lover.

Then the pain and rage that was building within him reached a zenith. He grimaced, wanting to cry out but restraining himself in front of the onlookers. Instead, he burned the tires again, causing the bystanders to back away quickly. He turned the steering wheel sharply and released the brake to make the car spin in a 180-degree turn. The tires squealed as the racing car sped back up the street in the direction of the nightclub.

In the distance, the smoking body of Dmitri started to come into view. And standing over him, disrespectfully kicking at the body and poking him with the barrel of his rifle, was the man responsible.

Ares.

Not only had he been an adversary throughout several skirmishes over the course of the war between Gorgons and humans, but he was now his archenemy, the murderer of his beloved Dmitri.

And he was going to die.

The car revved on and its speedometer pushed over 200 kilometers per hour within seconds. Alexei's vision narrowed and he saw nothing but his target. Ares stood in the middle of the road, defiantly raising his rifle high and pointing it straight at the oncoming car. There were no bullets as he expected, no rain of steel flying at him. Instead, the evil red lightning that helped bring the end to Dmitri shot forth, enveloping the car.

The Ferrari began to shake and tremble and Alexei struggled to maintain control. Despite barely being able to steer he refused to let up on the accelerator as he bore down on his target. Finally, the vibration was too much and the Formula racer careened to its left regardless of Alexei's best efforts to keep it on course. To Alexei's discontent, he completely missed Ares and instead the front wing of the car struck Dmitri's body, shattering half of the front wing. Carbon fibre shrapnel sprayed across his face, with one of the larger pieces tearing a deep horizontal gash across his left cheek. Blood gushed forth, but Alexei's rage displaced any pain.

The back end of the Ferrari flew up and the car went into an end over end flip, smacking the other American agent in the process, sending him flying through the air and into a nearby building.

Miraculously, the car slammed down right-side up and kept rolling, partly from the still running engine and partly from the inertia of its forward motion. Alexei tried the brakes but the car didn't respond. The steering was just as dysfunctional. The car continued, out of control, down a side street and headed straight for the nearby marina. Alexei held the wheel tight as the broken car shot off the end of the short street and splashed nose first into the water, illuminated only by the brightness from the early morning full moon.

███████ ● ● ● ███████

CARLOS Correa, Ares, did his best to keep up with the doomed Ferrari. He made it to the side street just as the racing car flew out of control and into the water. He ran down to the end of the street and joined other onlookers just in time to see the back end of the Formula One Ferrari dip down below the surface of the dark water. He looked on and surveyed the area for a couple minutes but never saw Alexei surface. Once he heard local police sirens approaching in the distance, he knew it was time to go. He had evidence to clean up, including the bodies of his fallen comrades, the scorched Gorgon, and the unfortunate fashion designer caught in the crossfire. A few people called out to him in French as he moved away from the scene but he ignored them. He had work to do and a story to spin.

11

PANTELLERIA

PRESENT DAY

THE boat's captain had announced the imminent arrival to Pantelleria and Maris Correa made her way to the upper deck. She stood on the bow with the representatives from Canada, South Africa, and Zimbabwe, along with their host, Alexei Volkov. For once, Alexei did not have a drink in his hand. The sun was nearing the horizon when the trimaran *Almaznyy Glaz* pulled into the private dock on the secluded yet popular island.

Pantelleria was a small thirty-two square mile paradise in the Strait of Sicily mostly reserved for the wealthy. Located just forty miles off the coast of Tunisia, which one could clearly see from the island on a clear day, it was the largest volcanic island in the area. Although the last eruption took place in 1891, fumaroles and hot mineral springs were common and current testaments to ongoing volcanic activity. Jagged lava cliffs dotted the windswept landscape, disguising ancient ruins and small historic stone habitats known locally as *dammusi*. A rich history including occupation by Carthaginians, Phoenicians, and Romans, as well as the Allies during World War II, opened the door to some of the finest dining in all of the Mediterranean. A small airstrip accommodated flights to and from Sicily and other nearby regions.

There was also, of course, the premier resort owned by Hexatetron called *Roskosh'*, which in Russian literally translated to "luxury." The opening of *Roskosh'* two years ago put the island's original lush and ultra-sophisticated hotel *Sikelia* to shame. With fifty plush suites, *Roskosh'* could accommodate nearly two hundred guests. Its architecture paid homage to the island's Tunisian, Lebanese, and Roman history, while incorporating aspects of its volcanic landscapes. A large natural spring was the centerpiece of its vast courtyard where guests could dine, socialize, and ultimately relax in the warm waters. The place was as eclectic as it was luxurious. None of the other island hotels could come close to the opulence of *Roskosh'*.

Upon their arrival, they were greeted inside the main entrance by a hotel attendant who had each of the summit attendees provide a thumb print onto a portable reader. This registered them into the hotel and linked their print to a pad outside their respective rooms, which would be used for room entry rather than a traditional hotel key of any kind. Maris had never visited such a beautiful extravagant hotel, and was inwardly in awe of its extravagance. The lobby didn't have a traditional registration or concierge area, and instead was decorated with fine sculptures and statues on pedestals. There was a high ceiling with magnificent glass chandeliers and curtains of pearl strings that added to the overall ambiance. A recirculating waterfall took up nearly the entire length and width of one wall.

Alexei gave his guests a tour of the resort while their luggage was taken to their rooms. The lobby served as a nexus for many of the hotel amenities including spa and sauna rooms, access to two open-air exercise rooms (located on opposite sides of the hotel so guests could view the sunrise in the morning and sunset in the evening while doing yoga, Pilates, or a number of other hosted activities), a salon, and three fine-dining restaurants. He took them through a glass hallway that branched off the lobby and ran through an immense aquarium, providing amazing 180-degree views of the multiple fish and undersea life inside. This corridor ultimately led to a wing of the hotel where the conference rooms were located.

The hotel was currently filled only with invitees to the upcoming summit, with one representative from fifty different countries registered to each of the hotel's suites. During their tour, Maris and the others were introduced to representatives from Botswana, Australia, and Brazil.

When the tour concluded in the lobby where it began, Alexei had attendants escort the other representatives to their rooms, while he insisted on accompanying Maris to hers himself. Maris politely obliged, though she wondered about his intentions, especially after their altercation on the boat.

The two upper floors of the hotel consisted solely of guest rooms. Alexei showed Maris to an elevator right off the lobby and they ascended to the top floor where Maris' room was located. The elevator doors opened revealing a long straight corridor. Her room was halfway down on the left. They conversed pleasantly as they walked.

"I've been doing some reading up on you, Alexei," Maris said. "It seems you have a knack for coming back from the dead."

"Oh, you must mean the Monte Carlo incident," Alexei mused.

"It's quite a story," she confirmed. Maris knew the story from an account of it in the dossier she received. She had refreshed up on it during the voyage to the island from Sicily.

"It was nothing, really," Alexei said, dismissive. "Reports of my death that evening were very premature and highly exaggerated. I had an unfortunate night out drinking and took my racecar for a joyride. It was nothing more."

"That's an understatement. You sunk a ten million dollar Formula One car into the Mediterranean. That's a bit more than an unfortunate night."

Alexei laughed. "Cars are just things, Scarlett. And things are easily replaceable. I, on the other hand, had to take some time to recover."

"I bet your people put quite the spin on everything. You know, to make sure the truth didn't get in the way of..." She paused briefly to come up with the right words. She definitely didn't want to say anything that would tip him off to how much she actually knew. "...your reputation."

"I laid low for a bit on the advice of my public relations people," was all he had to say on the matter. His broad smile returned. "But you can't keep a good Russian down." They stopped in front of her room. "Here we are. Room 23."

"Thank you, Alexei." Maris put her thumb on the reader and the door unlatched and opened slightly.

"If you would," Alexei said, "I would love it if you would join me for dinner. I am intrigued by the great Scarlett Caso and would love to learn more."

"Not tonight, thank you. I'm very tired from all the traveling the last couple days. I need some good rest before the summit tomorrow."

"Another time, then, perhaps."

"Yes, Alexei. Another time."

Her Russian host walked away as she entered the room and locked the door behind her.

Maris' room – which was more like an apartment with separate living room, bedroom, kitchen, and bath – was certainly based on Tunisian architecture and influences. The ceiling was arched and there were no inner corners where any of the walls met. Rather, every corner was rounded and smooth giving the room a very fluid look and feel. Most of the surfaces were painted in yellows and browns, while the furniture was mostly a bright aquamarine color with some reds and oranges. The floor tile had a slight tinge of sea green color to it and was made up of various sizes arranged without any discernable pattern. There was a wide private balcony off the main living space that overlooked the Mediterranean and all its beauty and tranquility.

Her suitcase was sitting at the foot of the bed. She inspected it carefully and determined it had not been tampered with. Good. When she went to put her clothes away, she noticed the closet was already half full with dresses both casual and formal, ladies' suit pieces, and other clothes and accessories, all from high-end designers. All the items were in her size – she hoped that was mere coincidence, but figured it probably wasn't. Alexei definitely was not frugal in making his guests, or at least her, feel welcome.

She hung her own clothes next to the clothes left for her by her host, and placed the smaller items onto open closet shelves. She left the briefcase of weapons and spy items attached to the inside of the suitcase then slid the luggage under her bed. Next she took a long, hot shower before putting on her nightwear, a two-piece silk pajama set provided by Alexei. She used her phone to send a confirmation message to NPDIA headquarters that she was safely settled in; then, even though the night was still young, got some well-deserved sleep.

■■■■■■■ ● ● ● ■■■■■■■

MARIS rose early the next morning, grabbed a light breakfast consisting mainly of fruit and juices comped by one of the restaurants, and partook in the sunrise yoga session before cleaning up and changing into casual island-influenced attire. The summit wasn't set to start until four o'clock in the afternoon so she did some exploring of the island. A driver was provided by the hotel to show her around and act as a tour guide explaining the history of the island and identifying prominent landmarks and other fascinating points of interest. During her excursion she grabbed a light lunch at a local bistro and frequented some of the local shops on foot, interacting with the islanders and taking in the local culture.

Maris returned to her room with plenty of time to prepare for the summit. She decided to put on one of the dresses provided for her – a long, free-flowing, sleeveless black Gucci dress – instead of one she had brought. Her Glock was nicely concealed underneath via the ankle holster provided in the "standard issue" items briefcase. She decided to keep her hair down, using a curling iron in the bathroom to just slightly curl it at the bottom. Taking great care, she put on the hoop and column earrings given to her by Galaxy. After a final touchup of her makeup, she set herself off to the convention room downstairs, grabbing her summit credential on the way.

● ● ●

THE entire hotel felt like it was in some sort of covert lockdown. The entrance to the lobby was locked, and "hotel attendants" were positioned at every access point. All the summit attendees were already guests of the hotel, so there was no need to allow entrance to anyone else. Nevertheless, the presence of employees at the entry and exit ways ensured no one could enter the premises who was not already invited. Security only increased as Maris approached the convention rooms. She had to show her credential at the entrance to the underwater glass corridor, and again when she reached the end of the corridor. It was incredible overkill in her opinion, but only heightened her expectation of what was to come at the summit.

The summit itself was not held in the largest conference room as there was no need due to the relatively smaller size of the gathering. Maris followed the stream of other attendees to Conference Room 3, and had to have the QR code imprinted on the backside of her credential scanned upon entry.

"Seat number A-17," the man who scanned her code said. "Just about front row center. Have a nice evening."

"Thank you," said Maris, before continuing down a short hallway that opened up into the conference room.

The room wasn't immense, though it was a spacious elliptical shape. The curved walls, ceiling, and floor were all black. Two curved rows of twenty-five seats faced a stage taking up nearly the length of one of the longer sides of the room. The seats themselves were not the generic, ordinary four-legged armless chairs one would normally find in a convention or large dining hall setting. Rather, each stand-mounted chair was a high-backed wraparound racing car style seat manufactured by and embroidered with the Ferrari logo. Three large monitor screens provided a backdrop to the stage itself. Maris thought the room looked more like it was set for some sort of E-gamers' gathering rather than a private convention.

Her seat was easy to find – with row A being the front row and seat 17 being just off-center among its twenty-five seats. As she made her way to her seat she noticed everyone in attendance was dressed to the nines. She was glad she decided to wear something in her room closet over any of the clothes she brought. Once seated, she exchanged pleasant "hellos" with the people seated on either side of her, Embry Beaulieu from Canada on her left and the representative from Australia, a woman named Lisa Willadsen, on her right. As the time ticked down to four o'clock, Maris noticed more "attendants" – a dozen in all – position themselves at the ends of the two rows of seats, near the stage, and other areas around the room.

A small tone pinged through the transmitter hoop in her left ear.

"Scarlett, this is Galaxy." The voice came through clearly even though its source was nearly half a world away. "Clear your throat or cough if you can hear me."

Maris put a hand up in front of her mouth and gently cleared her throat.

"Copy that," Galaxy responded.

A digital timer flashed on the center screen above the stage, starting at sixty seconds and counting backwards. The summit was about to begin. When the timer showed twenty seconds, the lights in the room went off, leaving the only light at that point coming from the glow of the countdown clock on the overhead screen. When the timer reached ten seconds, multiple spotlights began cycling and spinning around the room while a dubstep drumbeat sounded from multiple speakers. The crowd began counting down along with the clock while they clapped in time with the beats. Maris looked around as discreetly as possible as she took in the experience of what was happening in the room. The voices and clapping grew louder and louder until the timer reached zero, when the crowd erupted into a loud cheer as lights flooded the stage and the circulating spotlights all stopped on the lone figure standing in the middle: Alexei Volkov, wearing a silver-sheen suit with black tiger stripes, looking down unmoving with his hands clasped in front of him.

He certainly has a flair for the dramatic, Maris thought.

The crowd jumped to their feet and Maris made certain to follow along. Grinding electric guitars joined the drumbeats, squealing along in a hard rock overture. Alexei came to life and played to the crowd, scooping his arms up again and again to encourage everyone to cheer louder. He moved from one side of the stage to the other, putting a hand up to his ear to keep the audience riled. The spotlights followed him wherever he moved. His big signature smile never left his face. After several prolonged theatrics, the Russian motioned to the people to sit and the music faded away.

"Welcome, everyone!" he called out in English, his voice picked up by a small mic attached to a transmitter wrapped around his ear and broadcast through the room. "Welcome to Pantelleria and hotel *Roskosh'*. Thank you for joining me today for this once in a lifetime summit. You are all here on the cusp of history in the making. I am fortunate to know most of you, although there are some here who have been afforded invitations who previously have not had prominent dealings with us. Many of you are from the world's largest diamond producing countries. But this meeting is not solely about diamonds, as you will see. So let me be sure everyone is up to speed on what exactly this is all about."

Alexei's speech was completely in English. Maris guessed all the attendees must have a shared grasp of the language.

"First, know that if you hear anything today you question on any personal, professional, moral, or ethical level, that is fine, but you cannot explicitly or publicly disagree. What you are about to see and learn here stays here. No one outside of this room is privy to any information presented to you today."

He paused before continuing. His demeanor grew more serious as he continued speaking.

"Now you may wonder, how can you be held to such an agreement? After all, none of you were explicitly approached about signing an NDA at any time. That is true. However, each of you did electronically sign an NDA when you provided your thumb print upon your arrival to this hotel. We spare no time nor expense to get that signed agreement immediately out of the way."

That's a pretty shitty thing to do, Maris thought as she looked around casually trying to get a read on the room. No one questioned the action, at least not outwardly. The payoff Alexei had to offer was certainly to be bigger, Maris figured, than what could be individually gained by going public with what they were about to hear. In addition, the cost of breaking any such agreement may also be beyond what one was willing to pay. She knew from what she had read about him that Alexei could be a ruthless businessperson, among other things.

The large displays behind Alexei came to life, showing the familiar Hexatetron logo of five interlocked circles inside a hexagon. As he continued to speak, the images changed frequently to provide visuals that reinforced the subjects he spoke about. The next images showed many of Hexatetron products before dissolving away to show piles of uncut diamonds.

"As you know, Hexatetron is primarily involved with the design and distribution of various software, file management systems, and firmware. What you may not know, however, is that we are also in the diamond industry, specifically raw diamonds – the uncut spoils of the Earth. Much of this money exchanges hands beyond the scrutinizing eyes of bankers and financiers, let alone nations and their various investigative departments.

"So you may wonder, why? Why is Hexatetron dealing in the underground diamond industry? To put it bluntly, financing can be tricky. Our public products and investments are easily financed and those books maintain a degree of transparency. But there is much more to what Hexatetron is and what we do. For years we have been involved with the diamond trade, procuring money from the industry and stockpiling our resources to fund a, for lack of a better term, a 'project' that is ready to be revealed to the world. And that leads me to all of you."

A map of the world came up on the screens. All but fifty of the countries were in a subdued beige color. Thirty-five of the fifty countries not in beige were colored green, with the remaining fifteen shown in red.

"You are all here because you are in some manner connected with governments, financially or politically, that we are either already involved with or are seeking involvement with. I guarantee that by the time I am finished showing you what I have to offer, you will be raised to prominence in each of your respective countries. You are the leaders of the future. And I don't mean that figuratively, but literally.

"The fifty countries you see in red and green are represented in this room today. Those in green are countries that are already directly involved with our underground diamond trade sales and have already agreed to the opportunity I'm going to offer. The countries in red – those are the countries we need to get involved with to ensure the project goes forward as planned."

The map dissolved to show just the fifteen countries in red, one of which was the United States. Maris began to have an uneasy feeling inside. Alexei stopped speaking and scanned the crowd, as if picking out the fifteen representatives one by one. The final set of eyes he met with were Maris'. She stared back at him with a steadfast determination to show she was focused and unafraid.

"If you see your country in red, I would like you to join me on stage."

The fifteen representatives stood and made their way to the stage. While Maris' apprehension was certainly due to what she had learned from the NPDIA, no one else appeared to be anxious. Everyone appeared to be eager to join the Hexatetron owner as they spared no time rushing onto the stage. They were directed to stand shoulder to shoulder, facing the remaining crowd as Alexei addressed them. Maris was third in line from where Alexei stood, and to her left was Lisa Willadsen, the Australian representative she had been sitting next to.

"Ladies and gentlemen, Hexatetron is more than just a computers and software company. We are certainly more than diamonds. What we are is…Fifth Dimension."

The maps on the displays faded away, leaving a large glowing white dot on the center screen.

"There are races in this world that are beyond human. To those of you seated in this room, this is no surprise. But to those of you on this stage, I am here to enlighten you to the world *beyond* your world, to the world of the Fifth Dimension. As you know, there are four dimensions in physics. It starts with a single dimension, which is a dot or a line. A second dimension comes into play when width is added. Three-dimensional is what we see, that is length and width with the addition of depth."

The dot on the screen stretched into a line, then became a square, and finally a cube as Alexei continued his dissertation. The cube morphed into a standard round clock with numbers one through twelve in a circle in Roman numerals, its two hands spinning quickly as it showed hours rapidly passing.

"The fourth dimension is commonly referred to as time, or space-time. Discussions on space-time could take up an entire convention in and of itself, but I am not here to bore you with that!"

Attendees both seated and on stage chuckled. Maris laughed along as well so as not to stand out.

The image of the clock went away and the Hexatetron logo returned briefly, before the hexagon on the symbol disappeared, leaving just the five interlaced circles. The circles then separated and lined up horizontally.

"So that takes us to the Fifth Dimension, and to why you are here today." He looked at the fifteen representatives on the stage.

The first circle glowed white.

"There are five races beyond human that are collectively known as the Fifth Dimension. I represent one of these races, the Gorgons." No one onstage knew where this was going, but Maris thought she might, and her anxiety grew. She shifted as she stood, brushing one ankle discreetly against her other to feel the gun hidden under her dress. The feeling provided her some, though not total, reassurance.

"Mythology has commonly mistaken Gorgons to simply be Medusa and her sisters, three beings with snakes for hair and the power to turn people into stone. What if I told you, that the Gorgons weren't just three sisters, but a race of people from another dimension – the Fifth Dimension – and we have lived among you for centuries?"

Uneasiness now began to grow among those on the stage. Maris glanced up and down the line of people standing with her. She saw some begin to shift as the disquiet made its way through them.

"For countless lifetimes we have lived in hiding and fear of humans. But we no longer need to live in an oppressed underworld. Humans are frail and weak, while the Gorgons are superior and strong." Alexei's tone grew assertive and more aggressive. He held a fist up to the crowd. "It is time we let ourselves be known to the world. And with your help, we will not only announce ourselves, but we will rule this world together."

The seated representatives applauded. Alexei looked at the line of people on the stage.

"You are here as representatives of your nations to join us. Join the other countries that are ready to fight for us and your rewards will be great! You will not only become the new leaders of your countries, but you will join us as leaders of the new world as the Order of the Gorgons takes over all of humanity!"

Alexei pumped his fist in the air. As he did, the thirty-five representatives on the floor stood and began doing the same, grunting in unison with each pump of their fist.

Alexei focused his attention to the person standing nearest to him on stage, a female representative from China. He grabbed her shoulders and turned her to face him so that she was sideways to the chanting crowd. His eyes turned completely white as he stared into the face of the woman. Maris tore her eyes away, but when she looked out at the crowd, what she saw frightened her in a way she had never experienced. All the thirty-five representatives' eyes had also turned white. She had to fight panic from building within her.

"The question I have for you is simple. Do you pledge you and your country to the Fifth Dimension and the new world? To join our order and see all your worldly desires come true under our rule?"

The Chinese woman nodded briskly. Alexei's eyes remained an opaque white as he stared at her.

"Yes," she said, quietly. Maris couldn't tell if she was speaking out of fear or actual dedication to his cause. Perhaps it was a bit of both. "Yes, I do."

"Louder, dear, for those in the back," Alexei urged.

He turned the woman to face the crowd and he grabbed her hand to have her pump a fist into the air.

"Yes! Yes, I pledge myself to you!" Her voice was loud and strong this time, and Maris had no reason to doubt her sincerity.

Alexei ushered her towards the far end of the stage. "You will not regret this, child! You may take your place in your seat on the floor." The Chinese woman rushed off the stage and joined in chanting with the others, pumping her fist vigorously in the air.

Alexei moved to the next person, a young man from Brazil. The motions were the same: taking the man by the shoulders, turning him to face away from the crowd, the eyes turning white, the questions.

"I do!" the Brazilian man exclaimed immediately with excitement. "I am with you, Alexei!"

Alexei briefly hugged the Brazilian before steering him to take his seat on the floor with the rest of the cult-like attendees.

Maris felt the Russian's hands on her shoulders and she turned to face him. She didn't expect to turn to stone, as the eyes never glowed with the first two representatives and they did not turn to stone. She didn't know, though, if there was some other magical power at play, a hypnosis or something else that was forcing the people to comply with Alexei's requests.

"Scarlett Caso, do you pledge yourself to my race and my cause? Do you pledge the people of the United States on your behalf to join us?"

Despite the absence of pupils, the white eyes cut right through her. But nothing else happened. No overwhelming desire to blindly join. No brainwashing or mind control took over.

"You need to agree, Scarlett." Galaxy's voice came through the earring. "If you don't, you might not make it out of there alive."

"I will join you, Alexei," she said before turning to face the crowd. Then she repeated loudly with her fist in the air, "I will join you!"

Maris had just taken her place back at her seat in the front row when Alexei turned the woman from Australia to face him. She pushed his hands away, unafraid despite the whiteness of his eyes.

"I don't believe this!" the woman exclaimed as the crowd fell silent. "What is this, some red pill, blue pill bullshit?"

The crowd around Maris started to chant again but Alexei raised a hand to silence them. His eyes returned to normal. "Lisa Willadsen, the esteemed representative from Australia." He shot her his signature smile. "I would implore you to rethink your position. This is an opportunity that will not repeat itself."

"There is no way I will be part of this. You and your cult can take the offer somewhere else. I'm not falling for it."

She tried to push her way past Alexei but he grabbed her firmly by her wrists. The Australian struggled as she tried to break free from his iron grip.

"I would implore you to reconsider," he began, his voice calm and smooth while his hold of her remained strong. "For the greater good. And for your sake."

She tried her best to get away but his grip was relentless.

"Let go of me!" She tried pushing and pulling but got nowhere in her attempted escape. "I'm going to make a full report to ASIS. There is no way you're going to get away with this."

Alexei locked eyes with her and his irises and pupils disappeared. The chanting in the room reignited.

"Lisa, Lisa. There's nothing the Australian Secret Intelligence Service can do to stop us. Our momentum is too strong, our reach too great."

His eyes began to glow. The chants developed into a roar among the original thirty-five representatives, almost deafening. Maris joined in to remain inconspicuous but her insides were churning, making her feel like she was going to throw up.

It looked like the Australian was about to exclaim something else in defiance when her body stiffened, and Maris could hear the sickening crack – even through the chants – as the woman turned into a solid statue of herself. Alexei gave the stone figure a solid shove and Lisa Willadsen fell off the stage and shattered against the hard floor. The crowd on the floor cheered while those remaining on stage watched in shock and horror.

"Such a shame," Alexei said. The crowd hushed. "I always thought I could rely on the Australians. But no matter." He looked down the line at the remaining representatives. "I'm suddenly not in the mood for any further theatrics, so let's cut this short, shall we? Anyone else care to not invest yourselves in the cause? If so, let it be known now."

The remaining people on the stage all shook their heads vigorously, not wanting to meet the same fate as the Australian.

"That's excellent news!" Alexei exclaimed. "Return to your seats so we can get on with what is needed. I'm done with the drama for today."

The representatives rushed to their seats.

"We still have much to present and discuss," Alexei continued as he adjusted his tie and straightened his suit. "Our plan is set in three phases. Phase One is to complete raising the funds needed for our organization to see our objectives to fruition. Phase Two will be the announcement of our organization through a global-scale event. I have people in Belgium putting the final touches on that phase together. You will become privy to those specifics as the time draws near. Phase Two will lead us directly into Phase Three, which is the takeover of major governments and financial institutions. By then each of you will be poised to assume the leadership of your respective nations. Rest assured there will be little resistance to this transition."

Alexei surveyed the room. Most of the representatives looked excited, while a few of those newly signed on fought with fear behind their complicity.

"Now, with everyone's allegiance secured, we are ready to commence."

The overhead monitors behind him turned off.

"I have a top financier in Hexatetron here to inform you how your countries will be involved with the established diamond trade moving forward. With so many more countries on board, we will have the funds we need to move onto the next phase in short order…"

The next two hours were taken up with the business and financial aspects involved in Phase One of the Gorgons' plan. Maris listened intently, as did Galaxy from NPDIA headquarters. Once that was complete, Alexei returned for some more grandstanding before the meeting came to its conclusion. They were all invited to a group dinner held in one of the larger conference rooms, where small talk took over among the tables of five that were set up for the guests. Maris found herself seated with representatives from South Korea, Israel, Luxembourg, and Botswana. No one mentioned the death of the Australian.

Maris was able to avoid contact with Alexei for the remainder of the evening, much to her relief, as he appeared to be wrapped up in talking with other Russian Hexatetron officials – or perhaps they were fellow Gorgons. She was eager to leave the island. During dinner, the guests were informed of when and how they would each be departing the island the next day. Some would have flights from the local airport, while others would be leaving on various boats throughout the day. Much to Maris' chagrin, she learned she would be taking the *Almaznyy Glaz* back to Sicily early the next morning.

Of course, she thought.

Once dinner was complete, everyone retreated to their rooms. Maris had barely made it into hers when a voice came through the transmitter from her earring.

"That was informative," Galaxy said without any precursor.

"You can say that again," Maris responded. She felt drained even though all she essentially did was attend a meeting. She took her heels off and lay back on her bed.

"After you return to Sicily tomorrow, you'll immediately head to your next destination. We've already got the travel arrangements worked out. Agent Vector will update you on all the trivialities."

"Where am I going?" Maris asked, though she already had a suspicion.

"You're going to Belgium."

■■■ • • • ■■■

WITH dinner complete and the residents having all retreated to their rooms, Alexei returned to the convention room where the summit took place. The room was dark, save for a few white stage lights. Alexei stood in front of the stage among the Australian's broken stony remains. He hadn't yet ordered them to be disposed of, preferring to leave them there during the remainder of the meeting as a reminder to the rest of the attendees of the fate that awaited any other naysayers. He reached down and picked up the woman's petrified head and stared into her lifeless eyes. Alexei had really hoped everyone was on board with the plan, but a single casualty would do little to derail his efforts.

He looked at his Rolex watch. It was almost midnight. Even for him, it had been a long day and he, too, was looking forward to getting rest. But there was one final matter to take care of.

Footsteps sounded in the dark in front of him. A large burly Russian with pockmarked skin stepped into the light reflecting from the stage. He wore a tightly-fitting maroon satin suit with white shirt sans tie. An intricate swirling tattoo went from one ear to the other, covering the lower back half of his shaved head.

"Thank you for meeting me, Viktor," Alexei said in their native Russian.

The big man gave a single nod but said nothing.

"I know it is late and it's been a long day for both of us, but there is a mission I need to communicate to you involving the American woman."

Viktor's eyes narrowed as he looked down on Alexei. Even though Alexei was just over six feet tall, he was dwarfed by the size of his comrade.

"*I want her dead, but not here. I don't want any suspicions connected with the hotel. She'll be returning to Sicily in the morning aboard my private yacht. Wait until she gets back to the main island. I want her far from here.*"

Viktor listened intently.

"*I don't care how it is done. But I want proof. There shall be no rest until I know she is properly disposed of. Is that understood?*"

The big man nodded.

"*I have always been able to rely on you, Viktor. You are the best man for this job. Do not let me down.*"

Viktor reached forward and took the stone head of the Australian out of Alexei's grasp. With his bare hands, he squeezed the head until it was obliterated into dust and pebbles, exploding from the sheer pressure from the large man.

Alexei smiled. He was certain Viktor would get the job done.

12

SICILY

THE uneasiness Maris experienced at the summit stuck with her the entire trip back to Sicily. And she couldn't shake the feeling that she was being watched. She suspected all the guests were being watched in some fashion, and probably would continue to be, at least until the Gorgons released their master plan upon the world. For her personally, it may have been the way the bartender on the yacht gave her the same looks that she did on the trip over – the sideways smile, the overcompensating of niceties. No matter. She kept to herself below deck and didn't do anything to raise any suspicions. Other summit attendees who were also on the boat left her alone, preferring to spend their journey at the bar and on the upper deck. She didn't blame them as it was another beautiful day of endless blue skies and pristine waters.

The only call she made was to Agent Vector when they were about an hour out from the big island. Once the *Almaznyy Glaz* docked, she couldn't get off the boat fast enough. She debarked coolly, though, wearing a yellow double-breasted pantsuit and flats, so as to not draw suspicion. Vector met her in the same car at the same roadside stop in the upper town area where he had dropped her off. He courteously opened the passenger door of the silver Alfa Romeo Giulia for her and then put her rolling luggage into the trunk. She held on to her wicker handbag. He slid into the driver's seat and drove away from the marina.

"I heard the summit was quite enlightening," Vector said in his usual dry manner.

"That's an understatement," Maris replied succinctly, knowing better than to try and respond in a way as to actually illicit some semblance of a real conversation.

Maris could feel the car accelerating quickly. She hadn't noticed the speed limits, but she was sure Vector wasn't paying any attention to them. The four-lane highway wasn't crowded this time of day, with cars in the two oncoming lanes passing only occasionally. Traffic flowing the same direction was also relatively sparse, with Vector smoothly weaving in and out of vehicles that got in the way. There was rarely a center barrier separating the opposing traffic lanes; rather, much of the time there was just a flat grated median that could easily allow a car to move into the oncoming flow. Maris was certain a few times that Vector was going to use that tactic when skirting other vehicles, but to her relief he never did.

To her surprise, Vector continued with their dialogue. "The Gorgons seem to be on the cusp of something big."

"World domination is more like it."

"We've dealt with them before," Vector said soberly. "We'll deal with them again."

Maris looked at the other agent curiously. She wondered what tales he could tell about past encounters but decided to keep conversation focused on the present.

"I don't know what type of reach they had in the past," Maris said, "but I think whatever they have planned this time is on a grander scale than anything they've done before. We're talking a global scale event of some sort."

"That's for you to find out, isn't it?"

Maris wondered if Agent Vector already knew everything she did from the summit. But as long as she wasn't being kept in the dark about anything that could benefit her mission, it didn't matter to her what he knew.

"I've got you booked on the next flight out of here to Brussels," he told her. "It leaves in just a few hours. We'll have a car reserved for you at the airport when you land." He glanced over at her. "Local rental. *Not* a company car." His eyes went back to the road. "You'll head into Antwerp's diamond district and pay a visit to Romilly & Ackerman, one of the world's premier diamond cutters. The facility is operated by a man named Xavier Dumont. Rumor has it he is a personal friend of Alexei Volkov's." Vector paused. "Alexei freely admitted Hexatetron's involvement in the blood diamond industry at yesterday's summit, along with announcing he has people in Belgium working on Phase Two of the Gorgon's plan. We figure Romilly & Ackerman is a good place to start poking around for answers."

Maris shook her head a little. "I can't just go waltzing into that place. If they are in fact connected to Alexei and Hexatetron, it won't take much for them to realize I was one of the people inducted on Pantelleria."

"You won't be going as yourself. There's a box for you in the glove compartment."

Maris opened the compartment and pulled out a black box. She opened the box and inside was a passport, credit card, two driver's licenses – one from Florida and an International Driving License, some makeup…and a choppy pixie cut black wig. She looked at the licenses then picked up the passport. The picture of the woman on the licenses and inside the passport was her, but with the black wig superimposed in place of her own hair. Her complexion in the photo was also much more fair compared to her own, and her eyeshadow was so thick it was almost raccoon-like. The name caught her attention next.

"Brandi Schiffer?"

"Fictional American diamond buyer out of Beverly Hills. We've arranged a meeting between you and Dumont tomorrow morning. He'll be expecting you."

"I'm used to the spy game," Maris said as she studied the box's contents. "But this look'll be a first for me."

"You don't like it?" The fact that Vector even asked her about it surprised her.

"I definitely don't hate it." She chuckled as she admired the passport photo. "Doesn't look like I'll have any trouble pulling it off."

She took the wig out of the box and studied it, thinking about how she would embody Brandi Schiffer. She set it back down and looked around the car.

"So do I get to learn more about this car yet?"

Vector looked mildly annoyed. "This vehicle isn't your concern. It's just your transport to and from the airport. Nothing more."

"But there *is* more to tell," Maris stated, much more than questioned.

"Stick to what you need to know. That's how these missions work."

Now it was Maris who was mildly annoyed. "So for all the talk about how hi-tech and advanced this agency is, all I get is some fancy earrings and a do-it-yourself emo kit?"

Vector grew more serious. "The tools match the job, Agent Scarlett. Your mission here is to gather information. The tools you've been provided support that mission."

"And what about you and your super-secret car?"

"My mission is to protect you. My tools support that mission."

Maris gave up. She returned the passport to the box and closed the lid, then put the box back into the glove compartment.

Vector changed the subject. "You'll find your flight information and all itinerary details have already loaded onto your phone. You should spend some time studying up on Romilly & Ackerman before we get to the airport."

Maris sensed the finality in Vector's statement. "Sure," she said as she took the phone out of her handbag and unlocked the screen. An NPDIA application indicator flashed on her home screen indicating the itinerary was downloaded. Opening it, she was provided a link to references on Romilly & Ackerman and Xavier Dumont.

Vector drove the Alfa Romeo along the A29 road through the Sicilian countryside, past the villages of Fulgatore and Ummari until they reached the E90 highway. Traffic increased some around the towns, but never backed up, and nothing slowed Vector's tenacity for breaking any speed laws. They were lucky to have not gotten pulled over. Maris studied quietly for nearly an hour as they cruised along. Not only did she read up on the diamond manufacturing company and its operator, but she also spent time memorizing details about Quintz & Deloitte, the fictional diamond buying company fabricated by the NPDIA that Brandi Schiffer represented. They had just passed the town of Terrasini when she locked her phone and attempted to strike up conversation once again.

"At the summit, Alexei mentioned something called the Fifth Dimension."

Vector looked at her for a moment.

"What did he say?" he asked. His curiosity seemed to be piqued. Perhaps Galaxy hadn't said anything about this in her briefing with him.

"Not a whole lot, just that there were five races collectively known as the Fifth Dimension. He said the Gorgons were one of those. What about the other four? What do we know about them?"

Vector shook his head. "Unfortunately not much."

"What do *you* know?"

Vector didn't answer.

"Come on. You can't keep all these secrets from me. Don't tell me about the car but tell me about this. Alexei brought it up. I have the right to know what I'm up against."

"I don't know much," Vector finally said. "Can't speak for the agency."

"Then just speak for yourself."

Vector sighed. "I know about the Gorgons, obviously, and yes, they are part of something called the Fifth Dimension."

"Alexei had attendees at the summit pledge themselves to the Fifth Dimension, but he never provided any details on anyone else involved."

"The Gorgons are a very self-serving and headstrong race. It makes me wonder if their relationship with the others is more precarious than they would have us believe."

"Maybe we can use that to our advantage."

"Except that we don't know much about the others. To my knowledge, our interactions with any of the others has been pretty minimal."

"So you're kept in the dark on some of these matters as well?"

"Like I've been telling you, we stay focused on what we need to know. But in this case I'm convinced there isn't much to tell. I've heard rumors about some group out of Mexico. Deities or something or other. I couldn't tell you much, though."

"Mexican deities?"

"I truly don't know anything about them. It's all very secretive."

Maris looked down while shaking her head. "This is all crazy. I mean, how are we supposed to –"

Maris' was cut off as their car was suddenly sprayed with bullets. The clanging and pinging of steel deflecting off the car sounded through the cabin as the bulletproofing of the exterior and windows held true. An alarm immediately sounded inside the vehicle. Maris saw two Maserati GranTurismos – one red, one black – keeping pace with them. The red one was on their driver's side while the other was in the rear. Each car had two men inside, with each of the passengers leaning out their windows and blasting machine guns at the silver NPDIA Alfa Romeo. There were no other cars around on their side of the highway at the moment. Vector accelerated and employed a weaving pattern to try and make them a harder target to hit.

"We have company," Vector announced. "You must've upset someone back on the island."

"Not that I know of," she retorted.

Maris tried to identify anyone in either of the pursuing vehicles but didn't recognize any of them. While three of the men between the two Maseratis looked rather nondescript – relatively thin, clean cut, dark hair, and wearing simple dress shirts – the driver of the red car next to them was a large, gruff-looking bald man with a tattoo that wrapped around the back of his head.

Maris reached down and retrieved her Glock from its ankle holster.

"You shouldn't need that," Vector said to her.

Despite the advice, Maris made sure the weapon was loaded and the safeties were all off.

Vector tapped the dashboard touchscreen and the GPS menu was replaced with an overhead diagnostic of the car. A green line ran around the outside of the car, indicating no damage had occurred to the vehicle. Yet, anyway.

"Hold on tight, Agent Scarlett," said Vector in a calm voice. "Be sure you're strapped in."

Vector jammed on the accelerator and the engine whirred like a jet as the car rocketed forward. The NPDIA issued Alfa Romeo GTA was obviously modified to operate at a much higher performance level than any standard version. Cars on their side of the freeway looked like motionless blurs as they sped past. The agent glanced into his rearview mirror while Maris looked back.

The Maseratis maintained their pace closely behind. The gunmen had retreated into their vehicles and the three cars raced along the Sicilian countryside.

"I don't think you're going to outrun them," Maris said.

Maris watched as the black Maserati moved ahead of its counterpart. She thought maybe its plan was to get close enough to bump them or otherwise force them off the road, when something unexpected happened. The black grate on the front of the car folded down. Unsure of what she was seeing, she focused on what the dropped grate revealed: the nose cones of six small missiles.

"I *really* don't think you're going to outrun them!" Maris sounded a bit frantic.

Vector tapped the back end of the car on the touchscreen and the rear spoiler on the display began to flash. A new alarm sounded and an alert on the screen shone in large red letters: INCOMING LOCKED ON.

Missiles fired from the front of the black Maserati in rapid succession. Not just two or three, but all six.

"Vector …"

The agent driving pressed the flashing rear spoiler on the touchscreen a second time.

Maris looked on, astonished, as the rear spoiler launched off the back of the Alfa Romeo and erupted into a spinning fiery target in the air between them and their pursuers. The heat-seeking missiles all honed in on their new target, exploding all near simultaneously in the conflagration of the swirling blazing countermeasures. The Maseratis themselves blasted through the disintegrating embers and continued their high speed pursuit.

"Holy shit," Maris uttered. She looked back at Vector. "If you have any other surprises, you better come up with them now."

The man didn't acknowledge her and instead remained focused on his driving. Traffic was beginning to increase and he had to let up on the speed as he led their attackers further along the highway. In a sudden move that caught Maris by surprise, Vector jerked the car hard to the left and tore across the grated median and into oncoming traffic. Oncoming vehicles blared their horns as they skewed and dashed in different directions. Maris braced herself, thinking she might have pulled a similar maneuver, but it was different being a helpless passenger rather than the one in control. She looked back over her shoulder to find, to her vexation, the Maseratis had followed them.

"I don't think this is working," she announced.

Maris looked forward again as Vector followed the highway through a bend in the road. Up ahead was another surprise: a tunnel tearing through a large hill in the Sicilian countryside. She remembered going through a couple of such tunnels on their way to Trapani, but had forgotten about them until now.

"There's no avoiding oncoming traffic if we go in there!"

"Tell me something I don't know," Vector snapped back.

The car whipped back across the median and onto their side of traffic, which only marginally made Maris feel better since their pursuers easily followed. The entrance to the tunnel grew closer at a frantic speed.

Maris held up her gun. "Can you open any windows? I can shoot back!"

"The windows don't open." Vector pushed the car even faster as they approached the tunnel. "Don't worry, I have some other surprises."

The Alfa Romeo slipped past three other vehicles then sped into the tunnel. Darkness enveloped them within seconds. Four rows of lights brightened the rounded tunnel – two overhead that ran parallel, along with one row on each of the side walls near the road. Vector turned on their headlights. Even though the tunnel wasn't extremely long, its end wasn't in sight yet. He put his attention again onto the diagnostic display on the touchscreen and pressed the areas of the rear passenger and driver side doors.

The lower rear door panels of the speeding silver NPDIA-issued vehicle slid out six inches away from the body of the car, while their adjoining windows remained in place. Maris looked at the diagnostic on the screen. The word ARMED flashed vertically over each of the rear doors on the display. The diagnostic on the touchscreen shrunk down to the lower left corner of the display, while the Alfa Romeo's back-up camera displayed a real-time image of the cars chasing them. A target and crosshairs appeared on the image and began tracking around the display as it tried to lock in on their pursuers.

Vector gently steered the car back and forth as the crosshairs moved smoothly on the screen. In just a matter of moments the crosshairs zeroed in on the front of the black Maserati. The weaponry flashed and the word LOCKED appeared on the screen. Vector pressed the small diagnostic image in the corner of the screen.

Two missiles, one from each of the rear doors protruding from the car, shot backwards from the Alfa Romeo and exploded into the front of the black Maserati, causing it to erupt into a fireball, disintegrating the vehicle. The tunnel shuddered as it was lit up by the explosion, and the sound from the eruption echoed like thunder. The red Maserati swerved to avoid getting caught in the inferno and quickly slid in behind the Alfa Romeo as it continued pursuit.

Vector pressed the button on the screen again and the crosshairs honed in on the red car. Again the display showed LOCKED. Another press of a button and two more missiles fired away.

The red Maserati had its own countermeasures, however, as red laser lights shot out from emitters next to each headlight and created a fan of lasers that moved rapidly back and forth in front of the car. The two missiles hit the red electrical fields generated by the Maserati and exploded harmlessly in the air, doing nothing more than raining shrapnel onto their pursuer.

Emptied, the side missile launchers withdrew into the frame of the car.

"Got any more tricks?" Maris asked.

"I'm working on it," Vector replied.

The red car pulled up next to them on the driver's side, sideswiping them and forcing the Alfa Romeo against the tunnel wall. Sparks flew and steel screeched as their car scraped along the passageway. Maris watched as her side view mirror was torn away. Vector struggled with the car, pushing the engine to its limit as the Alfa Romeo forced itself away from the wall, in turn causing the Maserati to scrape against the tunnel on its own driver's side. The two cars went back and forth, slamming against the tunnel walls several times before finally speeding through the end of the tunnel and back out onto open road.

Maris felt helpless. She still held her Glock and wished there was a way she could use it. Hopefully, Vector had something else planned.

The Maserati sped up until it was about half a car length ahead of them. At first, Maris wasn't sure what the other car was doing, until she saw a panel open near the trunk on the rear passenger side of the red car. A large barrel with the point of a thick spike protruding from it locked into place, aimed at their Alfa Romeo.

Maris barely uttered the words "Look out –" when the spike fired.

She immediately realized this was no mere spike. The object

trailed a cable as it punctured their driver's door – and through Vector's left leg. The man screamed in pain, yet somehow managed to maintain control of their vehicle. But then the end of the spike opened, revealing itself as a grappling hook. The grapnel yanked back hard, pinning Vector's leg against the driver's door. Maris reached over and grabbed hold of the steering wheel as the hook tore away the driver's side door out into the open road – and the man she knew as Agent Vector along with it. The door, with the NPDIA agent stuck to it, struck the ground behind the speeding cars as the cable released. The agent and the door tumbled countless times against the concrete before coming to a stop.

Maris scrambled into the driver's seat as the wind from the open door whipped through the cabin of the damaged car. She was thankful the car was an automatic, as it allowed her to keep hold of her gun while she took control of the vehicle. Glancing over at the Maserati, she saw the passenger level his machine gun at her through his open window.

Maris pressed on the brakes hard, not quite slamming on them as she was not belted in and didn't want to send herself flying through the windshield. The Maserati sped ahead. Maris pressed on the gas, not wanting any cars that may be further behind to come up too quickly, and rapidly caught up to her attacker. The passenger in the red car leaned out, pointing his large gun back at her. Bullets spat and sputtered harmlessly away against the bulletproof windshield. Maris took her gun by her left hand. Although she was right handed, she had proven herself to be a solid shot as well with her left. She put her Glock out the driver's side opening and fired two bullets. The first missed, but the second shot struck the assailant's forehead. The man collapsed back into his car as the machine gun clattered away onto the road.

Putting the accelerator to the floor, Maris crashed her car into the back of the red GranTurismo, pushing it forward. The driver seemed unfazed by the action as he kept control of the Maserati, jerking the car into the right lane, and then braking to let Maris fly past. Once again, Maris became the hunted, and she pressed on, trying to think of what to do next as they sped past other unsuspecting travelers on the highway.

With everything happening so quickly, Maris didn't notice the alert that had been sounding from the touchscreen display. The diagnostic showed red where the driver's side door was and the words HULL COMPROMISED flashed at the bottom of the screen. She wondered, though, if anything else still worked. She quickly hit the safety on her Glock and lodged it partway under her right leg to free up both hands. Wanting to see what sort of weaponry may still be at her disposal, while not knowing what to expect, she touched the display where the passenger seat was located. It flashed the word READY.

Maris held her breath and pressed the screen a second time, hoping for the best. Instead of a weapon, however, the roof of the car blew off over the passenger side seat, then the seat itself ejected up and out of the vehicle. She watched both the roof and seat in her rearview mirror as they landed on the ground far behind her pursuer. She exhaled as she was glad she didn't try to experiment with the driver's side seat.

Dammit! If Vector only would have given me the rundown of what this car could do.

The wind in the car was worse than ever, with not only the driver's door missing but now also from the opening in the roof. She kept an eye on her pursuer in her rearview mirror, and then exactly what she didn't want to happen happened.

The front grill of the red car dropped, exposing its six missiles.

Maris was certain the car's bulletproofing wouldn't hold up against those. Two of the missiles fired. The now familiar alarm sounded – still audible over the sound of the wind – and the INCOMING LOCKED ON display flashed on the touchscreen. A highway exit presented itself almost immediately, and Maris swerved onto it. The missiles didn't track the quick maneuver and sped on, exploding harmlessly against a large street sign in the distance.

Maris hoped her unexpected exit was quick enough to cause the Maserati to bypass the side street, but there was no such luck as the red car followed. Maris veered the car left to right and back again as much as possible to hopefully prevent any more missiles from locking on. The car alarm was sounding again, the wind continued to whip, the engine screamed as it pressed on, and the car's tires were screeching against the pavement.

To Maris' relief, this road was more barren of other drivers. They were on a short straightaway where two more missiles were launched. Luck was again on her side as the road turned into a roundabout. Maris tore into the traffic circle and the missiles impacted against a group of nearby trees. She kept the car screeching and squealing as it sped around the circular drive. The other car entered the circle and the two cars remained directly across from each other as they went around in circles. The roundabout wasn't very large, and Maris got a good view of the baldheaded driver. She grabbed her gun, released the safety, and fired – not a bullet, but a beam of red energy.

The laser-like pulse missed her target. Maintaining control of a vehicle while trying to aim and fire a weapon she wasn't entirely familiar with wasn't easy. She fired again. The red stream flashed across the hood of the Maserati, just in front of the windshield. She did her best to steady her hand, and fired a third time.

The crimson lightning struck the car and the Maserati immediately careened out of control, flying straight off the road and into the burning oasis of trees where the missiles had struck moments before. The car barreled into the mini inferno and exploded.

Maris stopped her car. With the wind no longer blasting in her ears, the sound of her pounding heart took over. She steadied her breathing, collecting herself. Her yellow suit was brandished with dust and dirt and her hair was a huge mess hanging in front of her face. She pulled her hair back and quickly tied it into a loose knot upon itself while she watched the Maserati burn.

A bulky shadow lumbered out of the flames, smoky and smoldering. It was the driver. Being silhouetted against the fire behind him, Maris couldn't make out his features to tell how injured he may have been. He was hobbling a bit, that much she knew. Gunshots rang in her direction from a handgun he carried, hitting parts of the car but missing her. She pressed the gas and sped away, leaving her unknown assailant amidst the burning rubble of his red Maserati.

■■■■■ • • • ■■■■■

THE Alfa Romeo limped into the valet drive of Palermo International Airport. All eyes were on the car that was missing its driver's door, scratched all up and down both sides, had part of its roof blown off, was missing its front passenger seat and side view mirror, and was scarred and dented with failed bullet holes. Miraculously, the trunk still popped open when Maris released it. She grabbed the black box from the glove compartment before exiting the car, then handed the car key fob to the young Italian valet that rushed up to greet her.

"Take good care of her, will you?" she said to the valet as she stepped out of the car.

The valet nodded, confused.

Maris retrieved her luggage from the trunk then entered the airport through its sliding glass doors. She had a flight to Belgium to catch.

13

BELGIUM

BEFORE boarding her plane at the Palermo airport, Maris entered the restroom and commenced her transformation into Brandi Schiffer. She washed up, changed into clean clothes, put on the wig, and did her makeup to match the digitally created images of Brandi that had been downloaded into her phone. When she emerged, very few would have recognized the former Maris Correa – or Scarlett Caso.

Also prior to leaving Sicily, Maris contacted Galaxy and asked to get a company car while in Belgium since she did not feel safe with a local rental. Galaxy denied her request, telling her the trip to Belgium came together too quickly to secure a private vehicle in time. Maris didn't like it, but had no other choice other than to accept it.

It was early evening when Maris landed in Brussels. She picked up her rental car – a very unglamorous and ordinary light blue colored Renault Twingo. Looking at the small, bulbous, 4-door hatchback – built very much more for practicality and economy than for sport or performance – Maris hoped she wouldn't need it to save herself in a pinch. If so, she was certain she'd be as good as dead. Before leaving for Antwerp (where her hotel was booked), she made a stop at a local shopping district and purchased some new clothes with the credit card Agent Vector gave her. The lighter, more tropical flair Scarlett Caso donned in Italy wasn't as fitting for the darker Brandi Schiffer. She needed to be better outfitted for her meeting the next morning with Xavier Dumont.

Maris checked into Hotel Rubens, in Antwerp's Grote Markt, which was situated in the heart of the old city quarter, just a few minutes' drive from the diamond district. Located just off the Scheldt

River, the area was filled with numerous elaborate 16th century guildhalls, along with many restaurants and cafes. The hotel, located on Oude Beurs 29 road, was built into a series of connected buildings whose designs complemented the 16th century architecture of the town square. Maris was glad to discover the hotel had its own parking, even though the reserved stalls were on a separate property a short walk away.

The room was quite appropriate for Brandi Schiffer, with dark wood floors, black furniture, gray walls, and black and white wallpaper behind the bed. Otherwise, the room was rather ordinary: there was a king-sized bed, a small table with two chairs, credenza, and bath area. It had been a long day and Maris was preparing to place an order for room service when her smartphone pinged a notification. It was a text from the NPDIA: YOU HAVE A RESERVATION FOR DINNER AT BISTRO 't HOFKE IN ONE HOUR. YOU WILL NOT BE SURVEILLED.

Maris had hoped to relax for the evening, but apparently the agency had other plans. Based on how information had been communicated to her so far during this mission, she assumed everything she needed to know was in the text. A quick GPS search for the restaurant showed it was about a ten minute drive away from the hotel. Accounting for the time it would take to walk to her car then drive to the restaurant, she would have a little over half an hour to get ready. She took a quick shower and dressed in some of her new "Brandi" clothes – a mid-thigh length black dress with stitched-on black vertical stripes, flowy lacy sleeves, and a neckline that met with an attached black collar. The outfit was completed by her short-cut black jacket – to hide the shoulder holster and Glock – and thick 3-inch high black heels. The wig and makeup made her good to go.

She took her smartphone but skipped wearing the transmitter/communicator earrings the agency provided her as the text had stated the NPDIA would not be listening in. She was a bit skeptical of the agency not surveilling the meeting, though she didn't entirely mind, as she wanted to know she was being trusted for this inaugural mission – a feeling she hadn't yet fully experienced. In any event, in this instance, the earrings would do no good so there was no point in wearing them.

Bistro 't Hofke was located in the oldest alley in Antwerp, called *de Vlaeykensgang*, in the middle of the city. The restaurant was not only unique, but considered by many to be idyllic and charming. Tucked away in a courtyard surrounded by old buildings, the bistro was cut off from the crowds and noise of the city. The place had a life of its own, breathing an old atmosphere while providing a menu filled with European tastes.

While Belgium had three official languages – Dutch, French, and German – nearly everyone spoke English to communicate between the varied dialects. The dull noise of the busy restaurant included not only the official languages, but spatterings of Italian and Spanish. The restaurant was bustling and Maris was happy to have a reservation. She approached the host stand and was about to introduce herself when the smiling maître d interrupted her.

"Ms. Schiffer, thank you for joining us this evening," the woman said in English, her Dutch accent coming through. "Your guest is waiting."

My guest? Maris thought, though she nodded in affirmation without revealing her surprise.

The hostess showed Maris to the open courtyard of the outdoor dining space. Tall brick walls provided a private ambiance, even with a dozen or so tables in the area. Lights dangling on strings overhead bathed the area in a warm yellow hue. Thigh-high brick planters with large green leafy plants were built into parts of the walls. One of the planters even had a tree that stretched up to the open sky above. Maris and her hostess crossed the cobblestone courtyard and stopped at a table for two against the far wall. The table and chairs were made of wooden slats, and the tabletop itself was covered in a maroon cloth.

The Englishwoman seated at the table wore a dark gray cutaway blazer and slacks, with a simple white pullover top. Her dark brown hair, short and choppy and cut over the ears, was parted on one side.

She looked up at Maris as she approached, her bangs flirting with her long eyelashes whenever she blinked.

"Your table, Ms. Schiffer," the hostess said.

"Thank you," said Maris, as she settled into the chair across from the woman.

"Your server will be right with you." The hostess gave the women a final smile before leaving.

"My name's Elsie Byrne," said the Englishwoman. "Glad to meet you."

"Mine's Schiffer, Brandi Schi –"

The Englishwoman cut her off with a dismissive wave and a smile. "I know who you are. Maris Correa, codenamed Scarlett. Former CIA now special agent with the NPDIA."

Maris' eyes grew wide. She glanced around at the surrounding restaurant patrons. No one seemed to be paying attention to them as they immersed themselves in food and private conversation.

"Don't worry," Elsie reassured. "This place has been screened and cleaned."

Maris was familiar with the term, which meant the place had been determined to be a safe place to speak openly without fear of unwanted ears overhearing their conversation.

"So who are *you* with?" Maris asked. "You're obviously affiliated with someone of importance."

"I was formerly MI6. I was recruited a number of years ago into SISX."

"SISX?"

"Secret Intelligence Service, X-division. British equivalent of your NPDIA. You must have known that you're not alone in this fight."

"It was mentioned to me, yes. I just wasn't advised I'd meet up with someone from another agency on this trip."

A waitress came to their table and asked for their drink orders. Elsie spoke up before Maris had the chance.

"I'll have a vodka gimlet. My friend will have a Four Roses bourbon over two cubes."

The waitress acknowledged the order and left.

Maris chuckled. "You'd think by now I'd be used to people I don't know knowing things about me." She shook her head. "But it still catches me by surprise."

"Your drink preference is just the tip of what I know."

Maris locked her eyes on Elsie's. "So then I insist we level this playing field." The levity evaporated as her look turned serious. "Tell me more about *you*."

"I'm thirty-five years old, not much older than you. My background is similar to yours, although I wasn't quite the child genius you were. I'm a career intelligence agency person. Joined MI6 when I was twenty-two and remained with them for eight years before I was recruited into SISX."

"Then Elsie Byrne is your codename?"

Elsie shook her head as she laughed. "You Americans and your codenames. We don't have codenames in SISX. We are who we are. Even though we deal with secret organizations, the public believes we're simply an offshoot of MI6, dealing with similar foreign intelligence issues, which I suppose, to a certain extent, is true."

"Have you been in the field the entire time you've been with SISX?"

Elsie nodded. "I've seen a lot of crazy shit over the years. My latest mission brought me right here."

Maris eyed the Englishwoman with a bit of suspicion as she studied her features. Her chiseled cheekbones underlined hardened eyes that rivaled the toughest agents she had ever known, male or female. "And what's your latest mission?"

"We've had our eye on Alexei Volkov for some time. We weren't able to secure an invite to the Pantelleria summit, but our intelligence uncovered a connection between Hexatetron and Romilly & Ackerman."

Maris sat back as she interrupted. "And I'm supposed to believe it's a coincidence that you're here the same time I am? I'm not a fool, Agent Byrne."

"It's *Commander* Byrne, if you're being formal," the SISX agent corrected. "But call me Elsie, Maris." Her features seemed to soften a bit with this assertion.

"Scarlett," Maris corrected with her own assertion. "If we're being formal."

Their waitress returned, set their drinks on the table, and asked for their dinner order. Maris waved her off, informing her they weren't yet ready to order. She took a sip of her bourbon and refocused on the SISX agent.

"I believe you were going to tell me about your latest mission?" Maris prompted.

"We believe something big is in the works. Something that will position Volkov and the Gorgons for some sort of dominance."

Okay, Maris thought, *so she knows about the Gorgons.*

Elsie took a taste of her drink. "I'm here to try and find out what. I've been assigned to assist you at the meeting tomorrow. Hopefully between us we can gather useful information for both our agencies."

Maris averted her eyes from the Englishwoman, frustrated. "You've been assigned to assist? By whom? Are our agencies working together on this?"

"To a degree. Our agencies share some information, but there's no guarantee that we're both privy to the same data at any time. SISX found out about your meeting and coordinated having me there. Just like that."

Maris rolled her eyes. "I feel like I'm being coddled. I can hold my own, thank you very much."

Elsie set her drink down. "Look, it's your first mission. I get it. But no one is coddling you. This mission isn't about you, it's about the future of the human race. The stakes are much higher. You'd be a damn fool to think you can take this on alone."

"I may not have dealt with worse, but I always find a way to manage." Maris took another drink. "The fact that I'm here alive in front of you is proof of that." She set her drink on the table, her hand still cradling the side of the glass.

"I'm sorry if you believe you alone should bear the burden of this mission. But this is a global situation. You should welcome all the assistance you're provided."

Elsie leaned forward, her hand brushing against the hand Maris was using to hold her glass of bourbon. Maris looked down at their hands then up at the English agent. Elsie was looking intently at her.

"You're fiercely independent, Scarlett." Elsie paused. "I like that."

Maris pulled her hand away from the glass and off the table. "What you already know about me is all you're going to know, Elsie. I don't mix business with my personal life."

"Fair enough," Elsie said, trying to come off satisfied. "You're gonna find this life to be a lonely one, though. Any pressures the CIA put on you were nothing compared to life in the NPDIA and fighting this secret war."

Maris picked up her menu. "We should decide on dinner."

When the waitress returned, Maris ordered the salmon with herb crust and vegetables, while Elsie ordered filet stroganoff and potatoes. During dinner, another round of drinks was ordered, and the mood lightened as conversation turned to college stories and early days in their respective CIA and MI6 agencies. The more stories they shared, the more Maris realized that Elsie was correct when she stated their backgrounds weren't too different. Throughout the conversation, though, Maris was mindful to not provide anything too personal that could potentially be used against her later. She kept her stories borderline superficial, telling just enough to be truthful without giving all the in-depth details.

Eventually, as dinner was winding down, the conversation circled back to the task at hand, and their meeting the next morning.

"Does SISX have any dirt on Xavier Dumont?" Maris asked. "Anything you'd like to share?"

"He's a pretty private person, not near the flair and flamboyancy of Alexei Volkov."

Maris took the final bite of her salmon. "That shouldn't be hard to say. Volkov is quite theatrical."

Elsie nodded and finished her stroganoff before continuing. "Dumont was born in a relatively small coastal town on the North Sea about an hour and a half from here called De Haan. His French father left the family while he was still an infant and he was raised by his German mother and other members of her family. Part of his family on his father's side is South African. Had a distant uncle who was actually part of the diamond rush in South Africa in the late 1800's. The family maintained their diamond industry connections for decades, though recent generations found other interests. Dumont harbored an interest in fine jewelry, though, and reignited the family's involvement in the diamond industry as he worked his way up through operations at Romilly & Ackerman."

"I'm waiting for something I don't know," Maris said, only partly in jest. Throughout the evening Elsie had come off as a straight-shooter, and gave no indication that she wasn't anything but trustworthy. But Maris knew to be careful of new acquaintances. In Maris' world, to a large degree, trust needed to be earned.

"How about this?" Elsie leaned in. "Not only are Dumont and Volkov good friends, but beyond that, did you know Romilly & Ackerman holds a large interest in Hexatetron?"

Maris raised an eyebrow. "Well, that's interesting."

"When Hexatetron was a startup, Volkov drew in the diamond company to help with initial funding. It's primarily diamond money that got the tech giant going."

"At the summit on Pantelleria, Volkov said something about Hexatetron taking money from the underground diamond trade to fund the Gorgon's operations."

"It's all blood money, or more precisely, *blood diamond* money. People are dying in small villages in Africa, being forced by local gangs to work the diamond mines. Those diamonds are being sold on the black market and that money is going directly to the Gorgons."

"Is Xavier Dumont a Gorgon?"

"From what we know about his background and family, we're as certain as we can be that he is human. We honestly don't have any reason to believe otherwise. Probably working with the Gorgons in hopes to be spared when their war goes public."

"From what I can tell about Volkov, I don't anticipate any humans being spared. I'm guessing there will be casualties among their ranks if the Gorgons win."

"Then for his sake, Dumont better hope we win."

"I'll drink to that," Maris said as she held up her bourbon. The two clinked their glasses together and downed the last of their drinks.

"Look," Elsie said, growing serious again, "these Gorgons and anyone working with them...they're no joke. I didn't mean to be so flippant earlier when I was telling you about my assignment to this job. There are really just a few good agents in this war. We need you to stick around as long as possible."

"You mean stay alive as long as possible."

Elsie sighed. "The reality is, in this job, very few retire by choice, if you get what I mean."

Maris nodded, hoping Elsie wasn't actually giving her a vague warning.

"I admit, if our sights are on the same target, we may as well be sharing the same scope." Maris crossed her hands on her lap and gave Elsie a content look. She needed to show Elsie she trusted her, even if she was still sizing her up. "If we're chasing the same prize, I'm fine running with you."

The waitress came and when desserts were refused, offered to take payment.

"It's on me," Elsie said as she handed the waitress a credit card.

The waitress left to get the women cashed out. Elsie smiled at Maris, coyly. "Next one's on you."

Maris stood and straightened her dress. "Thank you for dinner, but I have to call it a night and get back to my hotel. I've had quite a day."

Elsie got up from the table, her own heels putting the two women at nearly the same height, and they shook hands.

"It was a pleasure meeting you," Maris said. "I'll see you in the morning."

"The pleasure was all mine," Elsie responded, smiling. "See you in the morning."

Maris passed by their waitress as she was exiting the dining area courtyard. She glanced back at Elsie who was still smiling at her as she was watching her leave.

14

PANTELLERIA

ALEXEI Volkov stood facing the fireplace in the spacious living room of his ultra-lush suite in *Roskosh'* – his Hexatetron owned resort on Pantelleria. He wore silk pajama bottoms but remained shirtless under the matching silk robe that hung open. Despite it being a warm summer evening on the Italian island, Alexei, like many Gorgons, had a penchant for the heat put off by natural flames and had a raging fire burning. The overhead recessed lights were low, with the fireplace providing the majority of light in the suite. Dancing firelight reflected in the half-empty glass he held from his third cocktail for the night.

Above the fireplace was a granite wall onto which was mounted a large flatscreen monitor. A red light was flashing in the lower right corner of the black screen. Alexei picked a small remote up from the top of the stone hearth that surrounded the fireplace and pressed a button. The flashing red light on the monitor turned a steady green. No image appeared on the monitor, though a thin soundwave line ran across the dark display that bounced and squiggled as the unseen person spoke.

"I thought you were going to take care of her before she left Italy." The voice, speaking English, was altered and distorted, but was still distinctly female. She provided no introduction and spoke as if they were already in the middle of a conversation, though it had just begun.

"That was the plan," Alexei said to the faceless screen. He took a drink. "There were complications."

"You need to get rid of her, Alexei. You know the Queen Mother doesn't take well to failure. We can't afford to upset her."

"You don't have to remind me of that." The disdain he held for the woman on the other side of the screen dripped through. After taking another drink he asked, "Did you call just to harass me? Or do you have something useful to provide?"

"Relax, Alexei. I do have something for you. Maris is in Antwerp and has a meeting tomorrow morning with your friend Xavier Dumont." There was a pause. "You know I don't like the degree of Xavier's involvement. If he gives anything away –"

Alexei interrupted. "He won't. I've known Xavier a long time. I trust him." He thought a moment before continuing. "More than I trust you."

The faceless woman laughed. "The difference is you have no choice *but* to trust me, Alexei. Now run off and do your job. Get rid of Maris Correa, for good."

Alexei provided no pleasantries as he disconnected the call and slipped the remote into a pocket on his robe. His shoulders dropped as he sighed. He swallowed the last of his cocktail.

"Do you see what I have to deal with?" Alexei said in Russian. *"What you're putting me through?"*

As he spoke, Alexei turned and looked at the man sitting in the living room chair behind him. The large bald man sneered, unflinching despite the fresh burn scars that covered most of his face and wrapped around to the newly deformed tattoo on the back of his head. The man grunted as he stood. Both men's eyes glowed white as they looked at each other.

"I'm giving you one more opportunity, Viktor." He waved his empty glass in the air as he spoke. *"Are you sure you are up to the task?"*

The large Russian Gorgon gave Alexei an almost imperceptible nod, but it was enough. Alexei stepped up to him.

"I'm not sure your scars will heal any more than they have." Alexei reached up to the bigger man's face with his empty hand, but did not touch it. *"Those burns would have probably killed a mere human."*

Viktor exhaled a deep breath and said nothing.

"You heard her. Your target is in Belgium. Get there tonight. I'll let Xavier know you are coming, but you cannot involve him or Romilly & Ackerman. Understood?"

Another grunt.

"Now go. We can waste no time."

The large man turned to leave.

"And Viktor…"

Viktor stopped but did not turn back around to face Alexei.

"Don't fail me again. No more mistakes."

The big man left through the oversized doors to the suite, leaving Alexei alone.

Alexei moved from the central part of the living room and to a bar built off a side wall. He set the empty cocktail glass on the bar and grabbed a bottle of Patrón Silver Tequila. He pulled off the wooden cork and took a large swig straight from the crystal bottle. The Russian wasn't thrilled with what he needed to do next.

He took one more drink, replaced the cork in the bottle, and took the remote from his pocket. He turned back towards the flatscreen and entered a series of numbers into the controller. A string of horizontal dots appeared on the monitor blinking in succession as the device worked to make a connection nearly 2,000 miles away. After a few moments the screen came to life, and the familiar underground study in Moscow where Alexei first learned about Maris Correa appeared on the screen. The room was dark save for the fireplace fully aflame, as it almost always was.

He didn't see anyone, but he knew she was there. A faint hissing off-screen assured him of that.

"Well, Alexei?" she said in Russian. *"My sources tell me the daughter of Ares, Maris Correa, is still alive."*

"Yes, that is true." Alexei's tone was subdued. He didn't like that she was aware of this news already. He wondered if the female informant he had spoken to earlier was the one giving this woman her information.

"And she's going under the name Scarlett Caso," Alexei continued.

"Americansss and their foolish codenames. It troubles me that I need to hear the news of her survival from someone other than you. I don't like being put off or lied to."

"My sincere apologies. We suffered one failed attempt, that is all."

"YOU suffered a failed attempt. Do not bring others into the fold of your failure."

"I don't mean to hide any information from you. I anticipate the job to be done within the next twenty-four hours. I was merely waiting to report until I had something to truly report."

The hissing from off-screen grew louder.

"You are lucky I hold you in such high regard, Alexei. I trust you will not let me down."

"I will not, Anastacia. You have my word."

The image on screen turned completely dark for a brief moment as the camera on the other end was obstructed. The bone-chilling hissing was louder than ever. A blurry shadowy shape took up the screen, then pulled away, coming into focus.

The face staring at Alexei nearly filled the entire screen. The woman's features were youthful, like those of a female in her twenties. Looking at her carefully, one could see the beautiful vibrant person she once was, but that woman was long gone. Her skin was ashen, and though she did not have wrinkles, there were cracks in her face with no particular balance or pattern like those of an old statue. The sclerae of her eyes were completely black, cold and soulless. The most horrific part of her, though, was her hair – or rather, the lack thereof – replaced instead by dozens of thin, slithering hissing snakes. The multi-colored nest of serpents formed a macabre halo around her face, moving and flowing of its own volition like waves of wheat in a breeze. Their hissing subsided whenever Anastacia spoke.

"You are no longer needed in Italy. Return to Moscow. We shall be together when Phase Two takes place."

"I will be on the next available flight."

"You better arrive here with good news about Ssscarlett's fate. I expect nothing less."

Alexei nodded at the creature on the screen.

"You have nothing to worry about. The bitch is as good as dead."

15

ANTWERP

MARIS was not going to take any chances for her meeting at Romilly & Ackerman. After being woefully unprepared during the drive to Palermo International Airport, she would not let her guard down again. She procured several items from the briefcase Galaxy had prepared for her. The all-black business suit she purchased in Brussels for the meeting not only went well with "Brandi's" look, but was also effective in hiding many of those items.

She wrapped the flower print scarf that was in the briefcase tightly around her left forearm and tucked into it the two gold-plated folding pocket knives; being right handed, this would allow her to attain and use the knives more easily. The black analog watch she wore on her right wrist, and the chrome-plated flip top lighter slipped nicely into an outside pocket of her suit jacket. The black-framed sunglasses she placed on top of her head over the black wig. She left the black leather gloves in the case.

Last, of course, was her trusty Glock and its small-of-back holster. Maris was disappointed that she used three of her fifteen energy blasts taking out the Maserati, two of those shots being wasted. She promised herself to be more careful with her remaining twelve shots. Lastly, she put on the dangling gold transmitter/tracker earrings. They didn't quite go with her outfit, but she convinced herself they weren't terribly out of place.

It was less than a fifteen minute drive in the gray overcast morning from Hotel Rubens to Antwerp's diamond district, also known as the Diamond Quarter. The district itself was rather small, encompassing just about one square mile, but was the largest diamond district in the world with over 380 workshops serving 1500 companies sharing the area with 3500 brokers, merchants, and diamond cutters, resulting in an annual turnover of $54 billion dollars. Upwards of 234 million carats get traded in the district annually. Over 80 percent of all rough diamonds are purchased in Antwerp, with nearly 50 percent of those returning there for cutting and polishing.

Romilly & Ackerman had carved its own niche in the district as one of the world's most renowned diamond dealers and cutters despite the neighborhood being dominated by Jewish, Lebanese, and Armenian brokers. The company occupied every floor of the tallest building in Antwerp, a 35-story structure with rows upon rows of large arched windows framed in red trim. Despite being one of the newest buildings in the Diamond Quarter, its design fit comfortably with the centuries old ambiance of the city.

As Maris took the final turns on the streets leading to the building, a familiar tone rang in her left ear.

"I don't mean to put a damper on your morning," Galaxy said with no introduction, "but I thought you'd want to know Agent Vector is dead. We recovered his body and hoped for the best, but he passed away about an hour ago."

Neither sadness nor remorse rose within Maris. She had seen plenty of her fellow agents killed over the years. It came with the territory. There was a slight tinge of guilt in knowing that the first man she met at the NPDIA died while trying to save her, but the sentiment quickly passed. Even though she hardly knew him, she knew she would never forget him – another casualty locked away in her memories along with the names and faces of other fallen agents from over the years.

"That's unfortunate," was all Maris had to say.

"Where are you now?" Galaxy quickly changed the subject. The mission always took precedence.

"I'm pulling up to Romilly & Ackerman." Maris turned her rented Renault Twingo off the street and onto the diamond giant's company property. "By the way, thank you for the lovely car."

"Knowing how you treated the company car in Sicily, consider yourself lucky we even hooked you up with something from this century."

Maris supposed the snarky remark was warranted and given in kind, but she didn't necessarily like it. "And with that I'm signing off. I have a meeting to get to."

Maris drove the small Renault down a slope and into the building's private underground parking garage. She showed the Brandi Schiffer driver's license to the parking attendant who in turn matched her name to their guest list for the day. The black and yellow gate arm next to the attendant's booth lifted, letting her through.

She almost felt embarrassed driving her small, light blue colored rental past rows of much nicer Mercedes, Audis, and BMWs. She found an empty spot in the second underground floor next to one of the garage's large concrete support columns, near the elevators. After taking a moment to check herself in the car's rearview mirror, giving a slight adjustment to the wig and sunglasses and making sure one last time that her makeup matched her identification photos, she exited the car, affixed the Glock holster that she had taken off for the drive into the small of her back, and made her way into one of the elevators. The elevator deposited her at one end of the main lobby, providing her a view of an entry area that spared no expense in its extravagance.

In contrast with the building's more classically designed exterior, the interior architecture was elegant and ultramodern. The lobby stretched up three stories and was long, with a wide bank of windows and glass doors on her left affording unobstructed views of the busy street and sidewalks outside. Large 24-inch by 48-inch black porcelain tiles covered the floor and were coated in a high-gloss sheen that made the entire area look like a massive reflection pool. White chairs and couches, about a third of which were occupied, were peppered throughout the lobby, providing guests places to relax as they waited for their diamond representatives to meet them. Two rows of eight decorative golden floor-to-ceiling columns were spaced evenly from one end of the lobby to the other. The far wall was covered in red and gray bricks and had a nonstop cascade of water flowing down the face of it. Glass prisms and chains hung from exquisite chandeliers like diamonds floating in the sky.

On Maris' right were two wide check-in desks in line with each other. The front and sides of each desk were covered in 13-inch square marble tiles and topped with a shiny black-chrome countertop with curved edges. The opening between them led to an atrium with four elevators, two on each side. There were two wide corridors on the outer ends of the desks that led to foyers housing more elevators. Maris walked up to the nearer of the two desks where three female employees were busy talking on nearly inconspicuous earpieces and typing away at unseen recessed keyboards on their side of the counter. With their chiseled features, white blouses, navy blazers, and navy skirts, Maris thought they looked more like flight attendants than corporate reception employees. The woman closest to her immediately provided Maris her full attention.

"Welcome to Romilly & Ackerman," the woman said in German-accented English. "How may I help you?"

Maris displayed her International Driving License. "I'm Brandi Schiffer with Quintz & Deloitte. I have an appointment this morning with Xavier Dumont."

The employee took the license and studied it for a moment. She looked up at Maris, who returned the look, emotionless. The woman typed into her keyboard as she looked at a display only she could see through a smoky glass covered opening in the countertop in front of her. She handed the license back to Maris.

"Yes, thank you, Ms. Schiffer."

The employee typed more into her keyboard then put a finger on her earpiece. "I have Brandi Schiffer here for her appointment with Mr. Dumont." She paused and looked up at Maris. "Yes." Another pause. "Thank you." Taking her finger off the earpiece, she said, "Mr. Dumont's assistant will be right down to escort you upstairs. You may wait right over there." She gestured towards the nearest set of empty chairs and couches, just a few steps away.

"Thank you," said Maris.

Maris walked over to the waiting area but decided not to sit. As she waited she looked out the windows at the pedestrians and traffic. It was starting to rain a light drizzle and umbrellas began to shoot up among the passersby. She reached up and touched her wig and sunglasses, almost as a reminder to herself that they were there. Her life had already been put on the line for this mission, and she wasn't convinced that danger wouldn't follow her any less as "Brandi" than it did as Scarlett. The use of caution was paramount.

"Ms. Schiffer?"

Maris looked at the woman who called her from behind. The woman looked very much like the stereotypical secretaries she remembered seeing in movies and television when growing up: white blouse with dark skirt, heels, hair pulled back, and glasses. Maris guessed it was no coincidence that the woman was also very statuesque – it seemed Xavier Dumont had very specific requirements for his hired help. She put a hand out toward the assistant.

"Hello, I'm Brandi Schiffer."

The woman smiled and briefly shook Maris' hand. "Mr. Dumont is ready for you. Please follow me."

Maris followed the woman into one of the elevators located in the foyer between the lobby desks. Its doors were already open and waiting as they approached and closed swiftly once they entered. It made Maris believe they were being watched. The woman pressed the button for the top floor. The high-speed elevator rose rapidly and made no stops before reaching their destination.

When the doors opened, Maris expected to see a large open area of individual cubicles and workspaces, much like a generic office space. What she was greeted with, however, was a wide opulent walkway lined with offices – many with glass walls to where she could see employees in tailored suits working away at computers, or facilitating meetings with diamond buyers or sellers, or conducting who-knows-what diamond-related (or otherwise unknown) business. The walls and ceiling were trimmed in Ebony wood, and the floor was comprised of highly polished hexagonal pink and gray toned marble tile.

Maris was shown to the end of the hall and to a set of wide double wooden doors. The woman waved a hand over a black glass panel in the door on the right and the door glided open with hardly a sound. On the other side was a modest reception and waiting area. There was an empty desk, four wide chairs, and a long couch. A coffee table and end tables had copies of magazines on them dealing specifically with the diamond industry. Just past the desk was another door, this one painted bright red in glaring contrast to the gray and white colors of the room. They walked to this door and the woman opened it the same way as the last, by passing her hand over a built-in sensor. The woman did not walk through, instead gesturing Maris to move on ahead.

"Mr. Dumont's office. Please enter."

Highlighted in chrome, silver, and white tones, the office was nearly as wide as the entire thirty-fifth floor. There were a few singlewide doors covered in stainless steel panels in the side walls. Despite its size, the space was relatively sparse on furniture. A long conference table sat parallel to the left wall and was surrounded by thirteen high-backed chairs.

Standing in matching angles in front of the right wall were half a dozen chest-high crystalline cases filled with diamonds and jewelry. Spotlights in the ceiling shown straight down onto each case. This area of the office was a veritable museum for the array of charms, rings, necklaces, and bracelets on display. Several large plain white rectangular partitions were seemingly randomly placed between and behind the cases at varied angles, appearing to serve no purpose other than aesthetics, almost like art pieces unto themselves.

The entire back wall was a single tall, wide panoramic window providing unhindered views of Antwerp and the diamond district far below. Except for the spotlights over the jewelry displays none of the recessed overhead lights were on, allowing the natural light from the large window to illuminate the room. Even on the cloudy day, the light drew long shadows from the room's fixtures, stretching toward Maris and the office door behind her. A single desk and chair were centered in front of the window, dwarfed by the picturesque postcard view behind them.

Maris made the walk to the far end of the office as the door slid shut behind her.

Standing in front of the desk was Elsie Byrne. She wore a navy suit that accentuated her thin yet athletic build. Her smile was warm and inviting and entirely familiar, though she acted as if they had never met, giving just a casual nod as Maris approached. Maris wondered how long the SISX agent had been there, and if there was a connection between her and the Gorgon conspiracy that she hadn't yet been made aware – or possibly hadn't yet figured out.

Behind the desk, facing away from the women and silhouetted against the glass window, was Xavier Dumont. The man was tall and insanely thin, almost anorexic in stature, with dark hair slicked straight back. His slim-fitted white pinstriped suit made him appear almost skeletal in the light. Wisps of white smoke danced against the glass from a cigarette held by long fingers perched near the side of his face.

The air in the room was cool but not too cold, and Maris noticed she could barely smell the smoke from the cigarette. She deduced the office must have an exceptional air circulation system, though she didn't hear any fans or compressors.

"Brandi Schiffer, I presume." The man's voice was airy and flamboyant and carried a German accent.

Maris exchanged a quick look with Elsie as the man turned around. His face was long and gaunt, and she guessed he was quite a few years older than her.

"It's an honor to meet you, Mr. Dumont," Maris said. She would have extended a hand but the man wasn't within reach and he didn't step any closer.

Xavier Dumont smiled. His teeth looked large in his lean face. "The pleasure is mine."

Dumont took a long drag from his cigarette and was courteous in blowing the smoke away from the women. With that he stepped forward and tapped the clinging ashes from his cigarette into a tray on his desk. He gestured towards the Englishwoman.

"Ms. Schiffer, this is Elsie Byrne. She's with Addington Stone Investors, a diamond buyer from England." His English was good despite his heavy accent.

The two women shook hands and exchanged polite pleasantries.

"I understand you are both here to establish relations with our brokerage and production networks," Dumont said, then looked at Maris. "You've come a long way to this meeting. You are from the United States, yes?"

"Yes, I'm with Quintz & Deloitte sellers out of Beverly Hills, California."

"I've only recently heard of Quintz & Deloitte, so I am not completely familiar."

"We're new, working with direct local clients, mostly the wealthy. But we're at a point where we want to expand our operations and look at establishing a global presence."

"We're fortunate you afforded us this meeting, Mr. Dumont," said Elsie.

"Indeed." Dumont took a final drag before extinguishing the cigarette in the ashtray. "I am always interested in expanding our operations into new markets. In my pre-meeting briefings it was explained to me on good authority that your companies may make for profitable partnerships. If it weren't for that, we would not all be standing here right now."

Elsie raised a hand slightly to get Dumont's attention. "I think it's equally important that you convince me about Romilly & Ackerman. I know, I for one, want to know first-hand about your operations."

"Of course. This way, please."

Dumont showed the women to the side of the office with the glass jewelry cases. He had them move into the walk space between the cases and the erratic row of white partitions, while he remained on the side towards the middle of the office.

"These panels are set to deflect the lighting at specified angles on this side of the room to provide the best illumination to the jewelry on display," he explained.

They stopped at the first glass case. The display showcased a number of diamond encrusted necklaces. Dumont stooped down and examined the necklaces through the glass while the women looked on.

"I take pride in the exquisiteness of the standards we hold and the work we do. We only sell the best diamonds in the world. Our expertise in sourcing, manufacturing, and selling is unparalleled. Take these necklaces, for example. The diamonds in each of these necklaces were individually chosen for achieving the highest criteria in the six C's of diamonds."

"I'm sorry," Maris interrupted. "*Six* C's? I'm only aware of five."

Dumont released a light chuckle. Maris couldn't tell if there was a hint of condescension in the laugh.

"So the five C's," Dumont continued, "as you know, include carat-weight, color, clarity, and cut. The fifth, of course, is the confidence found in the accuracy of any associated diamond grading certificates."

"And the sixth?"

"The sixth that we employ here at Romilly & Ackerman is *conduct*."

"Conduct?" asked Elsie.

"Yes, Ms. Byrne. *Conduct* as in how each diamond has been treated. Treatments such as fracture filling, laser drilling, and high temperatures and pressures that would unnaturally enhance the clarity or color of a diamond are strictly forbidden. We take pride in knowing none of our diamonds have been subjected to unnatural conduct."

"I see," Elsie said.

Dumont continued admiring the necklaces without looking up

as he spoke. "The very foundation of our core values is steeped in our knowledge, passion, and honesty, and is what sets us apart from our competitors. Ethics are important to me, and this company adheres to the highest ethical standards in the business."

"Including your mining sources?" Maris challenged.

Dumont stood upright and shot Maris an annoyed look. Without immediately addressing the question, he moved to the next case. The women followed. This case had a flat velvet tray showcasing an array of raw, uncut diamonds.

Dumont sounded defensive when he spoke next. "I assure you, Ms. Schiffer, despite our diamonds being sourced from partners in the Democratic Republic of Congo, Botswana, and other African nations, all of our stones are one hundred percent conflict-free. Our mining companies are held to the strictest ethical standards in the business. They are afforded zero margin of error when it comes to their mining practices."

"Good to know," said Maris, trying to come across as relieved even though she knew better.

Dumont didn't react to Maris' newfound reassurance. The edge in his voice remained. "Due to our strong unforgiving standards in every step of the process – from mining, production, and finally, selling – Romilly & Ackerman is positioned better than anyone to give you the highest quality diamonds at the best prices on the market. Our standing as a coveted member of the Responsible Jewelry Council fully attests to our ethics and professionalism."

Dumont moved on from the rough diamonds and positioned himself in front of the next case. This display was filled with the most beautiful diamond rings Maris had ever seen.

"I can tell by the sheer elegance of this building that your company takes great pride in what it does," observed Elsie. "It's like a trophy in the middle of the city."

Dumont's demeanor lightened. His face beamed as he looked around his vast office. "You may have noticed this is the largest and tallest building in the district. Belgians prefer to keep architecture more muted and suited to fit in with local history. It wasn't easy getting this place built. But money talks."

"Only when something is for sale," remarked Maris.

"*Everything* is for sale, Ms. Schiffer."

Maris paused, letting the suddenly thick air in the room lighten before she continued.

"I wonder, Mr. Dumont, why haven't you added your name to the company's? I mean, at this point, aren't you essentially the sole proprietor and operator?"

Dumont reached delicately into his suit jacket and took out a thin silver case. His movements were fluid as he opened the case and removed a cigarette. He showed the open case towards the women.

"Would either of you care for a cigarette? Executive Gold Treasurers. The finest cigarettes money can buy."

Maris and Elsie politely declined, though Maris was quick to procure her lighter from her outer pocket and offered to light the cigarette in Dumont's hand. Dumont nodded, and Maris flipped open the chrome top and lit it.

"Thank you," Dumont said as he put the cigarette case away and blew smoke into the air. "I'm not used to having a woman offer a light."

"I'm not like most women," Maris said with the utmost confidence. The Englishwoman flashed her a slight smile.

"To answer your question," Dumont said, "Romilly & Ackerman built a reputation long before me. When I positioned myself into a controlling interest in the company years ago, I did not want to disturb the good name. It's good business, and I am a businessman, nothing more, nothing less. Despite what some may think, I'm not, as you would say, an egomaniac. I don't have a desire for world domination."

Interesting choice of words, Maris thought.

The next case he showed them was filled with diamond encrusted bracelets.

"Mr. Dumont," Elsie said, "it was my understanding when this meeting was booked that there would be a tour of the facility."

Dumont took a puff from his cigarette, then pulled a small, slightly curved chrome saucer from a pocket, set it on the glass case, and tapped ashes into it.

"All in due time," he said without any hint of emotion. He pointed at a set of matching bracelets and was about to say something when Maris interrupted.

"I'd like to know about Romilly & Ackerman's investments in other companies. For instance," she feigned pondering on a name, "how did you get involved with Hexatetron? Does Romilly & Ackerman have any sort of controlling interests in it?"

Dumont answered without missing a beat. "When Hexatetron was a startup, its founder, Alexei Volkov, drew us in to help with initial funding. He was convinced, rightly so, that diamonds are a commodity that will never lose its, shall we say, financial luster."

"Interesting," Maris said. "Are you close with Alexei Volkov?"

"We are business acquaintances. Outside of business we've shared a few meals, but our relationship is purely professional." Dumont paused. "Tell me, Ms. Schiffer, are you always concerned about the personal lives of your business partners?"

Maris looked Dumont straight in the eyes. "I believe the company a person keeps says a lot about the person themselves."

"Do you have concerns with Alexei Volkov, Ms. Schiffer?"

"He's been known to be reckless on occasion. I would hate for that to have an impact down the line on Romilly & Ackerman and, in turn, any business relationship we may have."

Dumont straightened himself as he took two long drags of his cigarette and then tapped their ashes into the saucer. "You should have no concerns about our dealings with Hexatetron. Our business partnership is sound and secure, and is sure to lead to great advances in the businesses of both technology and the diamond trade."

"Do you have any joint operations on the horizon?" Maris asked.

"Nothing exclusive, though Hexatetron is one of several sponsors at the upcoming G50 summit in Dubai."

"G50?" asked Elsie. "I'm not familiar."

Dumont took two more successive drags before answering. "Yes, the first convention attended by some of the highest ranking officials of fifty nations to discuss and hopefully establish international agreements involving diamonds, gold, and other metals. Organizers are proud to include many traditionally third world countries to get their input in creating and enforcing ethical global standards for mining, distribution, and production at every step in the processes."

"Being included in a summit like this has to be a real coup for some of those countries," said Maris.

"It is indeed. I recently spoke with representatives from the Democratic Republic of Congo and Botswana who are ecstatic about their involvement. They are excited to be treated as equals on such important issues."

"Will you be there representing Belgium? Or Romilly & Ackerman?"

"Not me personally, but my company, along with dozens of others, will have representatives there providing our perspectives, and hosting small workshops and seminars throughout the weekend. We'll also be present at the final conference on Sunday evening where all representatives from all fifty countries will attend. It's going to be a great celebration."

It was too much of a coincidence that fifty countries were involved with the G50 conference – the same number as the summit on Pantelleria. In addition, both conferences included at least some of the same diamond producing third world countries. Maris felt almost certain this would be the event that Alexei Volkov spoke of where the Gorgons intended to unleash their grand plan. What that plan was exactly, though, she still didn't know.

"Mr. Dumont," she pressed on, "I'm curious, why fifty nations? I find that to be an interesting number." *And entirely familiar*, she thought. *These pieces fit too well together.* "This seems like an ambitious undertaking for an inaugural convention."

Dumont inhaled deeply on his cigarette, burning it down to its built-in filter. He looked Maris right in the eyes as he blew the smoke directly at her.

"There is much you do not know, Ms. Schiffer." His voice was deeper, more ominous.

Maris noticed Elsie cover her nose and mouth as she took a step back from the display case. As Maris stayed focused on Dumont, the SISX agent fell out of her peripheral vision.

"I'm sorry," Elsie said. "The smell of cigarette smoke doesn't sit well with me."

"My apologies, Ms. Byrne." Dumont extinguished the cigarette. "I do not want my guests to be uncomfortable."

A shadow fell over Maris, and she figured it was from Elsie moving behind her.

A hard thud struck Maris on her right temple. Bright white spots filled her vision and her knees buckled as she fell to the side and struggled to hold herself up on the glass display case. Through her strobing eyesight she saw Dumont watching her without any reaction when a second wallop came even harder than the first.

Then everything went black.

■■■ • • • ■■■

Reality came and went in phases as small flashes of consciousness floated in and out of Maris' head.

"Take...far from here..."

A man's voice, familiar, speaking Russian. Xavier Dumont's? Maris tried to concentrate, translating the Russian in her head.

"...everything with you...destroy all evidence..." The voice seemed to be directly over her. *"I will dispose of the vehicles..."*

Maris opened her eyes into little slits. Her vision was foggy as she struggled to regain her full senses. She could feel the cold, hard floor beneath her sprawled body. A pair of shiny black shoes, touched by the cuffs of white pinstriped slacks, was barely a breath away. Definitely Dumont. But who was he talking to?

"No trace…"

She couldn't hear any other voices. Was he talking to Elsie?

"Ensure no resistance…I'll report to…"

Chaotic thoughts muddled through her head. It had to be Elsie he was talking to. No one else was in the room and the Englishwoman had stepped out of her sight just before something hit her, knocking her to the floor.

An intense pressure was suddenly on her head, and a cloth covered her nose and mouth. The sweet smell of sevoflurane filled her nostrils and the blackness returned…

16

UNKNOWN AIRSPACE

"SCARLETT? Are you there?"

What? A woman's voice. It sounded like someone was talking right into her ear. *What's happening?*

"Agent Scarlett? Come in, Agent Scarlett."

Maris' eyes popped open. The left side of her head was leaning against the interior glass of a luxury helicopter. Her body was facing forward, and in her current position all she could see at first was sky, which was mostly blue with sporadic clusters of gray clouds. She lowered her gaze and there was only water as far as she could see.

"Scarlett. Come in. This is Galaxy."

Maris' head was throbbing but it was no worse than the headache from the ECE charge that knocked her out in Africa, so she was certain she'd shake it off soon. Galaxy's voice was coming through clearly. Uncertain yet of her situation, she took care not to respond.

She continued to take in her surroundings without yet moving her head. The whir of the helicopter blades was muted in what was a mostly soundproofed cabin. Bright light poured in through the windows. Her hands were in front of her, bound by rope, and she realized her feet were also tied together. In front of where she sat was an empty space big enough to accommodate another row of seats. A tan leather padded wall with a closed sliding door separated the passenger area from the cockpit.

Meticulously, Maris moved her head away from the window and turned to look to her right. There were four matching leather seats in her row. On the seat next to her was her black wig and sunglasses. The pilot, whoever it was, most likely knew who she was – she deduced Dumont must have known the whole time as well. Maris continued looking down the row of seats and an unexpected sight greeted her. Propped against the glass in the seat on her far right was Elsie Byrne. Her hands and feet were bound like Maris' and she appeared to be unconscious.

Is she, though? Maris wondered, still uncertain of the Englishwoman's allegiances.

She thought about her agency smartphone and even though she expected nothing, she reached in and around all her suit pockets in search for it – but it was gone.

Elsie obviously was not flying the helicopter, but Maris had not ruled out her involvement in this kidnapping. She recalled the bits of conversation she heard back in the office after she was hit in the head. She remembered hearing Dumont speaking with someone, and it sounded as if he was giving instructions. Maris reasoned that Dumont was most likely not flying the aircraft either.

If not Dumont, then who? Perhaps someone had joined her, Dumont, and Elsie in the office after she was knocked out. Or had someone else been with them all along? Maris wasn't quite sure what to think, but knew she didn't fully trust Elsie among her confusion.

She reached up, slowly, and took hold of one of the gold columns dangling from her earrings and yanked it off. She slipped the tracking device between her seat cushion and the one next to her. It took just a couple moments before Galaxy sounded again in her ear.

"We've picked up on your signal. I'm assuming you aren't able to speak. We're zeroing in on your location."

It was a full minute – though it seemed much longer – before Galaxy came back through.

"I've got you. You're over the North Sea, between Belgium and England." There was a pause, then Galaxy added, "Looks like you're headed further out to sea."

That doesn't sound good, Maris thought.

Movement on her right caught Maris' attention. Elsie was stirring. She appeared to come to her senses as quickly as Maris did. Just as it was one of the fastest working inhalant anesthetics, sevoflurane afforded the speediest recovery, especially to anyone whose body had been trained to adjust to recover from anesthesia as quickly as possible.

"Where are we?" Elsie asked as groggily while she looked out her window. Her voice was low and barely audible over the sounds of the helicopter.

"Over the North Sea, I believe," Maris said, pretending to take a guess.

Elsie looked at her. "Are you okay?"

"You hit me," Maris said as a matter-of-fact, ready to gauge the Englishwoman's response.

"It wasn't me, I promise you. A man came out from behind a partition and got both of us."

"A man? Who?"

"He was large and bald. I just got a glance, but he seemed to fit the description of a Russian known to us only as Viktor. Gorgon strong-arm of Alexei Volkov."

The man in the Maserati?

Elsie continued, "I'm not sure, but it looked like his face was covered in fresh burn scars. Horrifying."

Most certainly the man in the Maserati.

Galaxy cut into the conversation. "We're making out another voice. Is that Elsie Byrne? The SISX agent you met at dinner?"

So Galaxy knew about Elsie. This made Maris feel much better about her. Perhaps she could be trusted after all.

"Yes, it is," Maris said, acknowledging what Elsie said while simultaneously answering Galaxy's question. Then after a slight pause, "I believe I had a run-in with him in Sicily."

"Then you know how dangerous he is. My guess is he's flying this helicopter."

Galaxy chimed in again. "We've been in contact with SISX. We've tied them into your signal. They have boats in the North Sea tracking you from the water."

"I wonder where we're headed," said Elsie.

Maris' eyes darted around the cabin, her mind racing. "My guess is we're pretty much where they want to be. I think our journey is about done."

Elsie looked out her window again at the endless sea below. "That's not encouraging."

"We need to act fast."

Maris shuffled herself over to the empty seat next to Elsie and held her forearms out towards the SISX agent. She looked and nodded at her left arm.

"Here, quick. Pull up my left suit jacket and sleeve."

Elsie grabbed the black suit jacket sleeve with her own bound hands. It was somewhat tightfitting, and Elsie struggled a bit, but she was able to finagle the sleeve until it was bunched up near Maris' elbow.

"I have knives hidden under my sleeve," Maris divulged in a rushed whisper. "Hurry, hurry."

The women worked together so Elsie could unbutton the blouse cuff and work it up over the jacket sleeve, exposing the flower print scarf wrapped around her forearm underneath. Sticking out from under the scarf, near the wrist, were the tips of the gold-plated folded pocket knives.

"Grab one and cut my ropes," Maris said.

Elsie slid out one of the knives, unfolded it, and went to work on freeing Maris' hands.

"You're like a fucking scout," Elsie said as she cut frantically. "Always prepared."

The frayed rope fell away onto the copter floor. Maris took the knife and cut away the ropes binding her ankles.

"Now me," Elsie said.

Maris took hold of Elsie's hands with one of her own to hold them steady. She slipped the knife between Elsie's hands and was about to begin cutting when a click was heard on the door latch to the cockpit.

"Hurry up," Elsie said. "Someone's coming."

Maris pulled the knife away without cutting the ropes, stood up, and moved over to the wall to the left side of the cockpit door.

"Wait." Elsie sounded panicky. "What about me? Cut me loose."

Maris furrowed her brow as she made a shushing expression with her lips. She pulled out the other knife and opened it. Holding an open knife in each hand, she pressed her back flat against the partition. There was another click and the door slid open.

From her vantage point, the first thing Maris saw come through the door was her Glock – her precious weapon – held by a large right hand covered in fresh burn scars. The big bald man that followed had scars on his tattooed head similar to the one on his hand. He glared at Elsie with eyes white, who quickly looked away for fear of making eye contact with the Gorgon. He then looked at the empty seat where he had left Maris, before settling his eyes on the cut ropes on the floor. He turned his head to his left, scanning the cabin for Maris.

As Viktor started to look back to his right, Maris struck. She thrust the knife in her right hand into the thick hand holding her Glock. She simultaneously stabbed the other knife into the small of Viktor's back. The gun fell to the floor as the large Russian bellowed in pain. He yanked his right hand away as he turned towards Maris and landed a heavy fist from his left hand into her chest, slamming her back against the partition. Elsie reached down to pick up the gun but the Russian smashed a knee into her face, knocking her backwards onto two of the empty leather seats.

Maris launched herself at the brute and plunged her right shoulder into the side of the Russian, catching him off-balance. The big man staggered onto the seats and partly onto Elsie. The SISX agent squirmed away, still smarting from the knee in the face, and rolled onto the floor. Maris was partially on top of Viktor, making quick jabs from both knives into the large body of the Russian. Her hands were covered in blood from all the cuts but the big man didn't seem phased.

Elsie grabbed the Glock off the floor and scooted herself away from the melee of the other two. She sat herself upright, holding the gun in her still-bound hands and pointed it at the big man.

"Viktor, stop!" Elsie commanded.

The Russian let out a loud grunt as he shoved Maris off of him and onto Elsie. The Englishwoman was able to hold onto the gun as she fell onto her right side with Maris on top of her. The Russian scowled at the Englishwoman, his eyes glowing white. Elsie looked away before she was drawn in to the gaze and turned to stone. Viktor jumped up from the leather seats much faster than one would expect of someone his size. Elsie was still looking away and unable to take an accurate shot. Viktor grabbed Maris and threw her against the seats, knocking the knives out of her hands and the wind out of her lungs. Then, with one hand, he tore the Glock away from Elsie while he wrapped his other hand around the SISX agent's neck. He tossed the gun into the cockpit and jerked Elsie to her feet.

"Scarlett!" Galaxy's voice cut through the commotion. "Listen to me. Come in, Scar –"

The transmission in Maris' ear suddenly went dead. She rapidly smacked the earring with her fingers but all that came back was silence.

The Russian wrapped his large hands around the Englishwoman's head and began to squeeze...and Elsie started to scream. The force from his hands held the woman nearly completely in the air, leaving the tips of her toes dancing on the floor of the helicopter. Elsie tried to scratch and tear her fingers into Viktor's hands in a vain attempt to make him stop. Even digging into the open cut in his hand didn't make a difference. Despite her efforts, the pressure on her head grew stronger...and she grew weaker.

Maris scrambled around the big man and into the cockpit. No one was flying the helicopter. The autopilot must have been engaged. She searched for the Glock, not sure of where it ended up when Viktor threw it. Elsie's blood-curdling clamoring echoed in Maris' ears.

There it was – on the floor of the copilot side. Maris leaned onto the copilot seat, stretched her hand toward the floor and grabbed the Glock. Ensuring the safety wasn't engaged, she turned back around and took aim. The Russian was partly facing her, with Elsie mostly out of view behind the partition on Maris' right. Unsure of what the ECE charge might do to Elsie if she used it on Viktor, Maris first quickly pumped three bullets into the big Russian, striking his right side and stomach. The man just glowered at her as he pulled Elsie towards himself, turned, and then shoved her toward Maris.

Maris fell backwards, twisting herself so as to not fall against any of the helicopter's controls, and instead ended up lying awkwardly on the copilot seat. Elsie was on top of her, thankfully alive, though weakened and helpless.

Elsie was suddenly hauled off of her, and Maris watched the man – with a limp Elsie in tow – disappear behind the partition on the left. Maris jumped up, still holding the gun, and rushed through the door to the passenger cabin.

A harsh wind greeted Maris as, to her horror, she realized Viktor had used one strong hand to pull on the locking handle of the helicopter passenger door and slide it open. The Russian's back was towards her, while Elsie – suspended in the air by her neck in the grip of the man's other hand – looked at her, the fight gone out of her eyes. The sides of her head were stained red with blood coming from her ears.

Maris levelled her gun at Viktor.

"Stop!" she ordered.

The man turned enough to put an eye on Maris and smiled.

"Let her go!" Maris' voice nearly cracked as she screamed at the Russian.

Viktor moved Elsie a bit towards Maris, then, without warning, he slammed her body twice against the jamb of the open door before throwing her limp form out of the helicopter and into the churning waters far below.

Maris' thumb slipped to change the weapon from bullets to ECE discharges.

The Russian took a step towards Maris with his glowing eyes as she let two red beams fly, both striking him square in the chest. The man recoiled, his body shaking and stuttering halfway between the open door and Maris. He didn't fall, though he didn't appear to have any control over himself. His skin looked like it was burning from an invisible heat as it began to turn black and peel away. An orange glow emitted from the Russian's eyes, nostrils, and mouth, and Maris felt a sudden sense of urgency to dispose of him for good.

She placed a strong forward kick into the man's midsection and he staggered backwards and fell out of the helicopter. She rushed to the open door and looked down. The body spun and flailed and it looked like actual fire was coming out of his head and hands. In the next instant the man exploded into a ball of flame. The burning and smoking pieces extinguished as they struck the blue sea.

Maris' situation was still dire. Elsie was most likely dead, there was no pilot, and she didn't know how to fly a helicopter. She stepped away from the open door when she thought she heard something…a voice through some sort of transmitter. Where was it coming from? She tapped on her earring a few more times but it was dead quiet. The voice was definitely not coming from there. She then went to the cockpit – the empty, pilotless, anxiety-inducing cockpit – but the voice trailed away as if she was now further away from it. She looked at the row of leather seats and at her black sunglasses, which were surprisingly still sitting undisturbed on top of the black wig.

The barely audible voice seemed to be coming from the sunglasses.

Maris scooped them up and studied them. The voice, sounding almost like it was coming through a transistor radio, was definitely coming from the sunglasses.

"Scarlett – put the sunglasses on. Scarlett, do you read? Get these sunglasses on!"

Maris put on the sunglasses and the voice was much clearer. Galaxy was practically shouting at her through audio transmitters built into the earpieces of the sunglasses.

"Agent Scarlett, I can't get you through the earrings."

"I'm here, Galaxy," Maris replied.

"Thank God," said Galaxy. "Are you okay? I can't explain right now, but we lost transmission through the earrings."

Maris rushed into the cockpit and settled into the pilot's seat.

"Elsie got thrown from the helicopter. Alexei's henchman Viktor is dead. And there's no one flying this thing."

"Do you know how to fly?"

"Airplanes? Yes." Maris' eyes scanned the controls. The autopilot was still engaged and the helicopter was flying straight – at the moment anyway. "Helicopters? Not so much."

She recognized some of the readings such as the airspeed indicator and altimeter. Many other displays and settings were unfamiliar, though, and the cyclic control stick between her legs and the pedals on the floor surely wouldn't control the helicopter like they do a plane.

"Scarlett, look at your watch."

Maris turned her right wrist towards her and studied the watch.

"Grab the outer edge and turn it counterclockwise a quarter turn. Then place the face of the watch against any digital readout on the control panel and hold it there until I say."

Maris did as she was told and the seconds ticked away like minutes. Several agonizing moments later her watch beeped and even though the face of it was hidden away from her, she could see it was glowing blue.

"Take the watch off and leave it sitting anywhere on the control panel."

Just as Maris was taking off the watch, the helicopter abruptly slowed its speed, and she lurched forward in her seat. Maris braced herself in the cockpit, her arms and legs splayed out as far as they could go. The copter quickly came to a stop and began to slowly rotate.

"There's something happening with the helicopter," Maris said, her heart racing.

"I have control of the helicopter remotely from headquarters," Galaxy announced.

The copter pitched a bit to its right and the rotating stopped.

"What the hell, Galaxy. You could have told me you were taking over."

"Relax, Scarlett, I've got you. It's a bit dodgy, though, because there's a delay from the time I initiate a movement to the time the chopper acts due to the distance between us."

"*Dodgy* isn't the word that comes to mind."

"Look down at the water. Do you see any of the SISX boats?"

"SISX boats?" Maris looked out and down through the cockpit windows but didn't see any boats. "Hold on."

She left the cockpit and went to the main cabin and looked out the open side door. Three narrow black arrowhead shapes were in the water not too far behind them in a triangular configuration.

"I see three boats headed this way."

"That's them. Now, Scarlett, since you're a Florida beach girl I assume you can swim?"

"Don't be a smart ass, Galaxy, and just tell me what I need to do."

"I'm going to get the helicopter as low as I can. Controlling it remotely I'm only comfortable with getting within maybe thirty feet of the water. All you need to do is dive in. The SISX boats will pick you up."

"Copy that."

Maris felt the copter begin to drop. She estimated it was a few hundred feet up, and it dropped quickly, listing in all directions without any sort of pattern while it fell. The movement wasn't enough to knock Maris off-balance, but she pressed herself against the partition to the cockpit to keep herself steady. It wasn't long before the descent ceased and the helicopter balanced itself.

"Okay, Scarlett, this is about as low as I'm comfortable taking it. You're on your own from here."

Maris peered out the side door. The drop looked much more than thirty feet. She kicked off her shoes and held her Glock close to her chest with both hands. And then she jumped.

Maris dropped straight down like a needle and plunged into the water feet first. The cold of the sea swallowed her. She quickly caught her bearings and kicked and propelled herself to the surface. Moments later she broke through and took a deep breath. Her knives, watch, and sunglasses were gone.

But she still had her Glock.

While she treaded water and waited on the approaching boats, the helicopter peeled off and once it was safely several hundred feet away, it crashed into the North Sea with a massive splash.

Maris didn't have to wait long before the boats were upon her. She noticed only two had made their way close to her, with the third hanging far back. Each boat was about twenty feet long, and was sleek and black with no markings whatsoever. Only two agents were on each boat. Maris swam to the side of the nearest vessel. A man dressed all in black extended a hand towards her to help her get on board.

"Welcome to SISX, Agent Scarlett."

17

MOSCOW

WHILE Maris was being kidnapped, another scene was unfolding in Moscow.

Hexatetron corporate headquarters was situated in the Moscow International Business Center, two and a half miles west of Red Square, in a twisting spire-like building near the edge of the Moskva River. Upon its grand opening two years ago, the skyscraper pierced the Russian skyline like a needle and, with its 103 above-ground floors, was the tallest building in all of Moscow. With its stature and magnificence, the dark blue and black structure stood as a proud monument not only for Hexatetron itself, but as a symbol of Russian modernism and technology.

It was mid-morning when Alexei Volkov arrived at the headquarters. The city was alive with the heartbeat of its nearly 13 million residents, with 300,000 workers just in the one-quarter square mile area of the International Business Center itself. The pulse of Hexatetron headquarters coupled that of the city, and most of its employees were already present and engrossed in their daily tasks when Alexei arrived, making his approach onto the business property free of any traffic entanglements.

Alexei parked his silver-blue Bugatti Chiron Pur Sport car in his personally reserved spot on the first floor of the underground parking garage. His parking space was right next to a set of four private elevators for use only by executives, and he had to scan his thumbprint to enter the vestibule that housed them. His Magnanni leather monk-strap dress shoes echoed against the marble floor as he walked through the vestibule. Each set of highly reflective silver elevator doors was emblazoned with the hexagon and five interlaced circles of the Hexatetron logo. The nearest set of doors opened automatically upon Alexei's approach, picking up on a corporate fob he had in his pocket.

This day, Alexei wore a two-piece blue sharkskin-sheened wool Giorgio Armani suit with a white shirt and sky-blue silk tie. He always dressed as if he was expected onstage wherever he went, though today his audience most likely couldn't care less about his appearance. Instead of pressing any of the floor buttons, Alexei placed his thumb onto a nearly inconspicuous scanner next to the elevator car's operating panel. The elevator immediately began to descend.

Alexei's phone rang. He pulled it out of an inside jacket pocket and recognized the call coming through on an encoded line. To answer the call he had to access a keypad on the screen and enter a code. The phone stopped ringing and the dark silhouette of a woman appeared.

"I'm fucking pissed, Alexei," the familiar yet electronically distorted voice of the woman said in English.

"What is it now?" Annoyed, Alexei was not in the mood for a senseless confrontation.

"Your friend, your idiot confidante in Belgium, told Scarlett about the G50 conference. This is getting out of control. He should have never been trusted."

"He is one of the few humans I do trust. I don't understand how this is a setback."

For a few moments the woman said nothing. Alexei stared at his phone screen, his amber eyes narrowing on the silhouette of the woman.

"Scarlett is sure to let her people know about the conference. What if they plan some sort of disruption? Phase Two must go off without any problems. The future of my people depends on it."

"You mean the future of *my* people depend on it." Alexei grew serious. "The few of you that are not killed or enslaved will be dependent on us for a life of luxury and excess. I would be careful not to do anything to fuck that up. You wouldn't want the Queen Mother to…question your loyalty."

The woman laughed. "You wouldn't dare do anything to disrupt her trust in me. I've been helping you all along. I was the one who secured the NPDIA the pass to the Pantelleria summit. And ever since then I've kept you up to speed on all her movements. Fuck, *I'm* the one who told the Queen Mother about Scarlett in the first place."

"And I am very grateful for all you've done. I just don't see any sense in getting upset over her knowing about the G50 conference. If anything, we may be able to use that to our advantage."

"By then it may be too late. You've failed in killing Scarlett. I'm sure the Queen Mother is none too thrilled about –"

Alexei interrupted. "That situation will soon be rectified. I have my man on it right now."

"You mean the man you sent to kill her in Sicily? The man who was left broken and scarred while she boarded a plane to Belgium?"

Alexei's mind swirled with angry retorts, but he swallowed his emotions and maintained his composure. "He will not fail again. It will be different this time."

"I know it will." Alexei had barely uttered his words when the woman seized control of the conversation. "I plan on doing whatever I can to ensure her death is imminent."

"And how do you plan to do that from a world away?"

"There are actions I can take. Even from a world away."

"Like what?" Alexei sounded skeptical.

"Don't question me, Alexei. If I were you, I would stay more focused on your upcoming meeting with the Queen Mother."

Alexei couldn't help but raise an eyebrow.

"Yes, Alexei, I know you are on your way to see her. I keep up on all the intricate workings in your organization. You better hope your man doesn't fail you while you're in her presence. That may not bode well for you. She can be very unforgiving."

Alexei scowled. "You know nothing of the relationship between the Queen Mother and myself. You pathetic human. Our connection goes well beyond before you were even born."

The woman laughed.

"My man is on a helicopter with Scarlett now," Alexei continued, ignoring the woman's seeming dismissal of his importance. "It's only a matter of time now before she is dead."

"And just like you need to focus on your own matters, I must focus on my own. I'm going to do what I can to ensure Scarlett does not survive that flight. If there is good news to be had to the Queen Mother, it will be because of me. You can trust me on that."

The screen went blank just as the elevator stopped. Alexei closed the securely encoded app he used for the call and slipped the phone back into his inside jacket pocket. The elevator doors slid open and the maw of the brick tunnel to the Queen Mother's lair opened wide, prepared to swallow him into its shadows.

Alexei started down the tunnel, his thoughts on Scarlett and how Viktor could not afford to mess things up again. He knew Viktor planned on disposing of Scarlett into the North Sea, and it was just a matter of time before he got word that the deed was done.

And it better be done, Viktor, Alexei thought. *For your sake.*

18

NEVADA

"**SCARLETT?** Are you there?"

Galaxy was shouting into the thin microphone that stemmed from the Bluetooth earpiece lodged into her right ear. She was huddled over her workstation – a large desk with three wide monitors and dual keyboards, attached wirelessly to a nearby tower of super processors with blinking red and green lights – located in the weapons development facility of Level 7 of NPDIA headquarters. It was close to 3AM in Nevada and Galaxy was the only one in the room. She felt like she had been living in the weapons development facility ever since Scarlett left for Italy, tasked with keeping tabs on her day and night, with few breaks except for when she would have someone step in for a few minutes here and there as she took micronaps in an adjoining break room rest area. This night, though, she was awake, alert, and focused, as she listened in on Scarlett's meeting with Xavier Dumont – and the deafening silence that suddenly shocked her.

It was obvious to Galaxy that something bad had happened. She pressed a button on her earpiece and disengaged the microphone, then frantically typed commands into her computer in an attempt to boost the signals – both outgoing and incoming – desperately trying to get in touch with Scarlett. One moment she easily heard Scarlett speaking clearly with Xavier Dumont, and the next, the signal went full of static and feedback, before dropping altogether for several moments. When the transmission came back online, she heard Dumont talking to someone but could not tell to whom. She had no reason to believe it was Elsie Byrne, as she was a well-respected SISX agent who had been tasked by her agency, in conjunction with the NPDIA, to work with Scarlett in Belgium.

"Take them far from here," she heard Dumont say. Her Russian wasn't the strongest, and she was better at understanding it than speaking it, but she knew enough to translate what Dumont was saying. *"Take everything with you, all their belongings, and destroy all the evidence. I will dispose of their vehicles."*

She heard rustling as if Scarlett was being moved or dragged.

"Dispose of their bodies into the North Sea. Leave no trace."

More muffled sounds of movement, coupled with footsteps. The one-sided conversation continued as the she heard sliding doors and the familiar dings of elevator controls.

"Ensure no resistance. If need be, give them a second dose of sevoflurane once they get situated into the helicopter. I'll report to Alexei and let him know the deed is as good as done."

The voice stopped but the sounds continued. Before long, she heard the muffled rotors of a helicopter. She waited several more minutes, before making the assumption the copter was in the air. Since she never heard any other voices, she figured whomever Dumont was speaking to was alone. And if the helicopter was in the air, chances were that Scarlett and Elsie were in a cabin separate from the pilot. Hoping it was safe, she decided to try and get Scarlett's attention. She put a finger back onto the earpiece and reengaged the microphone.

"Agent Scarlett? Come in, Agent Scarlett."

More silence, but Galaxy was not going to give up and she worked harder to try and boost the signal.

"Scarlett. Come in. This is Galaxy."

Still no response. Galaxy released the microphone button from the earpiece and began to enter a new set of commands into her computer when the sound of the glass entrance doors sliding open caught her attention. She looked up and saw Associate Deputy Director Carrie Berglund enter the room. Galaxy made eye contact with the woman and gave her an acknowledging nod.

"Agent Ursa, I didn't expect to see you here so late."

Carrie looked reticent in her slim dark suit. "I understand Agent Scarlett had a meeting today with Xavier Dumont. Is there any news to report?"

"Actually, I think Scarlett may be in considerable trouble. I had her on audio just fine then the signal went dead for a bit. Next thing I heard was Dumont giving commands to an unknown third party at their meeting. It didn't sound good."

"How so?" Carrie had made her way up to Galaxy's workstation.

Galaxy looked up at the other woman. "I believe she's been kidnapped."

Carrie didn't say anything and instead moved to the workstation that was pressed up against and facing Galaxy's. She unlocked the system with a security code and began typing into the keyboard.

Galaxy paid no attention to the Associate Deputy Director. It wasn't unusual for higher ranking personnel to come into the facility from time to time, assessing productivity and taking notes, and occasionally doing work on the other computer station when it was not already in use. She had long since given up asking what they may be doing as she was never provided a straight response. So she just let Carrie continue on with whatever she felt she needed to do.

A dialog box suddenly opened on Galaxy's left computer monitor. Recognizing the command prompt as a signal from one of Scarlett's earring column tracking transmitters, Galaxy opened a program onto her center computer screen. The program showed an outline of Belgium and the surrounding coastline. A large swath of dark blue represented the North Sea. She reached out to Scarlett again as she worked on tracking the transmission.

"We've picked up on your signal," Galaxy said into her mic. "I'm assuming you aren't able to speak. We're zeroing in on your location."

After a minute a pulsating red dot appeared in the area of the North Sea.

"I've got you. You're over the North Sea, between Belgium and England." She studied the trajectory of the signal, then added, "Looks like you're headed further out to sea."

"Where do you think they're headed?" Carrie asked.

Galaxy looked at the other woman across the top of the computer monitors and shook her head. "I don't know but I don't think it's good."

"I'm tapping into the signal so I can hear along with you," Carrie said as she entered commands into her computer. She then picked up a small receiver off her desk and nestled it into her right ear.

Listening back in on Scarlett, Galaxy could hear her talking to another woman. After a few moments she and Carrie exchanged another look.

"We're making out another voice," Galaxy said. "Is that Elsie Byrne? The SISX agent you met at dinner?"

"Yes, it is."

The sudden response to her question surprised Galaxy, but it seemed to double as a response to Elsie and what they had been discussing: Scarlett's attempted killer. She quickly entered new commands into her workstation. All three of her computer monitors were filled with a mix of tracking imagery, columns of code, and other applications providing real-time data related to the situation, including an image of a work room from across the world. The room was similar to the NPDIA control center with its bevy of monitors, workstations, and bustling personnel.

"We've been in contact with SISX," Galaxy said to Scarlett. "We've tied them into your signal. They have boats in the North Sea tracking you from the water."

Carrie raised an eyebrow. She pulled up a separate program that showed a radar scope from SISX. The area covered was a portion of the North Sea, with Scarlett's helicopter blip in the upper left of the image, along with three other blips far behind and to the right representing three boats in the water. She lowered her head as she studied her computer screens for a few moments, then brought her eyes up to where she could barely see Galaxy over the top of their center monitors.

"Dr. Choi," Carrie said calmly.

Engrossed in studying her displays and intently listening for any further clues from Scarlett, the little Korean woman didn't seem to hear the Associate Deputy Director, or if she did, was ignoring her.

"Here, quick. Pull up my left suit jacket and sleeve," Carrie heard Scarlett say. Then a moment later, "I have knives hidden under my sleeve."

Carrie's right hand slipped behind her back and under her suit jacket, where she discreetly removed a black and silver M48 Cyclone 8-inch spiral blade from its custom sheath. The glass-fiber-reinforced handle felt good in her hand, weighted but not heavy. She brought her hand to her lap, where she rested the weapon that had the reputation of being "the world's deadliest knife."

"Dr. Choi," Carrie said again, though louder and more firmly. "We need to stop this."

Galaxy glanced up at her, annoyance evident in her furrowed brow. She looked back down at her monitors, dismissive. "Stop what?"

"We've got to let Scarlett go. She cannot survive any longer."

"What do you mean?" Galaxy looked up again, confusion washing over her face.

"Scarlett and her family have been a thorn in the side of the cause for too long. I'm going to put a stop to it."

"*Cause?*" Galaxy's full attention was on Carrie now. "What cause? What are you talking about?"

Carrie typed an entry into her keyboard and Galaxy's monitors went black as her system immediately shut down. "I'm taking control of the situation. I suggest you sit there and stay out of the way while I do what I need to do."

Galaxy crammed codes and commands into her keyboard but her workstation wouldn't get back online. The darkness of her screens exemplified the gloom of her situation. She banged her fists on her keyboard then stood up and leaned forward, seething.

"What the fuck are you doing? And I demand to know what *cause* you're talking about."

Carrie looked up at the woman, glaring at her from across the desks with a shrewd look in her eyes. "I'm talking about the Gorgons."

Galaxy blinked and tersely shook her head. "Fuck you, the *Gorgons*? Are you one of them?"

Carrie smirked. "No, but I've been working with them for some time."

In that moment, Galaxy realized the only way she was going to make it out of this situation alive was if Carrie didn't. There was no way Carrie – Agent Ursa whom she had known, worked with, and respected for years – would have revealed that information without the intention of it never being repeated. She remembered a rule from her agent training: if the bad guy tells you what their plan is, then your survival is not part of that plan.

Sounds of a struggle came through Galaxy's earpiece. Even though Carrie had killed her workstation, the earpiece worked on separate frequencies and servers since it was tied in with global satellite surveillance systems.

"Stop!" she heard Elsie shout out to their assailant.

Carrie heard the commotion, too, and resumed her rapid keystrokes. "I've about had enough of listening to this nonsense. Time to cut the precious Scarlett loose."

Galaxy pressed the transmitter on hear earpiece. "Scarlett! Listen to me. Come in, Scar –"

The earpiece went dead and Galaxy could no longer hear anything. She pressed the transmitter button frantically. "Scarlett! Can you hear me? Scarlett!"

Galaxy marched around the desks, her white lab coat practically billowing in her haste, intent on confronting the Associate Deputy

Director. Carrie kept typing without breaking concentration from her computer.

"What did you do?" Galaxy demanded. She smacked a hand flat onto the desk. "Listen to me, you bitch!"

Carrie swiped the knife off her lap and stood up fast, causing her chair to fall back onto the floor. She pointed the deadly blade at Galaxy, just inches from her face.

"No, you listen to *me*," Carrie said as she took a step towards the other woman, forcing Galaxy to backpedal.

Galaxy kept her eyes on the knifepoint held steadfast in front of her as she took cautious steps backwards. Her hands were up with her palms facing towards Carrie, but she was careful not to bring them up near the knife so as to not let the Associate Deputy Director believe she would make any unexpected moves.

"The end of civilization as you know it is happening soon," Carrie said. "The Gorgons will soon rule over everyone, and I intend to be around long after that happens."

Galaxy found herself backed up against one of the long steel tables that peppered the room. Carrie was just a couple steps in front of her, close enough to easily plunge the knife into her without hesitation. Keeping her eyes on the knife, Galaxy brought her hands slowly down to her sides, touching the cold steel of the tabletop behind her.

"Killing me won't do you any good. How would you explain me being found with knife wounds in me for no apparent reason?"

"Easy, really," Carrie said, smugly. "Someone in the NPDIA has been spying for the Gorgons, letting them know of Scarlett's existence and whereabouts. Scarlett is supposed to already be dead, to strike fear and dread into our Deputy Director, and to weaken our resolve as the Gorgons ready themselves to take over the world at the G50 summit."

Galaxy's eyes widened as she looked away from the knife and locked eyes with Carrie. "You. You're the spy?" Her blood boiled to the point where she thought her glasses might fog over. "We had suspected they had someone on the inside. I would have never thought it was you."

Carrie smiled. "But as far as everyone here is going to be concerned, it was you. And I did the agency a favor by killing you before you could do any more harm. It's a shame they'll barely recognize that little face of yours once I'm done with it."

The Associate Deputy Director moved fast, jabbing the knife at Galaxy's face. The smaller woman was expecting the attack and ducked to her left, while her right hand brought a metal clipboard she had found by touch on the tabletop around from behind her, smacking the cold metal edge of it into Carrie's knife hand. Carrie let out a yelp but she didn't lose grip of her weapon. Galaxy dropped to the floor, scrambled backwards under the rolling table, and popped up on its other side.

"You're not going to get away," Carrie said, the menace in her voice not going unnoticed by Galaxy. "There's nowhere to run, and you've got to go through me to get to the exit door."

Carrie smacked the edge of the table in front of her causing it to slam into Galaxy's midsection, knocking her to the floor. The Associate Deputy Director leaped onto the table, sliding sideways across it and knocking various computer parts – motherboards, processing units, and casings – along with dozens of tiny screws and an open screwdriver set crashing on top of Galaxy. Carrie slid herself off the table and stood over the smaller woman cowering on the floor.

"You can't win," Carrie said. "The Gorgons are going to rule the world. Humans are either with them or against them. I choose to be with them."

Galaxy looked up at her attacker, resolute. "And I choose to be against them."

The pain in Carrie's foot was instantaneous and she cried out in pain. Sticking straight up from the top of her right boot was the handle of a screwdriver. Blood was already soaking out onto the smooth rock floor as the tool had gone completely through her foot and punctured the outsole of her ankle-high black boot.

The Korean woman was on her hands and knees, clambering away. Carrie reached down and yanked the Phillips screwdriver out of her foot and tossed it aside. She limped towards Galaxy, who was back on her feet and racing towards another nearby table. The distance wasn't far and Carrie caught up to her in just a few, though painful, strides. Carrie thrust her knife towards Galaxy's back, but the smaller woman turned and was holding a weapon of her own – a stainless steel spiked-back Bowie knife – that she had scooped up off the table. Galaxy twisted her body to avoid Carrie's deadly strike, while simultaneously using her own knife to parry the attack.

Galaxy continued her motion and brought her vicious Bowie knife up and jabbed it towards Carrie's chest. The Associate Deputy Director took a step back while completing a counter-parry, knocking Galaxy's blade away. The two women stared at each other for a moment, sizing each other up and calculating the fight that was about to ensue. Then it began.

Like a well-choreographed duel between Errol Flynn and Basil Rathbone, the battle was fierce, fast, and ferocious. But instead of fencing with swords or sabers, the women had only their knives, dramatically increasing the danger while reducing the margin of error due to the close proximity of their clashing short, metal blades. Every attack, parry, and riposte was dangerously close to either their faces or bodies, not to mention the hands that held their respective weapons.

Carrie's attacks were straightforward and ruthless in their nature, using all her strength and brute force as she fought to make her mark on the smaller woman. Not terribly nuanced or sophisticated, Carrie grunted and shouted as she battled and did her best to break her opponent down, eager to get back to her task of seeing Scarlett's demise.

Galaxy's style was more elegant and refined. She almost appeared to be in a "zone" as she focused solely on Carrie's knife. She employed more defensive moves than offensive, taking quick mental notes as she studied Carrie's attacking patterns, catalogued them, and searched for holes and mistakes.

Carrie advanced rapidly, the steel of their knives clashing and clanking, and Galaxy weaved backwards around various tables before finding herself pinned on the inside corner of where two long tables came together in an L-shape. The taller woman lunged and stabbed again, with the strike coming within an inch of Galaxy's face before it was blocked. Carrie jabbed a second time at her opponent's face, and Galaxy countered to block again with her knife, but Carrie feinted and instead dropped low, stabbing Galaxy in her left side.

Galaxy screeched in pain. Carrie used her free hand to grab the wrist of Galaxy's knife hand, forcing the weapon up and holding it away from any immediate danger. The Korean woman cried out louder as Carrie twisted her spiral-shaped blade, tearing into Galaxy's innards. The white lab coat splattered with red swaths of blood.

Galaxy reached her empty hand onto the table beside her, searching for something – anything – to use as a weapon. Grabbing hold of a large empty glass beaker, she smashed it into the right side of Carrie's face, creating several deep cuts along with multitudes of scratches and abrasions. Shards of broken glass and streams of blood sprayed in all directions, and Carrie, screaming, instinctively brought both of her hands to her mutilated face, pulling her knife out of Galaxy's side in the process.

Galaxy hobbled away as quickly as she could and headed towards the glass entrance doors, holding her left side as blood seeped out between her fingers. She stopped and half-leaned, half-fell onto another of the steel tables in the room, knocking awry several seemingly random items such as a deck of cards, a white and red china dinner plate, and a ball-point pen, among other things.

Carrie tossed away her knife and reached inside her jacket, pulling out a 9mm Taurus PT111 handgun from its concealed holster. She turned and set her eyes on Galaxy, half a room away and holding herself up against a table. Their eyes met, Carrie's filled with rage and Galaxy's looking nearly defeated.

"That's it, you bitch," Carrie said, her hand shakily trying to take aim as she fought the pain growing in her foot. "I wanted to be more discreet but fuck this noise!"

Galaxy had a hold of the deck of cards from the table and she tossed them in the air in front of her as Carrie let loose a barrage of bullets, emptying all twelve shots from her pistol. The cards were not ordinary plastic-coated paper like they appeared. The cards separated and spun in the air, and the bullets pumped in her direction were drawn to them, exploding as steel met the loose flying pieces of the deck. Sparks erupted as the bullets disintegrated on face cards and numbered cards alike, and in an instant the remaining cards fell to the floor.

Ignoring the pain in her foot, Carrie ran at Galaxy, slamming a fresh magazine into her 9mm. Galaxy grabbed the china dinner plate off the table and flung it at her attacker like a Frisbee. The plate turned orange-red in the air as it instantly superheated and became a fiery projectile. Carrie dropped to the floor and the flaming discus narrowly missed her head, smashing against a tower of databanks and computer processors, and erupting into a swarm of infinitesimal glowing embers that rapidly burned themselves out as they fell to the floor.

The Associate Deputy Director was on her hands and knees, exhausted with pain, but still holding her gun and intent on killing the woman who not only stood in the way of her goal of seeing Scarlett die, but also undoubtedly had left her face scarred for life. She reached up and gingerly touched the cuts on her face, and fresh adrenaline surged through her as she leapt to her feet and rushed again at her target. Her gun was raised and she held it with both hands, steadying it as best as she could. She was just about five feet away from Galaxy and, this time, she knew she wouldn't miss. Galaxy's back was to her as she leaned onto the steel table.

"Turn around slowly, Dr. Choi," Carrie demanded. "I want to see your face before I pump it full of bullets. The cuts you gave me will be nothing to what you're about to experience."

The small Korean woman, her short black hair disheveled, glasses slightly crooked, and lab coat saturated with blood, slowly turned to face her assailant one last time. Her eyes no longer showed pain, but hatred for the woman who had betrayed not only her but also the agency that had trained, supported, and nurtured her for so long.

"Any last requests before you die?"

Galaxy held up her right hand and displayed a small black plastic cylinder that looked like…

"Lipstick?" Carrie asked, incredulous. She started to laugh but pain like white fire shot through her face, reminding her of her wounds. "Your last request is to put on lipstick? Well, by all means, indulge yourself."

Galaxy weakly pulled the cap off the small tube. She held the cylinder in both hands and went to twist the bottom. She showed the open end to Carrie.

Carrie dismissed looking at it. "I hope it matches the red of your blood, because that's the only color that you're going to be covered in."

"This shade is called *Fire Red*," Galaxy said, and she twisted the bottom of the tube.

A stream of fire instantly shot out at Carrie. Not just an ordinary flame, the fire was attached to flammable droplets that sprayed all over Carrie's arms, chest, and face that spread and burn as they struck. The gun went off, firing three shots in various directions as Carrie involuntarily pulled the trigger in a panic as she burned. None of the bullets were in Galaxy's direction. Carrie dropped her gun and fell to the floor, curling up into a twitching, burning mass.

Galaxy reached below the table and grabbed a fire extinguisher from a lower shelf and exterminated the flames, leaving a grotesque, blackened, smoking corpse that no longer appeared human. Galaxy moaned, and even she didn't know if it was from the pain in her side or from being grossed out by the look and stench of the carcass on the floor. She didn't have time to be concerned about either, though, and holding her side, staggered over to the workstation Carrie had been using. The traitor may have rendered the earring transmitters useless, but Galaxy had other ways to try and get through to Scarlett.

First thing was first, though, and she pressed a button on the underside of the desk. Red siren lights began flashing through the room as an emergency signal was sent to other components, as well as the command center, of NPDIA headquarters. Help would come for her soon.

After a few keystrokes, the monitor on her right showed an image of a pair of black sunglasses, with blue dots flashing near the ends of the earpieces. Initiating the workstation's built in audio hardware, sounds from the helicopter erupted from the system's speakers. There was the sound of rushing wind, followed by two familiar pulses from Scarlett's ECE device built onto her Glock. A few moments later she heard what sounded like a faint distant explosion. Mustering all her strength, she shouted at Scarlett, hoping the agent would hear her from the earpieces of the sunglasses.

"Scarlett! It's Galaxy. I'm calling you through your sunglasses. Can you hear me?"

She paused a moment and waited. No response.

"Agent Scarlett! You need to put on the sunglasses. Come in, Scarlett."

More silence. She took a deep breath and yelled as loud as the pain in her side would allow.

"Scarlett – put the sunglasses on. Scarlett, do you read? Get these sunglasses on!"

The flashing blue dots on the outline of the sunglasses turned green. Someone had put on the sunglasses. She hoped it was Scarlett.

"Agent Scarlett, I can't get you through the earrings."

"I'm here, Galaxy." The sound of Scarlett's voice brought a wave of relief through her.

"Thank God. Are you okay? I can't explain right now, but we lost transmission through the earrings…"

In the following moments, Galaxy instructed Scarlett to use her watch so she could synchronize with the helicopter and control it remotely. Once the agent a world away had jumped to safety, she controlled the helicopter to plunge into the water, where it would settle into a watery grave at the bottom of the North Sea.

The glass doors to the weapons facility slid open. Galaxy looked weakly at the agents and medics rushing into the room, led by Deputy Director Carlos Correa. She produced a faint smile in his direction, then promptly passed out.

19

MOSCOW

ALEXEI Volkov stared nervously at the silhouetted back of the Queen Mother.

They were in her throne room, located several floors beneath Hexatetron corporate headquarters. As with most of the Queen Mother's chambers, the throne room had subdued lighting and dark corners. The namesake of the room – an opulent pewter and silver chair with wide arms and a high back that radiated twisting snake bodies and heads sculpted in chrome – was placed at one end on a short dais with three steps leading up to it. A dark open archway that led to the Queen Mother's private quarters was bored out of the rock behind the chair. The room was much longer than it was wide, and the long side walls hinted at the natural underground rock from behind magnificent tapestries that dated back several centuries. The floor was covered in 24-inch long black and gray tiles, antiqued with high and low spots that gave them a weathered, worn feel. There were two entrances to the room, one each in the side walls at the far end away from the dais.

A dozen stone statues lined up along each wall, six on each side, in front of the tapestries and were amply spaced. These were no ordinary statues, however; they were people: men, women, and one child approximately ten-years old, who had been victims of the Queen Mother throughout the decades. They were turned to stone for a variety of reasons – stealing, dishonesty, lying, or betrayal. Each of their bodies and faces was twisted in a combination of fear and agony, eternal reminders of her fury and unrivaled rule.

It wasn't the statues, though, that commanded the most attention in the room.

Made of clear glass over a foot thick, the entire wall opposite the throne was a giant window into an immense aquarium. As wide as a movie screen, the window provided a spectacular view of hundreds of fish and a multitude of undersea life in a crystal-clear environment composed of sand, rock, and various live vegetation. The most impressive component of the display, though, was not the fact that a mechanical marvel created such a remarkable habitat so far underground in the first place, but rather, its unusual main occupants.

Three live mermaids swam in the water, each with long, flowing magenta hair and green eyes. The upper parts of their bodies were bare, exposing their small breasts and olive-tinged skin. Their midsections were covered in translucent scales that became pronounced, vibrant colors, that in turn ran the length of their sleek, tapered lowered bodies and into their wide flowing tails. Each of the mermaids' lower bodies had different colors: one a deep burgundy, one a bright teal, and the third an amethyst purple.

Anastacia Dimitrova, the Queen Mother, stood at the middle of the clear wall, facing her prized possessions. While mermaids were more prevalent in the seas than humans realized, very few were kept in captivity. There was an open top to the aquarium that could not be seen from the throne room, where handlers would feed the part-human, part-fish creatures along with the other sea life. Anastacia would sometimes visit her mermaids from that area, where they would come partway out of the water and allow their "owner" to touch their hair and skin in the loving way that she would. The part-humanoids could not communicate in any known language, and could not breathe air, so their time above water was always brief. They never feared the Gorgon woman, having no real comprehension of what she was, what she was capable of, or the pain and suffering she could bring.

The snakes on the Queen Mother's head intertwined among themselves as the Gorgon put a hand on the glass. The burgundy-tailed mermaid swam to her, blinking her green eyes then pressing a cheek onto her side of the glass as if she was being touched. The creature then swam away and joined the other two – Anastacia referred to the three as "sisters" to each other even though she had no reason to believe they were related in any way – swimming in figure eights and other patterns almost as if they were purposely providing entertainment to their owner.

Alexei had the news that Viktor was dead and that Scarlett was in the hands of the British agency known as SISX. He was about to provide the Queen Mother with the information but the woman spoke first.

"My contact in the NPDIA is dead," she said to him in Russian.

"That's unfortunate," Alexei responded.

Anastacia turned and faced Alexei, who stood near the center of the room looking down and away, and began walking towards him. As she approached and her silhouetted shape moved into a closer light, Alexei could see she wore a long, flowing, sequined emerald green dress that dragged on the floor a few feet behind her. As she walked her arms swung slightly from side to side as opposed to front to back like humans – or other humanlike Gorgons, for that matter. Her gait was flowing and smooth, almost floating. Alexei wondered if she had the legs of a human under the long dresses she wore or if there was something else. Despite knowing her for over a century, there were still some mysteries about her to which he did not know the answer – or perhaps, truth be told, he did not *want* to know those answers.

"It's been brought to my attention that Sssscarlett was informed of the G50 conference. Yet another failure on the part of one of your men. I hope, though, that fact is inconsequential. I trust you have better news to provide."

After a few long, silent moments, Alexei looked up and faced the Queen Mother. The solid black of her eyes bored into him.

"I'm afraid my report may not be the news you desire." Alexei's voice was unwavering, though a little quiet.

Anastacia said nothing as she moved closer to him. Her cold eyes kept a lock on his, and when she drew near she continued her pace and walked around him, slowly, looking him up and down. The snakes on her head seemed agitated as their hissing increased. Alexei didn't move, remaining steady with his head up, looking forward like a soldier at attention.

"Tell me, Alexei...what is your news?" Her words were slow, deliberate.

During their long time together, Alexei and Anastacia had become the closest of friends, having looked out for each other for over a century. But the Queen Mother's temper was well-known, and he knew she would cope with only so much failure. As she walked around him and out of view, he focused on statues across the room, knowing his next words could very well turn him into another of the throne room's adornments.

Alexei took a deep breath. He could hear the snakes behind him, and thought he could feel the Queen Mother's breath on the back of his neck.

"Scarlett lives," he finally said. *"She thwarted my man in Belgium and is now safe at SISX headquarters."*

Save for the snakes, excruciating silence filled the room as Alexei waited for a response. His mind raced as he anticipated her reaction. Would it be anger? Forgiveness? Understanding? Anything would be better than the countless moments that followed, the sound of the snakes pounding in his ears like high winds of a hurricane.

"Alexssssssei..."

He felt her hand on his shoulder, urging him to turn around. He complied, if not hesitantly, unsure of what was to follow. They stood face-to-face. The cracks in the white-gray of her skin didn't move and her look was expressionless. She grabbed him by both shoulders, not sudden, but sternly, and her long, black fingernails dug through his suit and into his skin. The Queen Mother possessed strength far beyond that of a mere human, or of any other Gorgon, and she was never afraid to use it. He stood strong – he knew the Queen Mother didn't like shows of weakness – and endured the pain in his shoulders as long as he could.

"You used to be the best, Alexei. The strongest and most reliable."

She pulled him closer and he could smell her foul breath as the snakes closest to him snapped at his forehead, just out of reach. Her black eyes turned gray, then white, and began to glow. No matter how Alexei tried, he could not take his eyes off them as her power took hold of him.

"I am done with failure." Her voice was stern and grew in intensity as she spoke. *"This woman eludes us at every turn. I will not abide her survival any longer."*

Anastacia had speed that rivaled her strength, and before Alexei could prepare himself, she released his shoulders and slammed her palms into his chest, sending him flying across the room and into one of the statues. The statue didn't move, while Alexei slumped down onto the floor, coughing as he fought to gain his breath, and preparing for a fate he knew he would not be able to avoid.

But to his surprise, instead of unleashing her wrath on him, she turned and faced the aquarium with her arms outstretched to her sides as she let out an unholy shriek. Small flashes of lightning sparked around her eyes, and then white, opaque beams shot out of them and went through the glass, and struck the mermaid with the blue-green tail. The red-haired beauty stopped swimming and a grimace of pain appeared on her face. Her green eyes turned gray, quickly followed by the rest of her, as she turned to stone and dropped to the bottom of the aquarium.

A cloud of sand bloomed through the water while fish and other marine life scattered away. The other two mermaids, though, were curious at first, approaching their fallen sister with confusion. They swam to her and each touched her cold, stone skin. It was then they realized she wasn't the same and that something was terribly and irreversibly wrong. Horror washed over their faces and they released unheard wails in the water that cut through Alexei's heart more than he expected. The Queen Mother always seemed to consider the mermaids to be more like family than pets, and Alexei could only imagine the amount of anger Anastacia must have felt to kill one of them.

Still… *Better them than me,* he thought.

Before Alexei could otherwise react, Anastacia was upon him with her superhuman speed, and lifted him in the air by his throat using both of her hands. He clawed and grabbed at them, but the Queen Mother's strength was beyond anything he could fight against.

"We will use Ssss.carlett's knowledge of the G50 conference to our advantage."

Alexei struggled to listen just as he struggled to breathe – not the most ideal of positions to be in while being provided direction. He did his best to remain calm and listen to the Queen Mother's words. He knew they would not be repeated.

"You will head up a task force and set a trap to capture Scarlett in Dubai. I am certain she will be there and you will bring her to me. We will use her to get to Ares and bring his organization down once and for all. And then I will do what you have failed to accomplish and kill her myself."

Anastacia threw Alexei against the nearest wall and then immediately stood over him.

"I am done with your games – I'm taking full control now."

She bent down and brought her face to within inches of his. He turned his head away, keeping an eye on her with a sideways look.

"May the Gorgon gods have more mercy on you than I if you fail again. You will make a sad yet necessary addition to my gallery of statues, but not before experiencing pain unlike anything I have unleashed in a hundred years."

Anastacia stood and walked away, leaving Alexei clutching at his throat and regaining his breath as he silently thanked the gods for sparing him.

This time, anyway.

20

LONDON

MARIS was in what looked like an extra-large single occupant hospital room. She had no grasp of how long she had there after being brought to SISX headquarters following her rescue from the North Sea. There was no clock in the room. The place was immaculately clean and smelled of sterilization, and was sparse despite its spaciousness. There was a rolling hospital bed that she slept on, next to which stood a tower of equipment to monitor her vitals, though they were not connected to her at the moment. Next to the tower was a rolling cart of relatively shallow drawers, each with a key lock to keep their contents safe from unscrupulous eyes; and next to the cart was a simple rolling chair with a plastic seat and seat back. Across from the bed on the other side of the room was a dresser, and attached to a wall in a far upper corner was a television that was never turned on as there was no remote to operate it. A single forest green contoured chair sat on the floor facing the direction of the television. There was a large rectangular window, though it was completely shuttered by a set of vertical steel blinds that kept out any hint of light and had a lock on them. A small restroom with a lavatory, sink, and shower was through a doorway on the opposite side of the room from her bed.

The SISX agents were extremely polite, without the usual "rough edges" she was used to from Americans. Despite being treated cordially, Maris couldn't help but feel like a bit of a prisoner. After she was plucked from the water, she was laid out on a padded bench inside the boat. Exhausted, she barely remembered her basic vitals being checked, or being given a brief non-invasive examination by a SISX medic. She remembered any questions she had asked that were related to SISX were ignored. Conversation remained pretty stagnant throughout their trip.

The boats docked in a seaport in Dover, England. From there, she was taken by a windowless van to what she was told was SISX headquarters, though she wasn't positive of the exact location as she was hooded as they approached London. Secrecy was understandably as vital to their organization as it was to the NPDIA. If they were above ground or below, she didn't know. If they were rooted in the heart of London or somewhere on its outskirts, she didn't know. The agents kept her hooded until she was released into her hospital-like room.

She was tired, incredibly sore, and hungry, but was not provided any sustenance until a female agent in a gray suit and skirt brought in a rolling steel tray with quite a variety on it – a plate of traditional bangers (sausages) and mash, peas, and gravy; along with a carafe of orange juice, a pitcher of ice water, and a half pint of Newcastle Brown Ale – about an hour after her placement in the room. In the meantime, she had taken a hot shower and dressed into a black sweat suit and fresh undergarments that were in one of the dresser drawers. In fact, the dresser was filled with several days' worth of the same matching black sweat suits and sets of underwear. She hoped she wouldn't end up wearing through them all before being released. She was also provided a pair of black and white Adidas. No other clothing was supplied. Her Glock was nowhere to be found.

Despite her mouth being dry and feeling a bit dehydrated, Maris chugged down the beer first. It wasn't nearly as satisfying as her favorite Four Roses bourbon, but it was refreshing. She made short order of the plate of food, then guzzled half the pitcher of water. Satisfied, she actually drank the orange juice in smaller sips, savoring the sugar sweetness and citrus flavor of the beverage.

Shortly after finishing her meal, a male nurse paid her a visit and checked her vitals, then promptly left. After a few hours of restlessness in the room, she decided to get some sleep. She slept soundly, except for being awoken twice for vitals checks. It was always a different nurse who performed the screenings.

It felt as though at least a full day and night passed. She had been brought five separate meals, and it was always a different agent who delivered it. Everyone that visited her was always well-mannered but said very little, and insisted her questions would be answered in due time. She guessed it was mid-afternoon as she settled into the green contoured chair facing the television, staring at the blank wall under the black screen. She was growing evermore restless and impatient, and her mind wandered.

Elsie.

Maris barely knew her. And even though initially she wasn't sure she could trust the Englishwoman, they had made an indelible connection during their dinner that Maris couldn't ignore. Elsie didn't deserve to die at the hands of the Gorgon the way she did. Somehow, Elsie's death hurt her more than any of her fellow agents ever had.

Maris leaned forward with her elbows on her knees and buried her face into her hands. Her honey-colored hair draped around her forearms like a shroud, helping to block out the world as she ran through her head everything that had happened in the last few days. She had barely had any significant downtime – no real time to fully process everything she had gone through. In many respects, she was used to these circumstances from her experiences with the CIA, but this mission was so unlike anything she had done before, and she had a feeling it was only going to get crazier before it got better.

The usual knock on the door before someone immediately entering interrupted her thoughts. Maris rubbed her face with her hands before standing and turning to face her latest visitor, expecting to see a nurse ready to check vitals. Instead, standing inside the room were three agents in suits.

In front was a woman who appeared to be in her fifties, with mid-length feathered salt-and-pepper hair parted to one side. She was shorter than Maris, even in the heels that clacked against the industrial tile floor when she entered. She wore a gray pantsuit with a white blouse, its top button unbuttoned. The woman was flanked by two larger men in dark navy suits, white shirts, and blue ties. The men stood at attention, looking straight ahead, and did not acknowledge Maris – not a side eye, blink, or anything. The posture of the three clearly placed the woman in front in a position of authority, and Maris could not tell if the men were truly agents, or the woman's bodyguards, or both.

The woman showed a smile that was broad and kind as she extended a hand towards Maris.

"Hello, Agent Scarlett," she said, her heavy English accent dripping from every word. "I'm Chief Dame X. Pleased to meet you."

"Scarlett Caso." Maris politely shook the woman's hand. She sat against the top of the contoured chair back which was just behind her and facing the opposite way, and crossed her arms.

"I'd like to say the pleasure is mine, but I can't say I've really felt welcome being locked up in here." Maris sounded irritated and did her best to not come across as disrespectful.

"My apologies for how you've been treated, Agent Scarlett. My people have been communicating with yours at the NPDIA over the last 24 hours, sharing information and coming up with our next steps. Unfortunately, you weren't privy to those discussions."

"So what *am* I privy to?"

Dame X looked up and behind to the brutes on either side of her. "Leave us," she commanded, and the two larger gentlemen exited the room and closed the door behind them. She refocused on Maris.

"Well, first, I thought you might like to know the condition of Commander Byrne."

"Elsie?" Maris' look transformed to a combination of worry and excitement. Her body stiffened and she put a hand to her mouth. "Is she alive?"

"For now," Dame X nodded, though her face was grim. "She's lucky to be. One of our boats rescued her from the North Sea. Your people had tied us into your locator beacon and we were tracking you when your signal went dead. Luckily, we already had your helicopter in distant sight when we saw her body fall."

"Can I see her?"

The Chief remained stoic. "Yes, but I warn you, we aren't sure if she's going to make it."

████████ • • • ████████

DAME X led Maris out of her room, past the two brutes who had been in her room but were now waiting outside her door, and to a higher floor in the building. As they traversed the building and changed floors via elevator, the Chief explained that they were in SISX headquarters, located on the outskirts of London. The building had 23 above-ground floors, with floors ten through fourteen being hospital wards and other medical facilities, and another eight floors that extended underground. Maris had been kept on the eleventh floor, and Elsie's ICU was on the thirteenth.

Maris' head was scrambled with questions about the next steps the NPDIA and SISX had come up with, but she was more focused on wanting to know about Elsie's condition. As such, she remained quiet in her thoughts and worry while she was led to the intensive care floor.

The Chief did not take Maris into Elsie's room itself, but rather to a dark observation area on the other side of a two-way mirror that peered into the modestly lit ICU room.

Bandages covered Elsie's head from her ears to the top of her head. Her eyes were black from the trauma her body had experienced. A ventilator was attached around her nose and mouth. She had a neck brace and her right arm was in a full cast, as were her legs. Metal braces came up from around her back and held her upper body in place. Monitors beeped and hummed, and the sounds of the ICU room could be heard through speakers in the observation space. No one else was in the room with Elsie at the moment, though she was being constantly monitored from a nurse's station remotely.

"This is as close as we're going to get for the time being," Dame X said, looking at her agent through the mirror.

Maris placed a hand on the glass, and stood so close to it her nose was nearly touching.

"She has extensive injuries and has been in a coma since she arrived," the Chief continued. "Internal bleeding in her head was putting pressure on her brain and we had to drill a hole in her skull to relieve it. Her windpipe was nearly crushed. Both of her lungs were collapsed and so the ventilator is doing all the breathing for her. Her arm and both legs are broken in several places. She has fractures in her neck and spine, and right now we aren't sure about the extent of any damage to her spinal cord. We don't know if she's ever going to walk or have use of her arm again."

The more the Chief described, the further away her voice sounded. Maris couldn't recount everything the woman said. All she knew was Elsie was barely clinging to life.

"I wish I could have done more to help save her from all this," Maris said, her voice low. She was talking as much to herself as she was to the SISX chief.

"Stop that," Dame X said, her voice unsympathetic. "It's the perils of the job. You know that."

Maris' gaze stayed on the broken woman while she answered. "I know."

"Take solace in knowing we found parts of the Russian. You made short order of him. That was nice work."

Maris finally tore her eyes away and looked at the Chief.

"That was just the beginning," Maris said, resolute. "There's more work to be done."

"There most certainly is, Agent Scarlett. And we've got your next mission."

■■■■ ● ● ● ■■■■

CHIEF Dame X's office was smaller than Carlos' back at the NPDIA, resembling a modest living room that didn't spare on the leather. There was a leather couch and matching loveseat, leather padding on the walls, and her desk chair was also leather. A glass-top coffee table sat in the middle of the room with the couches on one side and the chief's desk on the other. Two glass end tables matching the coffee table flanked the couches. Lamps sat on the floor in the two corners of the room farthest away from the double-wide leather padded doors. Each lamp post stretched up then separated into five individual overarching poles that shined light downward. A flatscreen monitor with a static image of the SISX crest was mounted to a side wall where it could be easily viewed from the desk or couches.

Dame X and Maris were the only ones in the room. They had relocated to the Chief's office after the disheartening observation of Elsie. The Chief sat behind her desk, while Maris was on the loveseat, still wearing her sweat suit and Adidas. She leaned back, getting more comfortable.

"I've been meaning to ask," Maris began, "what do I call you? Chief X? Just Chief? Or something else entirely?"

"Dame X will do, thank you."

"I thought SISX didn't use codenames."

"Dame X is less a codename than it is a title, Agent Scarlett, and is an acceptable shortening of Chief Dame X."

"How long have you been Dame X?"

"Five years. I took over when the last chief was killed on a mission in Singapore. And I have a long way to go. The position is essentially a lifetime appointment."

Maris sat upright. "Have you taken on anything like the Gorgons before?"

The Chief scribbled something on a notepad in front of her. "Small skirmishes, yes. And I've been involved with larger campaigns as an agent. But I've never overseen a large operation like the one we're about to undertake."

Maris tightened her jaw. She looked at the Chief, skeptical.

"You can wipe that look off your face, Agent Scarlett. We've got some assistance in this. From someone you know."

"Oh, yeah?" Maris was still more uncertain than curious. "Who?"

The SISX crest on the monitor hanging on the wall dissolved and in place was her father, sitting behind his desk in NPDIA headquarters.

"Hello, Agent Scarlett." His tone was dry.

"Deputy Director Correa," Maris returned, maintaining a strictly business manner. Not to mention she didn't know if Dame X knew of the kinship between the two of them.

Carlos' hands were clasped together and rested on his desk.

"Before we get into mission specifics," Carlos said, "you should know what's occurred here at headquarters."

Maris stood up from the loveseat. It sounded like something was wrong. She took a step towards the monitor.

"There was a spy in the agency. Associate Deputy Director Carrie Berglund, or Agent Ursa, as you also knew her."

Maris' jaw dropped. The shock was less about Carrie being a spy as it was about the fact the agency had been infiltrated in the first place. She knew things like that could happen – the Federal Government was no stranger to traitors and betrayal – but for some reason she held the NPDIA in a higher regard, if not the highest regard, considering their secrecy and importance.

"What happened?" Maris asked.

"While you were fighting over the North Sea, she revealed herself to Agent Galaxy."

"Galaxy?" Maris' head spun. Images of her fight in the helicopter flashed in front of her…in particular the moment the large Russian grabbed Elsie by the throat and the receiver in her ear went dead. She knew when she lost contact something must have happened. She never fathomed it had something to do with the Associate Deputy Director.

"Is she okay?"

"She required some emergency surgery to a stab wound in her side, but she's expected to make a full recovery."

"Thank goodness," Maris said, only partially relieved. First there was Elsie barely clinging on to life, and now the news of Galaxy. This was a game more dangerous than any she had ever encountered in the CIA due to how high it reached.

"Can't say the same for Agent Ursa," Carlos continued. "She was found burnt to a crisp by one of Agent Galaxy's special weapons."

Maris shook her head. "Served the bitch right."

"I would echo that sentiment," Dame X added.

"There was some good to come from this, though," said Carlos. "During their altercation, Agent Ursa revealed to Galaxy that the Gorgons are planning a large scale takeover at the upcoming G50 conference in Dubai. The world's leaders are going to be there. We suspect, between what Carrie told Galaxy and the information you gathered in Antwerp, that the Gorgons plan to eliminate those leaders at that event."

Maris blinked. Everything was becoming clear. "When I was at the summit in Pantelleria, there were representatives from fifty nations, all of whom were connected to high levels of leadership in their respective countries. And they're all working for the Gorgons. The G50 conference is going to be broadcast all over the world..." Her voice trailed off as a realization struck.

"What better way to announce themselves than to kill the world's presidents, prime ministers, and other leaders than on that global stage."

"We're not going to allow that to happen," Dame X said. "The G50 is in three days. We've had a special team prepping here already. The NPDIA has a team of Americans readying themselves as well."

"I'll be heading up that team," Carlos said.

Maris looked at her father. Outwardly she remained steadfast, but internally she was conflicted. Yes, she had become estranged from her father over the years, but knowing the scope and the danger of this mission, she wasn't sure she wanted him involved up close.

"With all due respect, Deputy Director," she said, "wouldn't it be better for you to oversee operations from headquarters?"

His eyes settled on hers. "Agent Scarlett, my fight with the Gorgons spans many years. We need to end this now and forever. I intend to be a part of that."

There was already too much death and pain in this fight, Maris contemplated. If her father was to get seriously hurt – or worse – in this, she didn't know what she would do.

Dame X continued the briefing. "The two teams will converge on the Madinat Jumeirah Conference Centre, located adjacent to the Burj Al Arab Jumeirah hotel. The teams will be there all weekend, disbursed among the conference grounds anonymously. But they will be particularly vigilant on the final night of the conference, which is when all fifty of the nations' leaders are to meet at the grand finale."

Maris looked back and forth between the two agency leaders before settling her eyes on the SISX chief.

"And where do I fit into all this?"

"First, at the request of Deputy Director Correa, we're going to take the next couple days to make sure you're fit for the mission."

"And what does that entail?" Maris shot her father a cursed look before looking back at Dame X.

"You'll be run through a series of tests, basic physical and mental exercises to make sure you still hit your baseline marks."

The Chief could see the irritation in Maris' eyes. "You've been through a lot the last few days, Agent Scarlett. Neither the NPDIA nor SISX are going to take any chances with you before making sure you're fit both physically and mentally."

Carlos chimed in. "It's standard procedure, Agent Scarlett. I'm sure it was no different in the CIA."

Maris couldn't argue that point. She kept her annoyance in check and looked back at the SISX chief.

"Assuming you're cleared for the mission, two of my best agents, Commander Snowden and Commander Laducer, will personally assist you in Dubai. Even though you're not SISX, Agent Scarlett, you'll be spearheading the SISX team because of your intimate knowledge of this case from over the last couple of weeks."

"I'll be in charge of the NPDIA team, under my codename Agent Ares," said Carlos.

Maris couldn't shake feeling again as though she wasn't being completely trusted, but in this case, she better understood the sentiment. "Is there anything else?"

"There is," said Dame X.

The Chief took a new smartphone out from her jacket pocket and handed it to Maris. "This arrived this morning."

Carlos added, "Standard NPDIA applications included, of course."

Dame X looked at Carlos and he nodded towards her. The Chief opened a desk drawer and Maris' concerns washed away as she was handed her modified Glock 19. The steel felt welcoming and reassuring in her grip. She couldn't help but smile.

"Let's get these tests going, Dame X," she said, energized. She held the gun up, aiming with one eye at a point on the far wall. "Then let's go kick some Gorgon ass."

21

DUBAI

THE Madinat Jumeirah Conference Centre rested near the foot of the world famous Burj Al Arab Jumeirah hotel in Dubai. Blue and white and designed to look like a giant sail cutting high into the sky, the hotel provided guests priceless views of the Dubai skyline and the Persian Gulf. Built on an artificial island off Jumeirah Beach, the fifty-six-story tall building boasted being one of the tallest – and most expensive – hotels in the world.

Madinat Conference Centre also spared no expense in its opulence. White and gold colors infused the Arabian elegance of the buildings and rooms. Lavish meeting spaces and grand ballrooms were decked in enough Arabesque style to be stunning without being overdone. Date palms stretched into the sky in many of the outdoor spaces. Every area of the conference center was immaculately maintained and designed to make guests feel like royalty, despite their beginnings or social status.

The G50 conference was much larger than Maris had imagined. Representatives from the fifty attending countries included heads of government – presidents, prime ministers, chancellors, and chief ministers – along with their assistants and entourages. Other attendees from the countries included the nations' top diamond buyers and sellers. Politicians and private sector moguls mixed and mingled and wined and dined as they spent the three-day event brokering deals to increase their presence and power in the global diamond industry.

In all, nearly 1500 attendees took over every event space of the Madinat Jumeirah Conference Centre, turning the facility into a massive private event. Meetings were held from the relatively small Al Badir Boardroom, to the stunning Magnolia facility nestled amongst one of the inland waterways, to both the Majlis Al Salam and Murjaan Ballrooms, which had been refurbished to accommodate larger informational panels and brokerage spaces. The Murjaan and Majlis Al Mina Ballrooms had been transformed into rest areas where dignitaries could take a break from the high-energy, fast-paced business dealings and meetings and enjoy quiet spaces and refreshments.

Dubai's 100-degree-plus summer heat kept the formal daytime activities indoors, but the first two evenings came to life at the Summersalt Beach Club and Fort Island outdoor spaces, where attendees enjoyed al fresco dining, cocktails, and live music, along with flame spinners, magicians, and contortionists that would not be out of place in a Cirque du Soleil act.

The joint operation between NPDIA and SISX was given the green light by Dubai and UAE authorities when the agencies approached the state and local governments about a credible threat to the conference. The UAE didn't have its own version of the NPDIA or SISX, although certain high-level officials in the UAE knew of the existence of mythics. As a result, the American and British agencies were granted full access to the event as the *de facto* on site undercover security. A combined one hundred agents between the two organizations – men and women of various ethnic backgrounds so as to blend in with the varied nationalities in attendance – assimilated seamlessly among the fifteen hundred guests. They wore business suits, business casual attire, or for those mixed in with diamond traders, modern chic apparel, and had weapons, including electrical charge eruptors, hidden under jackets and in ankle holsters. None of the attendees realized they were all under constant surveillance by the agents who were literally hiding in plain sight.

The first two days were uneventful, with the various sessions and meetings occurring uninterrupted. The quiet of it all just increased the anxiety of what the agents anticipated to occur on the final evening of the conference.

Maris cleared all her baseline tests – as she knew she would – and, just as she was told, was in charge of the SISX team. Because of her attendance at the summit on Pantelleria, she found herself in disguise all three days to ensure she wouldn't be recognized by any of those attendees who were now at the G50. Outfitted by the support team at SISX, Maris sported a blonde bobbed wig and non-prescription opal tortoise rimmed glasses. Her makeup was muted, allowing her natural Cuban-American skin tones to come through. On the third evening she wore black designer jeans that went over the tops of her shiny black Dr. Martens ankle-high Chelsea boots. A fitted gray knit top was covered in a long black leatherette zippered jacket that hung open and went nearly down to her knees. The jacket did well to hide her Glock that was tucked neatly into its small-of-back holster.

Maris was constantly flanked by Commander Snowden and Commander Laducer, and on the final night the two broad and tall gentlemen wore charcoal gray suits with shiny twill shirts – Snowden's was maroon while Laducer's was forest green – unbuttoned at their tops, and no ties.

Carlos Correa, Agent Ares, was also in disguise with hair that had been bleached completely white, and he wore gray colored contacts to cover his deep brown eyes. His clothing on the third night was business casual, with dark gray tweed slacks, a white dress shirt with its collar unbuttoned, and a black bomber jacket. He hoped the look would be enough to disguise him if he were to be seen by Alexei Volkov, who the agencies had learned would be a key speaker at the final night's closing seminar.

Unlike the other events over the three-day conference, the final meeting took place in the Al Falak Ballroom on the twenty-seventh floor of the Burj Al Arab hotel itself. With inspiration from the majestic décor of an 18th century Viennese opera house, the ballroom was round with a large open floor space and an upper balcony that ran the circumference of the room. A beige carpet decorated with black, red, and white geometric shapes covered the floor, terminating at several 4-step staircases that led to a walkway that ran the perimeter of the room under the balcony area. Two grand stairways ran along the outer wall, positioned across from each other, providing access to the balcony itself. Several brass and marble columns offered decoration and gave support to both the balcony and the ballroom's recessed ceiling. An exquisite glass chandelier hung from the center of the ceiling, affording more ambiance than light, as the area was well lit by a multitude of recessed lights and sconces.

The final meeting was a relatively small affair as the event accommodated only 300 guests, and was reserved exclusively for the world's leaders and just one or two of their assistants, depending on the country. White table clothed round tables that sat eight dignitaries each dotted the ballroom floor and were filled to capacity. The undercover agents were peppered throughout the lower perimeter walkway and balcony. Only about thirty of the one hundred agents were in the ballroom, with the rest stationed in areas outside the ballroom doors and adjacent spaces within the hotel.

Maris and her accompanying SISX commanders Snowden and Laducer were stationed on the balcony, while her father stood vigilant near a column on the lower walkway across from her. She keenly scanned the ballroom floor. With everyone in such a confined space, she easily spotted many of the representatives she saw or met at the summit on Pantelleria. And they were all seated amongst the world leaders – the President of the United States and the Prime Minister of the UK among them. She knew from the Pantelleria summit that at least thirty-five of the summit representatives were Gorgons, and they were all here in attendance. How many more Gorgons were in this room seated near and around the global leaders, she did not know.

The closing seminar started at 7pm and included dinner, during which attendees were left to their own devices as they ate and drank and made political small-talk with others at their respective tables. At 9pm, the lights in the room dimmed to black, leaving only a few scattered low-lit lamps around the lower perimeter walkway to provide a dull luminescence through the event space.

A spotlight turned on, shining on one small section of the balcony. Alexei Volkov stood in the light in a royal purple Emporio Armani suit with his world-famous charismatic smile and his hands raised. Maris nudged Snowden and Laducer and gave an upward nod towards the man on the illuminated gallery, which was halfway around the left side of the upper floor from where she and her assigned agents were positioned.

The floor erupted in applause as everyone instantly recognized the Hexatetron mogul. Maris reached inside her long jacket and around her back and discreetly unholstered her Glock, dropping it down to her side. The safeties were off and her finger was ready to move to the trigger at a moment's notice. Snowden and Laducer readied their sidearms as well. Alexei lowered his hands and the room silenced.

"Dobryy vecher, damy i gospoda!" Good evening, ladies and gentlemen! Alexei exclaimed in Russian before switching to the more commonly understood English among the attendees. "I am thrilled to see you all here this evening. These last three days have been so very productive and informative. It is only fitting we end the event with this formal gathering of the most important people in the world under one roof. On behalf of Hexatetron Corporation and all of the organizers of this event, I would like to say it has been a great pleasure to see and conduct business with you all.

"For many years, our nations have been part of the world diamond trade. Unfortunately, the industry has supported an uneven playing field between the countries involved. First world countries typically held all the buying power and have traditionally been able to dictate the balance of power to control the prices and influx of diamonds into the market, despite third world countries being the ones to supply the product. I believe that power balance has been evened out quite a bit over the last three days, while still allowing the purchaser nations to maintain status in the global industry. Now, though, the provider nations can supply the product with the protections needed to ensure all diamonds are not only of quality, but free of the stigma of being blood diamonds.

"As I have reviewed daily the progress made over the last three days, I am proud to see that a new era in the diamond trade is being realized. Due to the standards and systems employed by a unique global partnership, we will enter what I have coined as the Standardized Policies And Radical Key Legacies, or SPARKLE for short. This agreement that you have all entered into over the last three days goes far beyond the Kimberley Process Certification Scheme, and has the full backing of typically apprehensive organizations such as Global Witness and IMPACT. What we have accomplished these three days is nothing short of miraculous, not to mention revolutionary. Never again will the buyer nations need to worry about blood diamonds. And never again will the seller nations feel like they are being abused and plundered by the modern world.

"The leaders of this groundbreaking achievement – that is, all of you – have contributed to what is sure to be a stable, growing diamond-based economy. The usual economic and political challenges that we have faced for decades have been wiped away, just like that. But it would not have been possible without the open-mindedness and cooperation of all of you. The stabilization we have created in this industry is sure to have a ripple effect in the world's markets that will ultimately help reduce deficits and debt, and even unemployment as we know it in several countries.

"All of you, the fifty countries that have worked so hard these last three days, have brought confidence once again to what traditionally have been suspicions and distrust in the industry. The strides we have taken will promote growth not only in the diamond industry, but residual growth in other industries as well. In short, the entire world is going to benefit. But again, it would not have been possible without you. You leaders in this room understand the stakes involved. And without you, we would not be celebrating success tonight.

"I am so very pleased about this progress, and about the positivity that the SPARKLE agreement is sure to bring. Tonight we take a turn, not only for ourselves, but for our respective nations, and for the world. After tonight, nothing will be the same. After tonight, everything you thought you knew will no longer exist, replaced with a radical new way of thinking and acting."

Alexei grabbed a drink off a table next to him and held it high.

"I ask everyone to raise a glass for this toast..." Nearly three hundred glasses were held in the air from the guests at the tables, as well as from others standing on the floor perimeter and balcony.

"Tonight is a night for celebration! To you, to me, and to all the great things we have accomplished! *Davayte vyp'yem za uspekh nashego dela!* Let us drink to our success!"

Glasses clinked throughout the ballroom and a resounding cheer of agreement erupted from the guests before everyone gulped from their glasses. Maris kept her eyes peeled, scanning the room for any usual movements or activity.

"Everyone stay vigilant." It was her father's voice coming through a micro transmitter lodged into her right ear. Every agent wore one, along with a slim transmitter strapped to their wrist, so they could hear commands and maintain communication.

"Now, my friends," Alexei continued. "It is because of you, the fine men and women from all over the world, that this event was possible. This occasion would not have happened without your willingness to come and work together, and to create a memory that is sure to never be forgotten as long as humankind rules this planet."

Alexei paused and eyeballed the room as he took in more applause and sipped his drink.

"And as such, I have a present for each of the leaders in this room. In a moment, the lights will all go out and I ask you to focus on your associates sitting at each of your respective tables. They have been tasked to give each of you a surprise gift that will last a lifetime." He let his words hang in the air as he further surveyed the crowd. "When the lights come back on, your lives will never be the same."

Maris was quick to react, and immediately shot a hushed command into her wrist transmitter.

"Goggles on."

Alexei took one more drink then raised his glass in salutation to his guests. Then all the lights went out. At the same time, the NPDIA and SISX agents quickly flipped on a pair of what looked like classic black Ray-Ban wayfarer sunglasses. Maris didn't replace the glasses she was already wearing, and instead, touched a discreet button on the right earpiece and her lenses immediately blackened over. The tech of her glasses – the same as that in the other agents' goggles – displayed a blue, green, white, and red digital representation of her surroundings. The image was far from photorealistic, but allowed her to see what was around her without needing to worry about the dark, or having to fear the Gorgon's stone-turning powers.

Maris tightened her grip on her Glock, and moved a finger to the trigger.

"Watch the tables," she said in a low voice. "Look out for –"

Dozens of pairs of eyes glowing white popped to life in the room. Most were from those sitting at the tables – some two or three per table – while others were from those standing around the room, both in the lower walkway perimeter as well as the upper balcony. Leading them all, his own eyes like white hot fire of hate, was Alexei Volkov, looking down at his children doing his bidding, admiring his handiwork. The ultimate operation, his ultimate accomplishment, finally unfolding before him.

Truncated screams and cries began to erupt throughout the room. As quickly as these began, so did the electric red ECE streams aimed at the whites of the Gorgons' eyes.

"Careful!" Carlos' shout cut through everyone's earpieces. "Don't hit the dignitaries!"

Maris watched the scene unfold in outlines of green, red, and yellow. She witnessed computer generated mayhem with real-life consequences as bodies scrambled and turned tables over for cover. On either side of her, Snowden and Laducer were already taking well aimed shots with their own electrical eruptors at Gorgons on the floor and across the way on the opposite balconies. Maris took her own shots, doing her best to conserve her limited remaining ECE blasts.

In the next moments, the air became filled not only with ECE blasts, but with bullets shot by both Gorgons and their human supporters. The high tech eyewear didn't provide any assistance with tracking bullets in the dark, making the chaotic altercation between Gorgons and humans all the more dangerous.

Maris, Snowden, and Laducer dropped behind the half wall of the balcony in front of them.

"This isn't going to work," Maris said. She shouted into her transmitter. "Someone get the lights back on!"

As she waited for her order about the lights to make its way through agency commanders and to the hotel management, Maris peeked up over the half-wall and set her eyes on Alexei. He was flanked by four Gorgons, two on either side of him, their eyes all aglow. Then Maris made out through her digitized vision something she didn't expect: Alexei was handed an Uzi machine gun. His white eyes narrowed as he began to randomly spray the floor and surrounding balcony areas with bullets, having little regard as to whom he hit.

What felt like hours was actually only about thirty seconds before the ballroom lights finally illuminated the room. Maris turned her digital dark-vision off and cautiously peered over the balcony wall while her SISX companions provided her cover. The ballroom was a fraction of the splendor it was just minutes before. Bullet holes and damage from misplaced ECE blasts riddled the walls and columns. From what she could tell, about half of the worlds' leaders were turned to stone, having not torn their gazes away in time from when they were initially drawn to the glowing white eyes in the dark. Several assistants and other attendees had also become statues. Dozens of Gorgons and humans – among them many of the humans who had pledged their allegiance to the Gorgons – lay dead or wounded, with only about a third of the agents who had been in the ballroom still alive.

Miraculously, both the U.S. President and U.K. Prime Minister had survived and were crouched together behind an overturned table with three NPDIA and SISX agents shielding them. Other survivors on both sides of the conflict were positioned behind many of the numerous upturned tables and perimeter support columns for cover, popping out to take shots at each other.

To her relief, she spotted her father crouched behind one of the lower columns, reaching around and taking shots with his ECE whenever he had a target in sight.

Carlos' voice cut through the chaos. "Keep an agent on each exit. Everyone else get in here now!"

Agents had ripped their eyewear off as they continued their fight in the light. Desperation was on both sides as humans and monsters tried to pick each other off. If nothing else, Alexei and his people achieved at least part of their goal – the world would now know of their existence.

On either side of her, Snowden and Laducer continued their up and down bob of taking shots over the half wall and dropping to cover. Maris dropped back down then realized that despite the sounds of screams and shouts, and ECE blasts and bullets, one sound was suddenly missing. The sound of Alexei's Uzi. She looked across the balconies to put her eyes on the Russian.

Alexei was nowhere to be seen.

She dropped back down, her back to the half wall, and spoke into her transmitter.

"I don't see Volkov anywhere. Does anyone have their eyes on him?"

"Negative." "Negative." "Negative..." came the responses.

An ECE beam suddenly crossed dangerously close in front of Maris, startling her. She heard a scream to her right and when she looked, four Gorgons were rushing toward them with guns blazing, while a fifth convulsed on the floor as it lay dying from Laducer's blast. Another dropped from a second shot from Laducer. Maris and Snowden quickly joined the melee. Laducer was crouched, while Snowden was standing, and Maris fought to press herself tighter against the half wall. Suddenly the blasts from Laducer stopped, and she glanced over to see him lying on his side with a bullet hole in his forehead. Snowden was firing as fast as he could, and two more Gorgons fell before he took several bullets to his upper body, with one well-placed shot cutting through his neck. The SISX commander fell backwards over the half wall and tumbled onto the ballroom floor below. Maris took two more shots of her own and the last Gorgon fell dead in front of her.

With that, Maris realized the room was eerily quiet. She once again carefully peered over the half wall. All the fighting had stopped.

"That's it," said Carlos. Maris spotted him standing out in the open on the ballroom floor. "All the Gorgons here are dead."

Maris stood up and she and her father made eye contact.

"Except for Volkov," she shouted down to him. "We need to find him."

"We have our eyes on Volkov," an unknown SISX agent's voice came through her transceiver. "He just turned two of our agents to stone on his way to the elevators."

"Kill the elevators," Carlos ordered. "We have to slow him down."

"Already done, sir," came the reply. "We cut them off as soon as the fighting started in the ballroom."

"Where do you think he's headed?" Maris asked.

The SISX agent answered, "We know he has a private helicopter on the rooftop helipad. It's been his only transportation since he's been here. We're almost certain that's where he's headed."

"Okay, everyone," Carlos began. "I'll be sure to –"

Maris didn't wait to hear any more. She ran around the perimeter of the balcony and to the nearest exit. She knew where the nearest elevators were, having used them to come up to the ballroom earlier, and was sure there would be stairways somewhere near them.

"Scarlett!" Carlos called up to her. "Wait for backup!"

Maris ignored his pleas and continued running, leaving the

ballroom and entering a nearby corridor. She paused briefly and quickly surveyed a floor plan posted in the hallway just outside the ballroom doors, and found the nearest stairs. As she raced down the corridor she glanced at the ECE readout on her Glock – she had just two shots left.

Adrenaline coursing through her, Maris crashed through the door that led into the stairwell. She had nearly thirty floors to climb to get to the helipad. She quickly shed her long jacket then began her sprint up the stairs.

■■■■■ • • • ■■■■■

"SCARLETT!" Carlos shouted at Maris again as he saw her race around the balcony. "Wait for backup. That's an order!"

He watched helplessly as Maris ran out of the ballroom.

Goddammit.

He pointed at the three agents – two from the NPDIA and one from SISX – standing closest to him. "You three stick with me." Then into his transmitter, "I want everyone to split up between all the ground floor exits and stairwells in case that bastard goes back down. I'm headed to the roof."

He looked back at the three agents. "Let's go get that fucker."

■■■■■ • • • ■■■■■

MARIS took two steps at a time as she reached the top floor. A sign in both Arabic and English read "Roof Access" on the door in front of her. She pushed through the door and realized it didn't open directly onto the roof. Instead, there was a short hallway that opened at the far end onto the roof. Hot fire pulsed through her legs after scaling so many stairs, and her feet ached from the ankle high boots, but none of that was going to stop her. Not now when she was so close to ending this.

There was no fatigue, no exhaustion, and no pain as she sprinted through the hall and out onto the roof. Despite the sun having set nearly an hour ago, the hot 90-degree heat still lingered and hit her full on. The area was flooded by rooftop lighting and the cloudless night sky was filled with stars. The space leading to the helipad was a large teardrop shape with tall walls all around. Ahead of her, at the apex of the rounded crest of the open space were two flights of open stairs that led up to the round helipad itself.

Maris assessed her surroundings as she ran towards the stairs. No one appeared to be on the roof, at least not in any of the areas that she could see. She could hear, though, the whine of the helicopter engines on the pad. The sound made her ever more desperate.

Her boots clanked on the metal steps as she zipped up the two flights and onto the pad where the chopper waited. The pad itself was built to only accommodate a single helicopter, and Maris was relieved that it had not yet begun to take flight. Maris recognized the chrome and blue Eurocopter EC 155 as being like one from an undercover mission she had with the CIA. The lavishness of the chopper interior definitely catered to the rich and elite. The CIA mission was more fact-finding at the time with far fewer stakes, and ended with the uneventful apprehension of a Chinese real estate tycoon. She had a feeling this mission was not going to end so pleasantly.

The helicopter rotors were just starting to turn when she reached its open side passenger door. Her breathing was heavy but she held her Glock steady with both hands, pointing it in front of her as her eyes darted around the interior. The only visible occupant was the pilot, who she could see through the open doorway leading to the cockpit.

Frustration washed over her.

What the hell? Where the fuck is he?

"Where's Alexei Volkov?" she called to the pilot.

The pilot glanced back over his shoulder. He shook his head and said something brief back to her in Russian, but she couldn't quite make out what it was. She was about to say something when a voice interrupted her from behind.

"Hello, Scarlett."

Maris turned around and standing not much more than an arm's length away was Alexei Volkov, completely composed, his purple suit not even wrinkled. She brought her weapon up with one hand while reflexively tapping the dark-vision mode on her glasses back on with the other. Alexei shook his head but otherwise didn't move.

"You don't have to worry about that, Scarlett Caso, or Brandi Schiffer, or Maris Correa. Or whoever it is you're calling yourself today."

"It's just Scarlett, to you. We killed your spy so your days of wondering who I am are over."

Alexei looked down and shook his head slightly. "That's unfortunate, for sure." He looked up at her through the tops of his eyes. "And I should kill you right now just for that. Lucky for you I need you alive."

Maris didn't flinch. "I don't trust you any more than I wonder why I haven't killed you yet."

"Tsk, tsk. A fully-grown woman, playing childish dress-up games." His condescending tone dripped down every word like moisture droplets on a glass of iced tea in the sun. "It's time you grew up, Scarlett. Time to play with the adults."

Maris was done.

"I've got nothing more to say to you, Alexei. Prepare to go to Gorgon hell."

Maris pulled the trigger and one of her last two ECE blasts erupted from her Glock. But just as she went to take the shot, Alexei turned sideways with extraordinary speed – not quite a blur but faster than any normal human could move - and slammed a sideways fist against her hands and her weapon, knocking it askew and causing the wasted ECE to shoot at an upwards angle, harmlessly into the sky. The fast, strong Russian punched her in the chest, forcing her backwards against the helicopter.

With one hand Alexei grabbed the wrist of Maris' gun hand, with his other he grabbed her by the throat. He squeezed and dug his fingertips into her wrist, and with his incredible strength, she couldn't help but drop her Glock onto the helipad deck. Alexei kicked the gun and it slid away from them, towards the edge of the helipad. With both hands, Maris clawed at the man's face, but he was just out of reach to be able to do any real damage. She then tore her glasses off and smashed them into the side Alexei's face, aiming for his left eye but just missing as he turned away. She still managed to cut his left cheek – just above his scar.

Alexei's grip loosened a bit, so Maris struck fast. She brought her hands over Alexei's arms and smashed them downwards and away from her, while at the same time kicking him as hard as she could in the groin. The larger man stumbled sideways, and she was relieved the move worked, being unsure of how his Gorgon anatomy may differ from those of humans. Maris ducked in the opposite direction, towards where her Glock was resting. To her disappointment, Alexei recovered quickly and immediately sprang at her, but she was already almost to her weapon.

Maris dove onto the helipad, scooping up the Glock and rolling onto her back, her weapon held fast with both hands and raising her arms to aim at Alexei. She had only one ECE shot left – she couldn't afford to waste it.

A split-second before Maris could get a clean shot, the Russian's eyes turned white. Maris quickly looked away, no longer protected by her eyewear. But it was all a ruse, as Alexei used the opportunity to grab Maris by both wrists and yank her to her feet. He freed one hand and punched her in the side of her head, knocking her dizzy. Maris didn't have to fight for consciousness, but her legs did buckle and she lost her footing. The Russian's eyes resumed their normal amber color and he dragged her by her wrists to the edge of the landing pad. The helipad didn't have a waist-high safety barrier as one might expect. Instead, there was an outer rail that ran almost the entire perimeter of the round helipad held out in place by a series of long poles. This rail was barely higher than the surface of the helicopter landing pad itself, and had metal netting with diagonal openings about the sizes of those in chain-link fencing stretched across the open spaces between the suspension poles, the helipad, and the railing itself.

A warm evening wind that already kicked around the top of the fifty-six story tall building was accentuated by the turning of the helicopter rotor blades that were rotating faster and faster. Alexei dropped himself down and sat on Maris' stomach. He stretched her arms out to the sides – and slammed the hand that held the Glock repeatedly against the hard helipad floor until she was forced to let go of the weapon. He grabbed the gun and threw it out and beyond the outer rail. The weapon sailed soundlessly into the night.

Her hand now free, Maris punched the Russian straight in the nose, and blood splattered over her fist. Before the man reacted, she got in two more strikes. He looked up, holding his nose with both hands, and his eyes flashed white just momentarily, most likely an uncontrolled reaction. Being so brief, the change in the man's eyes didn't affect Maris. She shoved the Russian off of her, and rolled to her side and onto her feet. The man was quick to stand as well, and he pumped bloody fists at his sides in anger. He pointed a finger at Maris as he seethed.

"If not for the Queen Mother's bidding I would kill you right now!"

Alexei took a big swing with one of his fists at Maris, but she ducked the undisciplined attack and she countered with a punch to his midsection. The Russian barely flinched. Despite her luck so far maiming and catching the Russian off-guard, she knew that if he got a strong hold of her she would be as good as dead. And a dead agent can't live to fight another day.

So she sprinted in the direction of the metal stairs.

Maybe if she could get away, they could track the helicopter and stage an attack on it in the air. She was nearly to the staircase that led to the lower rooftop area when two strong hands grabbed her from behind by her shoulders and threw her to the helipad floor. The Russian kicked her in the stomach not once, but twice, ensuring all the wind was knocked out of her.

Alexei picked her up, and while doing so, her blonde wig fell away, leaving just her bald wig cap. Despite his anger and the pain in his nose, which was already beginning to heal faster than any human's would, he couldn't help but snicker at the ridiculousness he found in it, and threw her to the ground again, in the direction of the helicopter.

Maris rolled onto her hands and knees, gasping. Alexei grabbed her by the back of the neck and shoved her forward, in the direction of the helicopter. The side of her face scraped against the helipad floor, giving her right cheek and part of her forehead a bright rash. Her wig cap went askew and strands of loose hair drifted out. She laid there for a moment with her eyes barely open, coughing and trying to get her bearings, when she was lifted again and hoisted high. She opened her eyes as she was flung over one of Alexei's shoulders. She mustered her strongest kicks and punches against his back and back of his head, but they weren't enough to slow the man down.

Alexei pitched her forward violently, and the whole back of her body banged against the side of helicopter. She began to slide down, the fight draining from her, when she was picked up again and slammed against the chopper a second time. On the third time, she smacked the back of her head hard against the copter and her vision turned hazy before narrowing to a deep, dark tunnel. She expected a fourth slam but instead the Russian tossed her into the helicopter before jumping in himself. He slid the helicopter door shut and she heard him shout something indecipherable in Russian, his voice echoing through the small cabin.

Then she felt a needle puncture the side of her neck, followed by nothing at all as all of her senses shut down.

■■■ ● ● ● ■■■

CARLOS and his fellow agents ran through the corridor leading to the open roof of the hotel. They burst into the teardrop shaped opening under the blanket of the starry Dubai night and Carlos felt himself pushing harder than ever as he ran across the roof and to the metal stairs that led up to the helipad. They were about halfway across the open roof when most of the lights flooding the area turned off, leaving what looked almost like a subdued emergency lighting barely illuminating less than half the area. In the distance, he could hear the sound of helicopter rotors reaching a zenith in their revving. He reached the metal stairs and scaled them in no time, and ran onto the helipad, the other agents right behind him.

The helicopter was already pulling high and away into the night sky.

The agent next to Carlos raised his gun to fire, but Carlos pushed the weapon down.

"Don't! Agent Scarlett may be on board."

From a side window, the scowling face of Alexei Volkov looked down and locked eyes with him. The anger in Carlos was so great that he didn't even consider looking away from the Gorgon. But the monster didn't do anything, other than continue to leer at him until the chopper banked away.

Carlos watched helplessly as the chopper flew away and appeared to blink out of existence in the dark, the fate of his daughter uncertain.

22

MOSCOW

MARIS awoke with a lurch. A cloud of disorientation blurred her vision and filled her head with fog. Her right cheek and forehead were tight with dried blood from the rash she suffered on the helipad. She was terribly thirsty and tried to swallow but couldn't get herself to physically perform the function. Her neck felt like rubber and her head bobbed to the left. All she could make out at first was a figure in a long gray coat moving away into a bright haze. Reality began to reveal itself in slivers that cut through the fog. As her senses started to return, her current predicament became evident.

She was leaning back just slightly, bound face-up to a wooden plank barely as wide and as tall as her body. Her wig cap was gone, leaving her honey-dipped hair draped messily in front of her face and spilling onto her shoulders. She was still wearing her gray top and black jeans, though the top was torn on the sleeves and down one side, and the jeans were scuffed and dirty, all from the fight on the helipad. Her arms were strained and felt like they were on fire, and she could feel a rough burning sensation on her wrists where they were tied together with ropes behind the plank. Leather straps from the backside of the plank wrapped around her chest and stomach, holding her tight to where she felt she could barely take a satisfying breath. Her legs were bound together with another strap around her thighs, with a final strap around her wet ankles.

And it wasn't just her ankles, but her feet and up to her knees were submerged in cold water. Looking down the best she could, Maris could see a large rectangular glass tank filled with water. Four bright lights shone straight up in a line through the clear bottom of the tank, illuminating her from below. The plank she was secured to was connected to a wooden A-framed apparatus with a vertical lever on her left. She had an idea of what the lever did and she really didn't like it.

Looking past the lever, she focused again on the large bright blur, and as her vision fully returned she was welcomed with a view of an immense aquarium at the far end of the large rectangular room. She quickly decided she must be dreaming – there was no way anything around her was real because she could have sworn she saw two mermaids with halos of dark red hair swimming slowly in the water, staring at her. The figure in the long gray coat came back into her view, just a few steps away. Maris deduced the thin bald man with round glasses was a doctor because of the stethoscope that swayed around his neck. He rolled a small cart up near the lever, but from her angle, Maris couldn't tell what was on it.

The doctor said something in Russian that, to her relief, she translated to "She'll be okay." Though she had the distinct feeling that assessment may just be temporary.

Her eyes moved away from the doctor and the awe-inspiring beauty of the mermaids in the tank, and focused on the stark contrast of the twisted faces on the horrific stone statues lined along the wall across from her. She recognized those expressions.

She started to look away when a heavy fist smashed into the right side of her face, jerking her head back the other way.

"Fuck!" she shouted and breathed through gritted teeth as she looked at the source of the blow.

Alexei Volkov stood there with a sneer. He was still in the same purple suit which told Maris not much time had passed from their encounter in Dubai until now. He said nothing to her, and instead turned away and spoke to someone else in Russian. Maris couldn't see who he was speaking to.

But she thought she heard snakes. And then Alexei's voice in Russian.

"Ares is alive and in Dubai. I'm certain it was him I saw on the hotel roof as we were taking off to come here."

Maris thought she saw a blur of movement out of the corner of her eye.

"Finally, the daughter of Ares in our grasp."

The woman's voice came from behind Maris unexpectedly and she would have jumped if she wasn't strapped down. The voice sounded like a thousand tortured female souls speaking in unison, creating a demonic chorus that shot through her veins like icy needles. A hand touched her right shoulder, ice-cold even through her top.

"Are you afraid?" Now the woman spoke English, and her voice was just that of a single person – though its low tone and cutting inflections still made Maris want to shudder.

Maris kept her game face on. "What's there to be afraid of?" Maris asked, baiting.

The woman leaned in to view. The skin like cracked porcelain, solid black eyes, and head of snakes that snapped and hissed at Maris made her want to scream, but she controlled it to just a slight gasp. Screaming shows cracks in your psyche, a break that tells the oppressor they have the control in the situation. As it was, Maris wasn't happy with the gasp she let out or the unintended look of fear that splashed across her face. The woman next to her was obviously not at all human, from the way she looked to the swiftness of her movements, and Maris dug deep into memories of the most awful situations she had experienced in the CIA and tried to convince herself she had encountered worse.

It wasn't working. Maris employed methods to control her breathing, keep her adrenaline low, and her nerves calm – basic anxiety suppressing techniques that surely saved her life in many situations. She intended to ensure this situation ended no differently.

"I'll give you plenty to be afraid of, Ssscarlet Caso." The decaying stench of the creature's breath made Maris want to gag. "Your apparent repulsion at the sssight of me will be the least of your worriesss."

The next instant the woman was no longer next to her and was instead seated on a throne resting on a platform that was opposite the aquarium and just a few steps away. Alexei marched to the platform and stopped at the top of the three-step staircase leading to the top of the dais. He tapped the fingers of one hand against the side of his leg. It was as if Maris regaining consciousness had interrupted something important– a conversation the two of them apparently were returning to.

"*My contacts in Africa are getting anxious,*" Alexei said. "*Once we get the funds to the guerrillas, they will easily take the local villages by force, and pay off authorities to be sure they look the other way and stay clear of the diamond mining territories.*"

Maris listened intently, translating the Russian words in her head as fast as she could. At least focusing on the rapid translation took her mind off the dreadfulness of her current situation.

"*Setting off your African revolution,*" said the woman.

"*Yes, Anastacia.*"

Anastacia… Maris repeated internally to herself. *Catalogue that name.*

The woman went on. "*The Democratic Republic of Congo, Central African Republic, Sierra Leone, and all the others, all they need is the cash, yes?*"

"*That is what is needed most, yes.*"

"*I'm going to make your dealings even easier.*"

Alexei's body shifted as he appeared more at ease.

"*How's that?*" he asked.

"*I am rewarding you for bringing in Ssscarlett. In addition to the cash, I'm also giving you the guns and cocaine your guerrillas would normally spend much of that money buying.*"

Alexei now stood straight, a sense of accomplishment beaming out of him.

"*It will be as if they are getting paid three-fold over the cash-only deal,*" he said. "*This will make matters much easier.*"

"A worthy investment. I trust everything will proceed as planned?"

"Most certainly."

Alexei looked back over his shoulder at Maris. With the frankness that he and Anastacia were displaying, they surely weren't going to keep her alive much longer. He turned his attention back to the Gorgon woman.

"With the diamond mines under our control, we buy the raw stones for relative pennies. The G50 agreements have empowered us to make our own determinations of what are to be considered 'conflict free' diamonds. And since we will have eliminated local conflict by taking control of the local governments, there will be no lying in the claim that our diamonds' sources are, in fact, 'conflict free.'"

"If anyone can take care of this with ease, it is you, Alexei. Other drawbacks aside, I have never questioned your business dealings."

"This is no different than negotiating with software developers and trademark owners," Alexei said, sounding triumphant. *"Only instead, we are dealing with diamonds, guns, drugs, and cash."*

"You will be pleased to know the cash and drugs are already on the plane, with the guns on their way. I expect the plane to be loaded and ready sometime this evening. Everything is under guard at our National Park airstrip. Once we get Ares here and deal with him and his daughter, you will be free to go and take care of business."

Alexei bowed his head. *"Thank you, Queen Mother."*

Maris was taking it all in, trying to memorize as many details of her surroundings as she could. She created separate mental files to catalogue as much as possible: Alexei, the doctor, the room, where the exits were (on each wall adjacent to the mermaid tank, and a shadowy archway behind the throne), the statues, what everyone was saying, and of course, Anastacia herself.

Anastacia is the Queen Mother Alexei was talking about on the helipad. Catalogued.

Alexei walked back over to Maris and put a hand on the lever connected to the contraption she was secured to.

"Now is the time for my ultimate revenge," he said to her. His anger pushed veins out of his forehead as spittle shot out from between his clenched teeth. "Now is the time for you to die."

He pushed on the lever and the board Maris was on steadily pivoted forward. Her feet trudged through the water then out as her face drew near the water's surface. The tightness of the straps made taking deep breaths difficult, but she inhaled as deep as she could as she prepared to be submerged.

"Stop!" Anastacia shouted.

Alexei pulled the lever back to its original position and the board stopped moving, leaving Maris face down, her body angled to where her head was a few inches lower than her feet. Her face was just two inches from the water. Alexei laughed and leaned in as close as he could to Maris' face. She looked at him, the uncomfortable pressure of her body compressing against the leather restraints had her still trying to take deep breaths she wasn't able to muster.

"Do not worry, Anastacia, I haven't forgotten. *Doktor!*"

The doctor came over, holding a small digital video camera and a tripod, and began setting up the recording equipment about ten feet away from the tank. Alexei stood next to the lever in camera view, just out of the way of Maris and her precarious position. Anastacia got up from her throne and moved to the edge of the dais. She didn't use superhuman speed like before; rather, she looked like she was gliding through the air under the long green dress that dragged behind her.

"*Remember,*" the Queen Mother said, "*our demands are for Carlos to come here alone.*"

"*You really don't think our demands should be greater?*" Alexei asked.

"*Not yet.*" Anastacia said as she glided down the steps and stood next to the tank.

The barely-human woman leaned over and made eye contact with Maris – at least Maris assumed it was eye contact; it was hard for her to exactly tell with Anastacia's eyes being solid black. Maris could see herself reflected in the dark glassy unblinking orbs that faced her. She wished she had the saliva to spit at the monster.

"You are an inconsequential rat," Anastacia said in her low tone. "You were able to find your cheese, but you are stuck in a maze from which you will never escape. I hope this has all been worth dying for."

Anastacia stood upright and moved next to Alexei.

"Sssscarlett is of no real significance to the NPDIA. She is just another field operative. Aresss, on the other hand…" Anastacia placed a hand on Alexei's shoulder as she spoke. "…isn't just a highly respected agent in their organization, but he is also their leader." She gestured with an ashen hand in front of Alexei's face, as if to help him see a future that she was foretelling. "Once Aresss is under our control, then under threat of his execution, we will demand the NPDIA surrender their headquarters to us."

"You know it won't be that simple. The Americans are too proud to give up so easily."

Anastacia smiled a macabre smile, with her cracked skin and black eyes, the grin she showed was a harbinger of nightmares.

"I don't expect it to be," she hissed. "If they refuse, then we focus on Ares and Ssscarlett. All we need are the security codes for their mainframe. From there it will be simple to infiltrate their systems virtually and dismantle them to where they have to fully surrender to us."

Alexei shook his head, though was careful in not taking too much of a mocking tone with the Queen Mother. He didn't want to anger her, but couldn't resist driving home a point after all her frustration over his own failures.

"I can't believe your contact in the NPDIA never gave you those codes," he said. "We could have ended this long ago."

"That bitch held onto them as leverage," Anastacia said, anger boiling just below the surface of her words. "But no matter. We will soon be in the position to extract that information."

Alexei spat on the side of Maris' face. "And what about this piece of shit?"

Anastacia smiled down at Maris and said her words in English. "She plays a mossst important role. We will sssslowly and painfully, very painfully, tear apart and dismember both her and her father, piece by piece, in front of each other until they give us the codes. It won't take long, I'm sure."

The Queen Mother did her magical glide back up to her throne and sat.

"You may commence, Alexei."

"With pleasure, Queen Mother." Then to the doctor, he said, *"Are you ready?"*

The doctor said nothing, only nodding as he started the video recorder.

Maris expected Alexei to shout out his demands, but instead of saying anything, he pressed the lever forward and she went face first into the cold water so quickly she could barely take a breath first. When she was completely vertical, with her head and shoulders completely underwater, the plank stopped abruptly. Maris closed her eyes and put some of her survival skills to the test.

When she learned how to freedive during that summer in Trieste, Maris could hold her breath for up to four and a half minutes. But that was under ideal circumstances where she was able to prep her body with proper breathing techniques ahead of time, then take a full, deep breath when she was ready. This was not that situation. The constrictive straps and sudden plunge into the cold water barely allowed her to take little more than a normal sized breath.

At first her body did fine with the circumstances. Maris was able to focus and hear what sounded like muffled voices reverberating through the water, though she couldn't make out what anyone said. She maintained her focus on the voices to distract her from her situation, but the technique provided short-lived relief.

Time ceased all meaning. She started hearing blood throbbing through her head and her brain began to feel foggy. She released air into the water in short bursts, trying to relieve some of the pressure she was feeling. Panic poised to take over. Her eyes felt like they wanted to burst through her eyelids. Fire took hold of her lungs and she struggled to maintain control through her body's natural urge to want to inhale.

Even though her eyes were shut tight, she thought she saw a bright light through the fog. Then the light turned into a distant pinpoint in a canvas of black. And the throbbing in her ears grew louder...and louder. Then suddenly there was silence. And Maris knew she had held on as long as she could. Her fight was gone.

She took a deep breath.

Just as her upper body pivoted out of the water and stopped when she was back to an upright position. Some water still made its way to her lungs, which she coughed up roughly, leaving her chest feeling like it was going to explode. She shook her head to get water off and to try to get the hair out of her eyes. She was only partially successful, leaving her peeking between strands of wet and matted hair as she looked at Alexei.

"That's all you got?" Maris goaded through strained breaths. Her voice was a gravelly whisper. "You're gonna have to do better than that if you're trying to break me." She tried to follow this up with a chuckle, though it was barely audible and quickly devolved into more coughing.

Alexei said nothing as he pushed the lever forward and Maris again found herself rotating forward. This time, with more of a chance to prepare for the plunge, she took two quick breaths in succession, followed by a deep third breath (as deep as she could, anyway), before her head sank once again into the water. Like before, she was stopped when she was completely upside-down with her head and shoulders in the tank.

Even though it had been a number of years since that college summer in Trieste, the freediver training all came back: the almost meditative preparation sessions, working with O_2 and CO_2 tables, and of course, the freediving itself. Maris focused on that Italian summer – hanging with her friends, sightseeing, the diving lessons – and the first two minutes underwater went by rather quickly.

The third minute went more slowly and her chest was starting to feel the pressure. Her body wanted her to exhale and take a breath, but she knew better from her training than to release any air until she was ready to breathe again. Her freedive instructor made it very clear that exhales include oxygen, and so releasing air was wasting oxygen.

The fourth minute found Maris ready to give up again. She didn't know how she had held on so long, but it was time to let go.

Then she was brought up out of the water again.

Alexei's timing was uncanny, affording her air each time she was about to give in. Water fell and dripped off of her as she pivoted upright. She quickly exhaled and breathed in deep as she spun around…then right back down into the water.

Maris held onto the one deep breath she took as she plunged back in. She didn't know how long she would be able to hold on, but there was no way she was going to get close to the four minutes of last time. Her lungs were already aching and her eyes felt like they wanted to roll back, nodding her off to a permanent slumber.

But then she was suddenly rotated out of the water again and she was able to take another breath of air. This time the contraption stopped when she was upright. She breathed heavily and was about to shake water off her head and out of her eyes when she felt something on her face. She peered through the tangled wet hair that covered her face and realized it was a gas mask. Alexei pulled the rubber straps on its sides, sealing the mask tight against her wet face.

Her eyes were wide as she struggled to see through the hair pressed against her face. It didn't help that the plastic visor around her eyes had smudges on it. She could make out a tube attached to the front of the mask in place of where the filter would normally be fitted. Her eyes traced the tube and saw it was attached to a device on the rolling cart that the doctor had brought up earlier. She couldn't tell what the device was, being nondescript from what she could see of its backside. And for the moment she thankfully could breathe relatively fine –

though the air coming through the mask had the slight smell of rubber from the tube.

The doctor on the other side of the cart looked at Alexei, who took a step away and made a simple gesture.

He held up the index finger on his right hand.

The doctor performed some sort of entry into controls on the device, and Maris felt fresh oxygen flow into the mask. Her breathing almost immediately stabilized and her head began to clear.

Alexei held his right hand up and made a fist, and the doctor completed another entry.

The oxygen stopped. But not only did the oxygen stop, all flow of air stopped entirely.

Maris looked around, not focusing on anything in particular as her mind raced and her lungs grew tight. She fought against panic, trying to reassure herself that they weren't going to kill her.

I'm no good to them dead... I'm no good to them dead... I'm no good to them dead...

Alexei approached her and stared into her eyes. She tried to focus on him, to show that she was still lucid and in control. But her vision blurred and she saw three of him, separate from each other, then blending together, then separate again. Then, just a halo around a single dark silhouette. He stood completely silent as he stared at her for several excruciating moments.

"My dear Scarlett," he finally said, "this is only the beginning."

Alexei made a gesture and oxygen flowed to her again. Maris' chest heaved as her air-starved body fought to pump oxygen through her again. Alexei turned away from her and focused on the camera, which had been recording the entire ordeal.

"This message is for Agent Ares of the NPDIA," Alexei began. His tone was smooth and calm, almost diplomatic. "What happens next is up to you. You alone will condemn your daughter to death. No one else will bear that responsibility. Our demands are simple: you and you alone will surrender yourself to us or Scarlett dies. Painfully." He paused for dramatic effect. "Once you agree, we will make arrangements to bring you here to where your daughter is. And then you will bow your head before me in eternal allegiance to us for your crimes."

Maris throttled her body against the straps that bound her. Her words were muffled as she shouted through her mask.

"Don't do it! Don't come here! They're going to kill me either way. Stay away!"

Alexei held two fingers up to the doctor. Maris didn't think anything of it at first, but in the next moment the clean oxygen she was breathing had a hint of something. Ammonia.

The sudden influx of the gas had caught her off-guard, and she had breathed in before she knew better. The air seemed like a mixture between oxygen and ammonia, but she guessed that wasn't going to be the case much longer. Her eyes had already begun to burn, and her nostrils and throat instantly felt irritated. And even though she tried to fight it, she coughed.

Which just made it worse. Alexei held up another finger and the ratio of ammonia to oxygen increased. Maris coughed uncontrollably and felt like she was going to throw up.

Then all air stopped. No oxygen, no ammonia. Nothing.

Maris tried to free her hands from behind the plank, succeeding only in tearing the ropes into her wrists, causing them to bleed. Her body felt like it was about to convulse. Her senses had never been so rattled, shocked, and confused in such a short period of time. Her head bobbled as she struggled to remain conscious.

The gas mask was suddenly ripped off her head and she promptly vomited.

Alexei held the gas mask up to the camera then threw it down onto the floor. He then planted a strong left hook into Maris' rashed right cheek and her vision went all spotty as her head jerked the other way. A blow into her stomach knocked what air she had out of her. She wheezed loudly as she fought to regain her breath. Alexei went and stood in front of the camera and leaned in close to its lens.

"Agent Ares, you have twelve hours to comply or your precious Scarlett, your precious Maris, dies."

23

DUBAI

AFTER watching the helicopter escape from the rooftop, Carlos set up a makeshift joint NPDIA-SISX command center in one of the smaller, more modest meeting rooms inside the Burj Al Arab hotel. The room, with its white walls, gold trim, and casino-carpet floor, was under constant watch by armed guard. Agents worked with two dozen laptops setup on long tables that were in rows in the rectangular room. Half of the computers acted as virtual blockades and extensive firewalls to protect the programs being used and sensitive information being accessed. The remaining computers were linked into NPDIA and SISX mainframe systems.

Initially, all the agents worked on trying to track the helicopter, but despite their best efforts could not locate it in any airspace. At one point, Carlos even wondered if the Gorgons had actually perfected a cloaking device, something his own agency had been working on fruitlessly for years.

After failing to find the helicopter, the dozen agents working on laptops with mainframe program accessibility were divided, with two continuing to scan airspace for the helicopter, while the other ten, including Carlos, searched websites, dark web channels, and chat rooms known to belong to or be frequented by international terrorist groups, Gorgons, and other underground criminal coalitions for any mention of Maris. An additional eight agents were setup with field operations radio workstations, busily scanning radio channels for any audio chatter that could provide clues to Maris' whereabouts.

For ten agonizing hours, nothing was found. Carlos never left his laptop workstation, except to use the bathroom twice, and never ate despite food – small sandwiches and other finger foods – being brought to the room. There were no mentions of Maris, no leads of any sort. No groups were claiming any sort of responsibility for Maris' disappearance, and at this point she was the only agent unaccounted for after the G50 operation.

Carlos was beginning to feel desperate. The entire time they searched, he never stopped worrying about his Maris, his Mariposa. He knew the longer the time ticked away, the less likely Maris could be found alive. He was fully aware of the dangers of the job, and of the situations his daughter could be put in, but he didn't expect something so serious, so soon. He clenched a fistful of his bleached white hair and felt like pulling it out. He hadn't changed clothes since the battle in the ballroom, though he had shed the bomber jacket, and he had undone another of the buttons from the top of the dress shirt and rolled up its sleeves to be more comfortable.

It suddenly hit everywhere at once, as the websites, social media outlets, and radio channels known to have applicable chatter were suddenly hijacked by Alexei Volkov. Video outlets showed the Russian's image without any precursor or warning. Agents at the radio workstations quickly gathered around laptops to see the video as opposed to just hearing it.

Soundlessly the image expanded to show Maris strapped to a board with her feet dipped in a tank of water. Alexei stood near the tank with a hand on a lever connected by a series of mechanisms to the board that Maris was strapped to. A person who appeared to be a doctor stood nearly out of view on the other side of a rolling cart that sat near the tank. Alexei pressed forward on the lever and Maris was submerged face first into the water.

Carlos watched, helpless, his wide, unblinking eyes frantically taking in everything that he saw on the laptop monitor in front of him. The energy in the room instantly went from anxious yet hopeful to ominous and dark, with a thick sense of dread weighing on the chest of every agent. No one approached Carlos, taking only casual glances at the NPDIA Deputy Director. No one had anything to say as they watched the several minutes long video, showing Maris being dunked in the water tank three separate times, before getting affixed with a gas mask and the horror of her air being cutoff.

Carlos felt himself breaking inside. It just couldn't end like this. *It just couldn't.* If he was alone he would have let his angry tears flow, but instead, he held onto his feelings as he saw the desperation in his daughter's face, even obscured through her gas mask.

"Don't do it!" she pleaded with him. "Don't come here! They're going to kill me either way. Stay away!"

Then something made Maris cough and choke, before Alexei ripped the mask off and Carlos watched his daughter retch. The anger flowed full on through Carlos when he saw Alexei punch his helpless daughter in the face and stomach, before approaching the camera. The Russian's face took up nearly the entire frame.

"Agent Ares, you have twelve hours to comply or your precious Scarlett, your precious Maris, dies."

The Gorgon moved back to the lever and dunked Maris again into the water before leaving her there as he walked off-camera. Carlos could see Maris growing weak and weary, and at three minutes in her body was trembling.

"Get her out, you son-of-a-bitch!" Carlos yelled at the computer screen, unable to contain himself any longer. "Motherfucker – get her out now!"

As if on cue, Alexei returned and pulled the lever, rotating Maris' head and shoulders out of the water and stopping when she was about vertical again, leaning back just slightly. Instead of reaching for the gas mask on the floor, Alexei held up a picana rod that he had with him when he came back into camera view. A wire trailed off one end of the electrical rod and into a box on a lower shelf of the rolling cart sitting near the water tank.

Alexei took a step towards Maris and jammed the two small prongs sticking out of the other end of the picana rod into a patch of wet skin exposed through her torn gray top, just below her left breast. The doctor looked like he was adjusting some controls on his side of the cart, then Carlos heard an electrical buzz just as Maris screamed.

The buzzing stopped after an eternity and Alexei pulled the rod away. Maris slumped as much as the straps holding her would allow. Her head dropped forward and she looked to be barely lucid as she fought against unconsciousness. Mucus flowed uncontrollably from her nose and saliva dripped from her mouth. Alexei looked over his shoulder at the doctor and nodded. The doctor returned the nod and made some adjustments on the control box on the cart in front of him. Alexei pressed the prongs back into Maris' skin. Her renewed screams were cut short as she lost consciousness.

Alexei lowered the rod and gave another nod to the doctor. The bespectacled man came around the cart holding a syringe. He put his stethoscope up to a few different spots on Maris' chest and listened. Satisfied, the doctor lowered the stethoscope then stuck the needle into Maris' neck and pushed the plunger in all the way. Maris gasped deeply as the world around her instantly returned. The doctor took his place back on the other side of the cart.

So many thoughts went through Carlos' mind, from basic expletives, to cries of agony and shouts of anger. The NPDIA Deputy Director choked everything back, seething through his teeth. He wanted to reach through the monitor and kill Alexei Volkov, to do what he should have done in Monte Carlo all those years ago, to snuff him completely out of existence. The torture video had gone on for several minutes, far beyond the agony that any father should have to endure watching his daughter suffer. During his years with the agency, he had seen people get tortured both on video and in person. Some of the torture was worse, and many of the recipients didn't survive. But none of those people were his daughter. None were his flesh and blood.

With the latest round of torture with the picana rod done, Carlos expected Alexei to make some more demands, or for the video to end. But it wasn't finished yet. The Russian went back over to Maris and replaced the gas mask over her face. Then Alexei faced the camera again.

"Watch your daughter, Ares. Watch her carefully…"

Carlos looked past Alexei, over the Russian's shoulder and at his daughter, whose head nodded with the gas mask again on her face. Maris suddenly shuddered and jerked as she fought to breathe once again. Alexei kept staring into the camera, acting oblivious to what was happening to Maris behind him.

"Only you can save her, Ares." Alexei's voice was like glass, in stark contrast to Maris' silent screams and violent quivering. "Only you have the power to release her."

Maris' eyes were wide. The veins in her neck bulged and she strained to try and break free from the straps. All of her energy was wasted as she struggled for breath.

"Remember, Ares, surrender yourself within twelve hours or she dies, slowly and painfully. You must be alone. If you are not alone, she dies. If we suspect you are being tracked in any way, she dies. And we will send her back over the course of several weeks in several pieces."

Carlos wanted to look away but couldn't as he watched Maris fight for her life.

"Surrender, Agent Ares."

Then the video ended as abruptly as it began, and the laptops displayed whatever function or program they had been showing prior to being hijacked by Alexei.

The air in the meeting room hung thick with tension, as if every agent was holding his or her breath as they waited for their Deputy Director to react, to say something. Anything.

The laptop monitor in front of Carlos lit up with the image of Dame X. She was sitting in her chair behind her SISX office desk.

"Agent Ares," the SISX Chief said, "we've been watching and listening from here in London." She appeared to look directly into Carlos' eyes. "Remain vigilant. You cannot give in to their demands."

Carlos shook his head slowly. "She's my daughter. I must go to her."

Dame X pursed her lips, dissatisfied. "We don't give in to terrorist demands, Agent Ares. You have to keep your personal feelings out of it. You know this."

"I'm sorry, Dame X." The words seeped slowly from Carlos' lips. The look in his eyes was distant and disconnected. "I know our directive and our mission. But I have to go."

Dame X shook her head, her frustration apparent. "She's as good as dead, regardless of whether you go or not. You must know this."

"It's a chance I must take," Carlos said, his voice low but strong. "I can't stand by and just let her die. Not like this." His eyes narrowed and his brow wrinkled. "Not by them."

"These are terrorists. You're willing to break the code of non-negotiation? Risk your life and the leadership of the NPDIA over this?" The woman's blue eyes were like icicles trying to stab Carlos through their virtual distance. "Your agency has already lost its associate deputy director. You want your agency to lose you, too? Because walking into their nest is going to end in both of your deaths. And nothing else."

"I understand the risks." Carlos held his words as he pondered for a moment, before adding, "And the possible outcome. But I must try and save her. I've been absent for most of her life. I can't keep my back turned in her greatest time of need."

Dame X sat back in her seat, her body language conceding defeat. "You will be unarmed. There's no way you're going to be allowed near her or Volkov without getting searched for weapons."

"You let me worry about that."

Dame X turned slightly sideways in her chair and waved a hand in dismissal.

"How is your giving in to their demands going to change anything?" she asked, lobbing a final attempt at reason with Carlos. "If anything, you may compromise the NPDIA even more than they already are with Scarlett's capture."

Carlos looked at the SISX Chief, his eyes ablaze. "I won't fail her. I will get to her, and I will save her."

24

MOSCOW

THE small and rather unremarkable four-seat helicopter completed a wide circle over the helipad on top of Hexatetron corporate headquarters before making its final landing approach. Carlos sat in one of the rear seats with a burlap sack cinched over his head, and his hands bound together in front of him with black nylon zip-tie cuffs. His black bomber jacket was back, just half zipped, and his white dress shirt had been replaced by a black one that was tucked into his gray tweed slacks and buttoned up except for the top button. The remaining front and rear passenger seats were occupied by men in smoky gray suits. Carlos didn't know if these men were Gorgons, but it didn't matter since the rear passenger kept a gun pointed at his side their entire flight.

After Carlos' initial conversation with Dame X about the Gorgon's video, he had the agents in the temporary command center inside the Burj Al Arab respond on all applicable channels with two simple words: "I surrender."

Within the hour, an anonymous sender established a secure online connection with the command center. Carlos was provided instructions on flying out of Dubai on a private jet – which turned out to also not be very extraordinary – to Moscow. There were eight hours from the time the instructions were received until lift off. Carlos fleetingly wondered if he was being given eight hours as some sort of strange courtesy.

During this time, Carlos privately contacted Dame X and detailed his plans. The conversation included a fair share of negotiating, or more accurately, *attempted* negotiating by Dame X, but her arguments fell on deaf ears. No matter how hard she tried, she could not dissuade Carlos from insisting he go alone, without any support.

"This doesn't need to be a suicide mission," she had told him. "Don't make it one."

"If they have any suspicion that I'm not alone or being tracked, she dies. I'm either going to save her, or we're both going to die. So we do this my way."

Carlos used connections through the NPDIA to have local authorities in Dubai provide him with resources he needed as he prepared to surrender himself. An hour before takeoff, Carlos took a Careem, a local Middle Eastern equivalent of Uber, alone as directed from downtown Dubai to a small side airstrip at Dubai International Airport where his plane waited. The two guards who were accompanying him on the helicopter met him at the private jet. Before binding his wrists with the nylon cuffs, they gave him a thorough pat down, from his arms, back, and sides, to farther up between his legs than he cared to experience. While in Dubai, Carlos had developed an irregular cough, and displayed a slight hunch as he moved from the car to the plane. They flew to Moscow Domodedovo Airport, where they transferred him to the helicopter and put the burlap sack over his head.

It wasn't very long before they landed and Carlos, still hunched over, was ushered to an elevator. He guessed it was at the top of a tall building because the elevator ride down was reminiscent of one on a very high skyscraper. The mechanical buzz of the elevator's brakes sounded through the car as they came to a stop. The doors opened and the pressure of a gun in his back nudged Carlos forward.

He heard a few sets of what sounded like heavy doors open and close – their loud, squeaky hinges and thick sounding deadbolts echoed through the corridors that they weaved their way through. Alternating patches of light and dark flashed through the sack on his head as he was guided along. No one had spoken to him since Dubai, which was fine because he had nothing to say. There was just the occasional nagging cough.

At the end, Carlos was guided by hands on his shoulders to stand straight and not move. There was the sound of a final door closing then almost complete silence...except for the faint sound of...*hissing.*

The burlap hood was ripped off. Standing in front of him, holding the hood, was Alexei Volkov. The guards flanked Carlos' sides and his wrists were still bound in front of him. The room around them resembled a rectangular ballroom, with stone statues lining the sides. Many areas of the room were concealed in shadow, though the immense brightly lit aquarium-wall behind him made up for a lot of missing light. To his right stood a camera on a tripod next to a short rolling cart with drawers and electronic equipment built into it. A single overhead spotlight shone down on a throne resting atop a dais at the opposite end.

"Anastacia Dimitrova," Carlos said, before coughing. "It's been a long time."

In an instant the Gorgon queen stood in front of him, her cracked ceramic face close to his, her black, soulless eyes piercing into him, her crown of snakes snarling at him.

"A long time, indeed, Aressss," the woman hissed. "You should have killed me when you had the chance in Barcelona."

Carlos smirked. "I didn't have a clean shot."

A closed fist slammed suddenly into the left side of his face, knocking him sideways. The guard on his right caught him, and stood him back upright. Unsurprisingly, it was Alexei who had thrown the sucker punch. The Russian stood there in a bright white suit with red pointed-toe dress shoes as shiny as glass, pulling his black leather gloves tight. He went to take another punch when Anastacia held up a hand.

"Pace yourself, Alexei," she said. "Aressss is confused, disoriented. He seems to think he can charm his way out of this. He is highly missstaken."

Carlos coughed and spat blood onto the floor. He scowled at Alexei.

"The only confused one here is the one matching bright red shoes with a white suit."

Alexei feigned a punch but Carlos didn't flinch. Anastacia turned and began walking towards her throne at a human-like pace.

"You two are like warring brotherssss," she said, indifferent. "I'm tempted to turn the two of you loose on each other, winner take all, loser dies. Just to be done with the whole thing."

Alexei sneered at the Cuban. "I would enjoy nothing more. The fight wouldn't last long, Queen Mother, I can promise you that."

Carlos remained focused on Alexei. "I agree. It wouldn't be long before I'd have you screaming like your boyfriend before he died."

Alexei shouted obscenities in Russian as he lurched at Carlos. The guard on Carlos' left grabbed Alexei to hold him back. Carlos struggled to take a step forward and the guard on his right went to grab him. Anastacia whipped around, her eyes white and surrounded by crackling electricity. Smoky white streams shot forward and into the guard on Carlos' right before the man had the chance to get his hands on the NPDIA agent. The guard tried to scream but turned completely to stone, his mouth permanently fixed in silent terror.

"Dostatochno!" Enough!

Anastacia uttered just the one word. And it was enough. The guard that had hold of Alexei released him and Alexei stepped back. Carlos stood fast, not wavering or showing any fear or surprise at what just transpired, though inside he was relieved to not be the target of the Queen Mother's fury. He gave the new statue next to him a sideways glance, wondering where in the lineup along the walls it would end up.

The Queen Mother looked at Alexei. "Get Sssscarlett."

"Right away, Queen Mother," Alexei responded, before heading off through one of the exits near the aquarium wall.

In a superhuman flash, Anastacia was back on her throne, lounging sideways with her legs up and crossed over one of the pewter armrests as she leaned back against the other.

To the remaining guard, she said, "Step away from that," as she gestured to her new statue.

A strong arm from the remaining guard pushed Carlos forward, putting more space between them and the stone figure. Carlos looked up, his glare shooting across the throne room and into the hideous face of the Queen Mother.

"You better pray my daughter's unharmed." Carlos coughed. "Or nothing will save you."

Anastacia sneered. "You are in no position to be making demands."

"I promise you," Carlos said, his voice low and his words measured. "If she is harmed in any way, you'll wish you never brought me here."

Refusing to allow Carlos the last word, Anastacia said, "You will be the one wishing you weren't here, Aresssss."

The room remained stonily quiet for the next couple minutes, save for the occasional cough from Carlos and the low hum from distant generators powering the aquarium and the few other electrical components in the room. Before long, the sound of approaching footsteps on the stone floor echoed from the exit Alexei had left through a few minutes earlier. A moment later Alexei came back into the room along with the doctor.

Between them, the two men dragged Maris by her underarms. Her legs were limp and did little to support her weight as she was pulled along. Surprisingly, her hands were not bound, but it was obvious to Carlos that Maris was in no shape to put forth any sort of fight, let alone having the wherewithal to escape. She looked weak, and her gray knit top and black jeans were tattered and torn from who knows what physical atrocities she had endured at the torturous hands of the Gorgons. Her hair was a stringy, tangled mess, and her face was swollen and bruised from both the bloody rash and the beating from Alexei. She was dropped face first on the floor a few steps in front of Carlos.

Maris' arms still burned from being tied back tight behind the wooden plank earlier, but she was able to push herself up partway. Bracelets of purple bruises encircled her wrists from the ropes that had bound them from before. She looked up at Alexei who had positioned himself between her and her father. The Russian reached behind his back and produced an ECE pistol out from underneath his white suit jacket. He leaned over, smirking as he brandished it in front of Maris' face, before rubbing the tip of its barrel against Maris' cheeks. She turned her face away in disgust.

"One of your prized ECE weapons. I picked this one up from one of your dead agents as I made my escape from Dubai. Used exclusively for the demise of my kind. Of course" – he tapped the tip of the barrel against Maris' swollen cheek – "its discharge would prove just as deadly against humans." He placed the open end of the gun barrel right between Maris' eyes. "A bit of poetic justice, don't you think? Dying by the very weapon designed to kill the likes of me."

Alexei shoved the barrel into Maris' forehead, forcing her head back, before he stood and aimed the gun at Carlos' face.

"This is it, Ares, your agency is going to turn itself over to us as we demand or you and your daughter are dead."

Alexei swung back around and clocked Maris' forehead with the butt of his pistol. Maris winced as her arms gave out from under her and she collapsed to the floor.

"Bastard!" Carlos exclaimed as he tried to shoot forward, but a heavy hand on his shoulder and the barrel of a pistol in the back of his head urged him to stop.

"Let him go," Alexei said.

The guard released Carlos and Alexei promptly smacked him across the side of his head with the flat side of the ECE pistol. Carlos fell to the floor and Alexei went to drop a heavy foot into his midsection, though Carlos managed to move his forearms up to deflect the kick.

"Get him to hissss feet," Anastacia commanded.

Alexei reached down and used the palm of his hand to smear the blood running from the fresh cut on Carlos' left temple all over the side of Carlos' face, and up into his bleached white hair.

"Doctor," the Queen Mother continued, "prepare to record our next demands."

The doctor nodded and repositioned himself behind the camera as Alexei took a fistful of blood-streaked white hair and pulled Carlos to his feet. The guard behind Carlos took a couple of steps back, though his gun was still pointed at Carlos' side. Alexei smiled as he put his face right up to that of the man whom he so despised.

"Don't worry. All the pain, all the suffering…it will all be over soon."

Carlos coughed. The side of his left eye was beginning to swell. He looked away from Alexei and spit, before slowly returning his gaze to the Russian.

"I respectfully ask, before we get started, if I can hold my daughter?" He made a point of looking at Alexei with soft eyes. "I understand this may be my last chance."

Alexei's nostrils flared and his brow wrinkled. His lips twitched and his eyes narrowed as he strained to find the right words.

"You ask me that after the lack of mercy you showed for Dmitri?"

He put the ECE against Carlos' bleeding temple, causing him to wince.

Anastacia called out from her throne. "Let them."

Alexei turned and glared back at the Queen Mother. "Anastacia, you would have me –"

Lightning sparked around Anastacia's eyes as she stood. Alexei could see the light flashes even from across the room. And he got the hint. He stepped away, though his blood was still boiling. He pointed the ECE pistol at Maris.

"Get up," he commanded.

Maris took a deep breath. Everything ached. She did her best to disguise the pain coursing through her as she slowly, and somewhat steadily, got to her feet.

Alexei used the gun to gesture towards Carlos.

"Go to him. Quickly."

Maris took a calculated step, then another and another, and she tried not to collapse her full weight onto her father as she threw her arms around him. Tears fell from Carlos' eyes as he kissed the side of his daughter's head. Maris breathed heavily as she pressed the side of her face that wasn't bloody and swollen against her father's body. She somehow managed to keep her tears at bay.

"I don't think I have an answer for getting out of this one, Dad," she said. Her voice sounded tired.

Carlos released a heavy sigh. His eyes were closed and he kissed his daughter again. "We don't always have the answers. Or at least not the ones we want."

Maris turned her head and looked at her father. He opened his eyes and smiled thinly.

"Do you have answers?" Her mind raced with possibilities. Not all of them ended well for everyone.

"My little Mariposa." His smile grew a bit broader. "I will always be right here, watching over you."

The memory of those words came flooding back. Back to Florida to when she was four years old. Back to the last day she saw him before he left her forever. Those precious words that meant everything yet nothing for so long. They had a weight of finality in them then. And, she feared, they had a finality in them now.

Carlos unzipped his bomber jacket and then hastily tore open his black dress shirt. Maris blinked rapidly and her eyes widened. A hideous fresh scar ran vertically down the middle of Carlos' chest to just below the bottom of his sternum. Stitches coated in dry blood held the skin of his chest together. But underneath the skin around the scar was a rectangular object, flat like a credit card, but noticeable. A green light glowed unblinking through his skin, while a red light flashed steadily next to it.

Alexei stepped forward. "What is that?"

The nearby guard moved forward to see what Alexei was talking about. Anastacia was still on her feet, but she moved away from her throne, slowly slipping behind it.

Carlos blinked and tears dropped heavy. He coughed.

"I love you. I always will, my little Mariposa."

Maris shook her head as she fought against her own tears.

"Run," Carlos said. "Now."

He shoved his daughter away from him. Maris knew better than to second guess her father and she turned away and started to run in the direction of the throne.

Alexei shouted, "You're crazy!" as he also turned away. The doctor looked at him, confused.

Carlos smacked his hands into the device sewn into his chest.

A high pitched hum emanated from Carlos' chest. The sound barely lasted a second.

———— • • • ————

"I will always be right here, watching over you."

The clack of Maris' shoes was off-time with the words that echoed through the dark surrounding her. She ran as fast as she could, surefooted despite not being able to see. Every part of her body ached, though, and she found herself surging on pure adrenaline. Her heart thumped loud between her ears, and her breathing was labored.

A crack of light appeared in the distance, like a bolt of lightning, yet unmoving. After a few moments of hanging suspended in the void, the crack splayed wide and a shadowy figure stepped through. It was her father.

His eyes streamed tears that turned to rivers, and decades of love and forgiveness washed over her.

"I love you. I always will, my little Mariposa."
Then he was gone.

■■■■■ ● ● ● ■■■■■

THE room erupted into a macrocosm of destruction; the guard and the doctor dying instantly due to their proximity to the explosion. The boom shook the entire throne room, causing the four statues nearest the blast to topple over and break apart as they crashed to the tiled floor. The tapestries twisted and billowed from the pressure wave that blasted through the air. Then the aquarium glass rapidly spiderwebbed, and any hope it would hold shattered under the pressure of over a million gallons of water.

Maris had just reached the dais when the wave of water knocked her down. She crashed hard against the platform steps, knocking her breath away (a state all too familiar to her lately). The flow forced her up and forward and when the water finally rushed away and out through various adjoining corridors, she found herself lying against the front of the heavy silver and pewter throne.

She coughed, catching her breath, and sat up, taking in the destructive scene around her. Nearly every surface was wet, with water even dripping from the ceiling. Various fish and sea life was strewn throughout the room, flopping and splashing in shallow puddles. Lying just a few feet in front of her was the mermaid with the purple tail. She stared at Maris with vacant eyes that were lost, confused, and sad. The half woman, half marine creature choked and her body shuddered as she gasped for breath. She raised a thin arm, reaching a hand towards Maris, before collapsing completely, her final breath gone.

Maris surveyed the rest of the room as she used the throne to help her get shakily to her feet. The Gorgon Queen Mother was nowhere to be found, though movement to her left caught her attention. Getting to his feet in the farthest corner of the dais away from Maris was Alexei Volkov. The two of them made eye contact, then almost instinctively both their sets of eyes moved to an object on the floor between them.

The ECE blaster.

Barely just two steps away, the weapon was much closer to Maris than it was to Alexei. Maris was certain she could get to the pistol and take a shot well before Alexei would reach her. It seemed as though Alexei had that same thought as, instead of making a move for the weapon, he bolted through the nearest of the two exits in the wall behind the throne.

Maris was not going to let her father die in vain. She was going to kill Alexei Volkov, or die trying. She plucked the pistol off the floor and checked the pulse meter. Seven shots remaining. With renewed vigor, Maris limped her aching, recovering body out of the throne room as fast as she could in pursuit.

The hallway behind the throne room was made up of black bricks and scant lighting. Water continued to slosh about as it worked its way through the hallways and other rooms unknown, before leaving the floors covered in standing water nearly two inches deep.

Her run splashing through the hall was short before the corridor split into a "T." A glance down the right, all there was to see was more poorly lit black hallway. Looking left, though, revealed the lithe frame of the Russian Gorgon running away in the distance. Maris leveled the weapon and took the first of her seven available shots. It barely cleared the top of Alexei's right shoulder, narrowly missing the side of his head before impacting against the wall in a bend in the hallway just ahead of him.

Alexei recoiled away from the sparks of the exploding energy blast. The next moment he was slammed against the wall as a second ECE blast tore into his left shoulder. He grimaced and internalized a scream as he shot the rapidly approaching Maris a look of hate before running on.

Maris resisted unloading the entire blaster out of fear of taking careless, emotionally charged shots and wasting them. Alexei disappeared around the corner ahead of her, but she wasn't far behind and she was hoping he was moving slower now due to being wounded.

She turned the corner and found herself in a small vestibule with a single set of elevator doors – a set of doors that had just begun to close. Alexei was on the other side, staring at her through the rapidly diminishing opening.

Maris launched herself forward, making it halfway through as the doors closed against her. The auto sensors in the doors caused them to reverse course. Maris felt a set of knuckles against the right side of her head, knocking her into the side wall of the elevator cabin. She glared back at Alexei, who was advancing towards her as the elevator doors closed. The elevator began to drop and the current of water that had entered into the cabin rapidly drained away, leaving just a thin sheen of water on the floor.

The strong Russian grabbed her by the hair on top of her head with his right hand, while launching a closed fist into the side of her body several times. Maris barely managed to keep all the wind from getting knocked out of her, again, as Alexei threw her against the wood-paneled back wall of the cabin. She slid partway down to the floor into a crouched position when Alexei grabbed her by her shoulders and yanked her back up. Maris used the momentum created by the sudden upward force to launch herself forward, surprising the Russian who bent backwards to adjust his balance as the weight of the smaller woman pressed upon him. Maris brought her feet up flat against the side wall, and twisted her body sideways in Alexei's haphazard grip. She took two quick steps, essentially running against the side wall, before Alexei maneuvered his grasp and tossed her to the floor.

Maris rolled sideways, somehow still holding the ECE blaster through the encounter. She swung the weapon up as she lay on her side and took a shot...narrowly missing Alexei's left ear. The Gorgon brought a heavy foot into Maris' hand and the blaster flew against the elevator doors. Maris scrambled for the gun but Alexei swooped down and scooped it up.

Maris raised her hands as she stared down the barrel of the blaster just inches from her face. The Russian shook his head.

"I really should kill you right now," Alexei said. "But I've decided a quick death by my hand would be too good for you."

A wry smile flashed across Maris' face. "What's it gonna be then? You definitely aren't gonna kill me with kindness."

She knew it was coming, but that didn't make it any easier when the butt of the ECE blaster slammed against the side of her head, knocking her to the floor where she lay unmoving.

The elevator came to a stop.

Alexei's footsteps shuffled in front of the elevator doors as they hissed open. Maris opened one eye ever so slightly as she continued to lay still. The open elevator doors were just out of her line of sight because of how she was positioned. No additional light came into the cabin through the open doors. She shut her eye as the scuttle of Alexei's footsteps came towards her.

The Russian pulled Maris up from under her arms and dragged her backwards out of the elevator. She felt herself get manhandled into a fireman's carry over Alexei's shoulders. A few steps later she was tossed onto a hard surface. Maris kept herself from letting out an audible "oof" as her body slammed down. She kept her eyes shut as she heard Alexei walk away from where she had been thrown down.

Taking the risk, Maris cracked open her eyes. She was laying on her side, facing out the back end of a flatbed transport not much larger than a golf cart. Opening her eyes wider, she saw they were in a shadowy concrete tunnel, barely wide enough for the vehicle and a narrow walkway on either side. She could hear Alexei out of view in the driver's seat power up the electric vehicle. A moment later, the even hum of the engine and the sound of the rubber tires running on smooth concrete echoed through the passageway. They traveled quickly and in mostly a straight line, which had just a couple slight turns.

Maris struggled to look around and see better without creating too much movement. Their journey lasted about a minute before the tunnel opened up into an immense brightly lit underground cavern.

Immense actually didn't begin to describe it. The area looked to be wider then a football field was long, and the end of it was beyond where Maris could see.

The space appeared to be a huge hangar bay. Cargo pallets full of crates separated based on their markings were lined in three rows: one row of crates was marked with "₽" on their sides (while Maris recognized this as the symbol for the Russian ruble, she guessed the crates were most likely filled with either U.S. dollars or a more widely accepted currency); another row was transcribed with "C17H21NO4" (the chemical formula for cocaine – *Can they be any more obvious?* Maris thought, wanting to shake her head); and the final row was painted with silhouettes of rifles, with the logo name "Supernova X Industries" beneath them. Some workers in jumpsuits milled about on foot, while others used pallet jacks or drove forklifts. The area was loud and the sounds of the workers echoed off the rock walls. The drive lasted just a few moments longer before they came to a stop. Maris shut her eyes.

There was the shuffle of Alexei exiting the transport, and a second set of footsteps approached.

"We've been compromised," Alexei said in Russian. *"Is the plane ready?"*

"Just about," replied an unknown Russian man's voice. *"My copilot just completed his preflight checks. And we're loading the last of the cargo now."*

"Good." There was a pause and Maris heard Alexei step closer to her. *"Load her onto the plane as well."*

"Why don't you just kill her here?" asked the unknown voice.

Alexei snorted in disgust. *"Too easy. I'm going to turn her over to the gangs overseeing the diamond mines in the Congo. They'll have their way with her and dispose of her when they're good and ready."*

"It's sure to be a fate worse than death."

"Exactly. But there's no time to waste. I'm boarding now. Get us in the air."

Maris heard the clack of heels snap together as the man said, *"Right away."*

She then heard footsteps, presumably Alexei's, walking away as unknown hands dragged her by her shoulders to the edge of the transport. Maris opened her eyes.

Surprised, the unknown Russian holding her unintentionally loosened his grip and Maris was able to easily knock his hands away. Maris pivoted on her back and brought her knees up to her chest. She kicked both feet forward as hard as she could into the chest of the Russian. The man staggered back and bumped into a stack of large wood crates as Maris got on her feet and stood behind the flatbed transport.

The two faced off, silent and unmoving for a moment, then the Russian charged forward. Maris sidestepped the raging pilot at the last instant, grabbed the loose clothing at the back of his gray single piece flight suit, and slammed him face first into the back end of the transport. The man dropped to the hangar floor, unconscious. The pilot was obviously, and thankfully, human and not Gorgon.

Maris looked around, surveying her surroundings. No one seemed to be aware of their brief scuffle. She noticed something, though, resting on top of a stack of nearby crates: a flight helmet. She quickly dropped to the floor and knelt next to the unmoving man, sizing him up.

■■■■ ● ● ● ■■■■

EVEN after learning about Gorgons and an entire supernatural world she never knew existed, Maris would still sometimes be surprised and in awe of what was happening around her. As she strode towards the plane, working hard to hide a pained limp from her injuries, dressed in the cargo pilot's flight suit, and wearing the flight helmet with its tinted visor lowered, she took in the true enormity of the hangar, both ends of which disappeared into distances the ends of which she could not see. The engineering and time it must have taken to create this was nearly beyond her comprehension.

The cargo plane itself was a camouflage green painted, massive four-engine, 226-foot long behemoth, with a 240-foot wingspan, resting on 24 large wheels. The tail section of the plane was rotated upward and its cargo door was lowered with its loading ramp extended, the large maw of the cargo hold gaping open. Maris casually ascended the wide rear ramp and walked through the vast cargo area towards the front of the plane. A long row of crates marked with the symbols of rubles, drugs, and guns ran down the center of the vaulted cargo space, covered in nets pulled tight and strapped to the floor of the plane.

The tail section began to lower shut as Maris approached the front of the cargo hold. The whine of the engines starting to power up gradually filled the air. At the fore of the cargo hold was an open passenger area comprised of five rows of three seats on either side of a center aisle. A set of parachutes was attached to the wall on either side of the doorway that led to the cockpit. There was just a single passenger seated, on an inside row, and Maris didn't give the person a second look as she coolly walked towards the cockpit.

"Get this plane in the air, pilot."

The Russian man's voice was instantly recognizable. Maris halted her stride and cocked her towards the source of the voice: Alexei Volkov, who was seated on the aisle in the row just behind her.

"We're behind schedule."

Maris nodded then strode into the open cockpit, sliding the door shut behind her. The cockpit was made for two, and the copilot's seat was occupied. Though his back was to her, Maris could see the copilot wore a flight suit like hers, and a set of thick headphones hung around his neck. Maris settled into the pilot's seat. The plane appeared to be Ukrainian, and the controls were labeled in Russian, but it looked much simpler than some of the Boeing cargo planes she had experience with.

"It's about time," the Russian copilot said. *"Alexei's not a very patient man."* He flipped two switches on the panel to the left of him and reviewed the readout on the controls. *"Here we go again to the Congo. From what I hear, these flights to Africa are going to get more frequent."*

Maris didn't respond, focusing instead on her own preflight checks.

"What's with the flight helmet, Slavik? Some fashion statement?" The copilot laughed at the absurdity.

Maris turned and looked at the copilot as she removed her helmet. The wide blue eyes of the copilot practically glowed in the dimness of the cockpit.

"Hey, you're not – "

Maris slammed the helmet into the copilot's face, then again against the side of his head, then again against the top his head. She pushed his limp body away leaving him slumping to his right. He was going to be out for a while.

Just a couple minutes later, the plane was barreling down the long underground airstrip. The activity of the hangar bay disappeared behind them as the plane gathered speed. Overhead lights and runway lights became increasingly long blurry streaks in the mostly dark tunnel. Maris kept her gaze forward into the seemingly endless passageway ahead of them, and she wondered how long the tunnel had to go.

As if to answer her, a crack of light appeared in the darkness about half a mile ahead of them. The horizontal crack grew rapidly wider as Maris realized she was watching a set of large bay doors ahead of them opening, the two halves disappearing into the tunnel rock above and below. Bright daylight poured in, and the plane rocketed forward, gaining lift just as the end of the tunnel neared, and jetting skyward once clearing the opening. Nothing but blue sky was ahead. Maris blinked and her eyes strained as they adjusted to the newfound light. Around them, all Maris could see was what appeared to be a vast unpopulated area with swaths of trees and vegetation mixed with vast grassy fields. Far behind them, the city of Moscow was rapidly disappearing.

The irony of the mission taking Maris back to Kinshasa where everything for her started was not lost on her. But Maris had no intention of going back to Africa on this day. She reached forward and updated the flight controls based on a new destination: London.

25

RUSSIAN AIRSPACE

THEY were about twenty minutes into their flight and Maris had just locked in the autopilot controls when the door to the cockpit slid open. Alexei Volkov barged in.

"We've changed course!" he shouted as he looked at the slumped copilot. *"What's happened? What's going on here?"*

He leaned forward and looked over at the pilot and locked eyes with –

"Scarlett!" he exclaimed.

The shock on Alexei's face provided Maris a momentary feeling of triumph, and she used the element of surprise to smack the flight helmet that was in her lap into the Gorgon's face, smarting his nose and causing him to flinch back. She jumped up from her seat and slammed her entire body into Alexei's, knocking him out of the cockpit. The Russian stumbled backwards between the rows of passenger seats as Maris rushed at him.

Alexei reached back and fumbled to pull the ECE blaster from where he had it tucked into his pants at the small of his back. Maris was on him before he could pull the gun out, wrapping both her arms around him and tossing him sideways. The two of them crashed onto the middle row of passenger seats, with Alexei on his back and using all his strength to pound his heavy fists into the smaller woman who still had her grip with her arms around him. Maris used all her strength and what leverage she had to absorb the blows as much as possible. Alexei changed his tactic and instead grabbed her body and hair and pried her away from him, tossing her backwards and away.

And there Maris stood in-between the seats on the other side of the aisle, pointing the ECE blaster at him.

Alexei moved cautiously and rested against the aisle seat and raised his hands.

"Scarlett, my dear," he said as he shook his head. "You know you can't win."

Maris nodded at the weapon outstretched in her hand. "It seems our definitions of who's winning differ greatly."

Alexei scoffed. "You think killing me ends the war. The war will only end when the fall of humankind is complete. Gorgons and mythics will rule the world, and none of this –" he gestured around the plane with his eyes. "– you, me, what's happening here and now, will matter."

Maris tightened her grip on the pistol.

"You may be right," she said. "Maybe killing you won't end it all. But every battle won is a step closer to winning that war. And this battle ends today, Volkov."

Maris leveled the ECE blaster at Alexei's chest.

When the plane suddenly pitched to its left in a steep turn.

Thrown off-balance, Alexei fell forward as Maris stumbled backwards. Alexei took advantage of his newfound momentum and tripped towards Maris, grabbing the ECE blaster with both of his hands. She fought back, also using both of her hands to keep possession of the weapon. As the two of them struggled, the plane leveled out on a new trajectory. The copilot must have come to and taken back control of the aircraft.

Remembering how a similar move worked during their fight on the helipad in Dubai, Maris brought a hard knee up between Alexei's legs and it definitely got his attention. Alexei grimaced and growled, and while his grip didn't loosen, his knees buckled enough to allow Maris to push him backwards and into the center aisle, where their fight continued.

Maris took a chance and released her hold of the gun with her right hand, using it instead to land fist after fist into Alexei's face. Alexei flinched from the blows while fighting to keep hold of the pistol. Their twisting and turning melee found the two of them tumbling through the open doorway of the cockpit.

"What is happening?" the copilot shouted.

The copilot continued yelling at them in Russian as they maintained their struggle. Alexei's back was against the center console and Maris was on top of him. Maris' hands were back together, and their bodies twisted back and forth against the plane's controls as they tangled over possession of the ECE weapon.

A shot fired.

The copilot fell dead against the controls in front of him and the aircraft immediately pitched forward. Maris and Alexei tumbled out of the cockpit, between the rows of passenger seats, and into the open cargo hold. The high pitched sound of the plane's accelerating engines filled the air, approaching near deafening. The cargo shifted under the nets, forcing their weight against the steel buckles and straps that tied them down. Creaks and groans mixed with the roar of the engines...then several of the steel buckles began to snap, unable to hold under the sudden strain from the weight shift. It took just a moment before enough of the straps broke free to allow all the cargo to come loose.

Then everything went "weightless," including Maris and Alexei.

As the downward trajectory lined up with the acceleration of the aircraft, the effect of a simulated zero gravity took over. Crates and loose nets floated aimlessly throughout the large cargo hold, bouncing against each other and off the interior plane walls.

Alexei found himself spinning slowly through the air horizontally, his arms and legs outstretched to his sides almost as if he was skydiving indoors. Maris' back slammed against a side wall, then she found herself gliding towards a crate. Unable to avoid the inevitable, she held her hands up in front of her as her upper body smashed against the wooden container. She bounded away as the crate crashed in the air against another container, causing both to crack, though they managed to hold themselves together.

Maris found herself spinning sideways rapidly. Reaching out, she dragged her arms against a nearby side wall to slow herself, before finally grabbing one of the cargo plane's exposed interior vertical steel beams.

Everything was happening so fast Maris was having trouble tracking it all. She saw Alexei manage to grab onto one of the floating crates, holding on as it spun slowly in the air. The remaining crates, Maris estimated there had to be a total of nine altogether, were flying and crashing about into each other and the walls. In all the commotion, she couldn't put her eyes on the ECE blaster anywhere.

The near earsplitting boom of the plane's engines was reaching a fever pitch. Maris pulled herself along the side walls using the exposed beams as hand holds. She continued to "float" over the side row of passenger seats as she made her way along the wall towards the front of the plane. Reaching the wall that separated the cockpit from the rest of the plane, she used the anchors that held the line of parachutes to the wall to pull herself towards the cockpit door. With her legs floating in the air behind her, her hands burned and her fingers ached under the strain as she worked herself along the wall. Hand over hand she pulled herself into the cockpit and managed to yank the dead copilot away from the panel. She made a quick adjustment to the controls in front of the copilot and the plane began to gradually level itself. Far from being out of danger, Maris worked her way into the pilot's seat and took over full control of the plane.

The crates in the cargo hold came crashing down onto the floor and into each other. Splinters went flying along with rifles, bags of cocaine, and bundles of cash including U.S. dollars, Russian rubles, and Congolese francs.

With the plane levelled out and the interior "gravity" returned to normal, Maris worked frantically to reset the autopilot. Piloting the plane, she would be an open target for Alexei once he regained his bearings. She pulled the plane into a steep climb to return to a more acceptable cruising altitude. The cargo slid and shifted and crashed about in the hold. Maris hoped that would also keep Alexei busy as she handled the controls. Every few moments she glanced back over her shoulder to see if she noticed any movement coming up from behind. She didn't want to get caught off guard by Volkov.

The plane achieved the altitude Maris was happy with and she set the autopilot. Time to check on Volkov.

Maris turned to get up out of the pilot's seat when she narrowly missed getting hit by a blast from the ECE pistol. It was a shot that originated from Alexei as he walked towards the open cockpit. It was also a shot that – having missed its intended target – detonated into the cockpit control panel. The panel exploded where the discharge slammed into it, and dozens of other dials and controls throughout the cockpit erupted into sparks.

The plane tilted forward again – and Maris knew there would be no using the controls to save the plane this time. Alarms sounded throughout the cockpit and smoke rapidly filled the air. One of the indicator lights still functioning on the panel showed that the aft cargo ramp was opening.

Maris found herself tossed out of the cockpit and into the passenger area. Between the weightlessness from the new parabola and the shift in the air pressure from the open cargo door, the cargo area beyond was a crazy mix of combining air pressures that created invisible vortexes. Broken wood planks from the crates, open nets, and innumerable splinters floated through the air, mixed with the guns, cash, and drugs. Some of the cocaine packages had split open and white powder wafted about like thin clouds. Maris could see Alexei again floating in the air, about halfway back between the passenger seats and the tail of the plane. And beyond him, daylight poured in from the open cargo bay door, providing a macabre glow to the topsy-turvy world occurring within the plane. Airborne debris cycled around in wind torrents that eventually led to the remnants and rubble being sucked up and out of the open cargo door.

The scream of the plane's straining engines blended with the howl of the turbulent wind. Maris was somehow essentially floating in place over the passenger seats and she tried to keep herself from colliding with any larger pieces of debris that blew around her. She could see debris being tossed around the large hold and she kept her eyes peeled for…

The ECE blaster by some miracle floated in front of her and she plucked it out of the air and tucked it tightly into the front of her black jeans.

Maris' reality warped again as bullets from an AK-47 sprayed around her, blasting passenger seats into bits, detonating wooden remnants of crates into multitudinous slivers, exploding white bags of cocaine into puffs of smoky clouds that immediately dissipated in the wind, and turning wads of cash into tiny bits of paper. Through it all, now near the back of the plane, Alexei was attempting to get an accurate shot at Maris from a loose rifle he had managed to grab. Maris did her best in her weightless state to avoid the shots and flying fragments.

As quickly as the shooting started, it stopped. Maris tried to get her eyes on Alexei. Her loose hair tangling around her face wasn't helping matters. But then there he was, in the distance, with his back to her and drifting towards the open cargo door. He had abandoned the rifle, appearing to instead focus on his escape. And she noticed one other difference about him: he was wearing one of the plane's parachutes.

Maris stole a glance behind her. The wall separating where she was from the cockpit was just a few feet behind her, and she could see one of the parachutes was indeed missing from its storage space. Her mind racing, she pushed and grabbed against the seat backs to force herself to the wall until her back was flat against it. She ran her hands frantically against the wall, feeling for the nearest parachute at her side. She pulled on the chute and from her awkward position she couldn't get it loose. Twisting her body around, she grabbed the chute with both hands, put her feet up on the wall, and pulled while she pushed with her feet. Maris flew away from the wall and towards the rear of the plane, holding the parachute tight.

She immediately realized she was being pulled uncontrollably towards the cargo hold opening. With no other options, she decided to give in to the forces around her, and rather than fighting against the wind she gave herself to it.

Maris found herself flailing out of control, and she was pelted by the rubble in the air before she was rapidly expunged from the aft of the plane. The cargo plane surged away as its engines pushed it full speed towards the ground below. The rumble of the plane's engines was immediately replaced by the sound of rushing wind howling in her ears. Fighting against the wind and other atmospheric forces around her as she tumbled aimlessly, she managed to put the parachute on and get the clasps around her midsection fastened. No longer in a life-threatening position, Maris righted herself to where she was face down, and slowed her fall by spreading her arms and legs.

She fought against the tears that her eyes unconsciously generated while trying to protect themselves from the rushing wind as she surveyed the air. The ground below was filled with trees and forested hillsides. She wasn't sure exactly where they were, but she knew their last bearing was approaching the Belarus border. And in the not too distant air below her was Alexei Volkov, he had yet to deploy his parachute, and he also had his arms and legs outstretched to control his fall.

Maris tucked her arms to her sides and controlled the pitch of her body, while subtly adjusting her feet and body position to increase her speed and aim her trajectory towards Alexei. The Gorgon continued his drop, none the wiser of the impending attacker bearing down on him from above. Maris tucked her body in tighter and straighter, falling like a needle towards her target. As she bore down, she splayed herself once again with arms and legs out wide.

Alexei grasped his rip cord, ready to deploy his chute, when Maris landed partly on his back and partly on his shoulders. The two of them entered into a freefall tumble. Alexei worked frantically to pry Maris' arms and legs from around his body. As their intertwined bodies continued to plummet, Maris found herself having twisted around Alexei's body to where they were face-to-face with each other. Maris tightened her legs around the Russian's midsection and her arms were locked around his upper body, pinning his arms partly to his sides. Alexei and Maris made eye contact, and the Gorgon's eyes instantly glowed white as his power raged through him.

Maris looked away at the last moment, sparing herself an eternity in stone, and brought her right hand around and forced it between their pressed bodies as she continued to hold tight with her left. Despite their awkward embrace and fall, Alexei managed to head butt Maris directly between her eyes, and for a moment blinding bright spots splashed in front of her.

She shook her head and her vision snapped into focus, and the bright red bloody spot from the ECE blast in Alexei's left shoulder from their encounter earlier caught her attention. She brought her left hand to his shoulder and gripped it, digging her thumb into the open wound. Alexei screamed.

The first ECE blast tore into Alexei's midsection as Maris pulled the blaster loose from the front of her waistband.

The second ECE blast went right between Alexei's eyes.

Maris tossed the expended gun away and pulled her rip cord. In the next instant her drop was suspended as her chute deployed. The bloody lifeless body of Alexei Volkov continued on to the forested canopy below.

26

NEW SMYRNA BEACH – FLORIDA

RAIN dripped from the branches of the tree and onto the white umbrella, creating a nonstop chorus of pattering in Maris' ears. Despite the wet day, the temperature was comfortable, if not a bit humid for a mid-summer afternoon. Somehow there had yet to be any thunderstorms, though the steady heavy rain provided enough of a downpour to put a further damper on the somber occasion.

Across a shallow grassy field from where Maris stood was a small group of people dressed all in black, standing in front of two gravestones. A priest was among the group, presiding over the occasion. From where she stood, Maris could not hear what anyone was saying, not that the pounding of the rain was helping with those matters much. She remained in the shadow of the large tree, watching the proceedings from a position of relative anonymity. Even from her distance Maris could read the sadness on the people's faces – a sadness that broke her heart.

Among those at the funeral were Maris' old CIA mentor Toni Trent-Eberhardt and her childhood best friend Rachel Roland. It pained Maris to only be able to see them from afar. She wanted nothing more than to run over and tell Toni and Rachel she was okay, that everything was going to be fine. She wanted to give them each a hug – a hug for her ex-CIA mentor, a hug for her best friend, and a hug for her…mother.

Maris' mother, Robin Correa, also wore all black, and Maris could tell she was crying near-uncontrollably. Witnessing the pain in her mother killed Maris inside. But she never tore her eyes away, taking in every bit of hurt her mother and friends endured.

Maris stood unmoving and, by contrast to all the funeral attendees, was dressed head to toe in white – a white suit jacket pinched at the waist by its single button, white skirt that went just past her knees, white three-inch heels, and white gloves. Her hair was tucked up into a wide-brimmed white hat that had a white lace veil draped in front of her face. The dark sunglasses she wore (the frames of which were also white) and the veil from her hat only partially covered the bandages taped to her right cheek and forehead.

"All white, huh? Nothing black?"

Galaxy stood next to Maris, propped up on a pair of crutches. She wore a black raincoat with a wide collar and hood, and was only partially covered by Maris' umbrella. Rain didn't bother Galaxy, though. It was just water. She was more bothered by Maris' lack of appropriate attire.

"For me it's not a funeral," Maris answered. "More of a rebirth. I felt white was more fitting." She paused a moment before adding, "I'm surprised you're even here, let alone walking, for that matter."

"The stab in my side was pretty clean. Won't say it doesn't hurt, but it's not keeping me off my feet."

Maris looked briefly at her fellow agent. "I'm glad you came."

"There was no way I was going to miss this. Even if we are stuck watching from over here."

Maris smirked. Here Galaxy was, all those miles from home, recovering from surgery from a stab wound, and standing in the pouring rain…and cynical as ever.

"Did you hear they changed our name?" Galaxy asked after they spent a few minutes watching the funeral in silence.

Maris responded though her gaze remained on the funeral proceedings. "No more NPDIA?"

Galaxy considered her next words carefully. "With the…shakeup of the NPDIA senior operations management, the directors felt it was a good time to consolidate global efforts in the fight against the mythics. With us and our companions in London leading the fight, it's been decided to put us all under the same…" Galaxy glanced up, snorting, "…umbrella. So we are now known as SISX-West."

Maris thought for a moment. "I actually like that."

Galaxy shrugged. "Meh. It'll grow on me."

"So then who's in charge of our branch?"

"West branch will be under the same leadership as London. I believe you're already familiar with a certain Dame X?"

Maris nodded. "She'll do a fine job."

"I'm sure she will. She better, anyway."

The funeral appeared to be winding down. Most of the people in the group were leaving, including the priest. Only Robin, Rachel, and Toni remained, waiting to pay their final respects in more privacy. Robin dropped her umbrella and collapsed to her knees, sobbing, as she set a small bouquet of flowers in front of one of the headstones. Rachel knelt next to her and placed an arm around her shoulders. Toni stepped in close, using her umbrella to keep them all dry. Maris kept her own tears from joining the falling drops of rain. She refocused on getting any information she could from Galaxy about what had transpired since her escape from the Gorgons.

"Did they ever find the plane? I'm sure the cocaine and cash is all but gone or incinerated in the crash. But what about the guns? There were a lot of weapons on that plane."

Galaxy shook her head. "We'll never know. The plane went down in a heavily wooded area of the Russia-Belarus border. Belarus officials are claiming nothing happened on their side, and Moscow is denying any knowledge of a downed plane. The matter is closed."

This information didn't surprise Maris. Something as trivial as a downed plane with no involvement with the Russian military and not having suffered any major casualties wasn't worth any investigation or real explanation.

"What about the monster who called herself Anastacia? Any leads on her?"

"Anastacia Dimitrova. The Queen Mother. There's been no sign of her."

"I thought the Gorgons would have leapt on the publicity of what went on in Dubai. Things didn't go the way they wanted, but there was enough damage for them to still make a statement."

"The Gorgons have remained quiet. And the leaders who survived the Dubai incident created a makeshift agreement to not release any of the, umm, supernatural details to the public. They blamed the entire incident on some made-up terrorist group then quietly swept it all under the rug."

"And that's working?"

"You wouldn't think it would, but crazy as it sounds, it is. The lines between truth, evidence, and belief are more blurred, or should I say they are more easily blurred, than ever."

The pitter patter of thick drops on her umbrella again took over. Maris watched as her mother, best friend, and CIA mentor slowly made their way away from the gravestones. Their respects were done, though their pain was as fresh as ever. Maris watched as they walked away, taking in their silhouettes as they slowly disappeared into the gray of the afternoon rain. She burned the image into her brain, knowing she would never see any of them again.

Once they were alone, Maris and Galaxy went and stood over the graves. Two rectangular blocks of polished marble with rounded edges marked the places where the deceased were laid to rest. Although in this case, no bodies were actually buried.

The epitaphs on each were brief:

CARLOS CORREA
Born 1957 – Died 2021
Loving Father

MARIS CORREA
Born 1988 – Died 2021
Loving Daughter

Maris picked up one of the flowers from the bouquet of white mariposas sitting in front of the headstone with her name on it. She stood upright, staring at the flower, its beauty radiating along with the memories she had of being called "Mariposa" by her father when she was a little girl.

"Is it weird?"

Maris shook away the childhood memories as Galaxy's voice jarred her back to the present.

"I'm sorry, what?"

"Is it weird?" Galaxy repeated. "Seeing your name on a tombstone?"

Maris paused, staring at her name engraved in the marble. "I would have thought so, but now that I'm here, seeing it in front of me, I feel disconnected from it all."

"Your mission with us was a success. It was bonus that we were able to use the plane crash to officially kill you off in the process."

"And just like that..." Maris took a deep breath. "Maris Correa is dead."

"It's a clean break. Makes it a lot easier with public records and for loved ones."

"I suppose it does."

Maris placed the flower she was holding on top of her father's headstone, resting her hand there for a moment before pulling away. The rain gathered on her gloved hand, each thick drop creating a sensation reminding her that even though Maris was dead, she was at the same time more alive than she had ever been.

27

ANTWERP

FIVE MONTHS LATER

IT was just 5AM. Dawn had yet to crack the morning sky, but light from a full moon washed over the city. Traffic on the Antwerp streets was scarce but steadily building. The Diamond Quarter would soon have the activity of a beehive, filled with customers, cutters, dealers, and brokers going in and buzzing about their daily business. The Romilly & Ackerman tower stood at the apex of the district, a beacon of wealth and affluence in a city filled with the rich and elite.

Xavier Dumont pulled his Apollo IE sports car into the parking garage, turning immediately to the right into an inconspicuous side concourse. The lane was barely wide enough for his vehicle, with sharp turns as it led to a personal parking space next to a private elevator. Dumont climbed out of his car, closed the driver's gullwing door, and entered the elevator. The lift provided a straight shot to his office on the top floor.

The elevator deposited him into a short hall that led to an opening near the end of the office where the large bay of windows overlooked the city. The spotlights shining on the diamond display cases along one wall were on but had been lowered to barely being perceptible. Moonlight filled the immense but sparse office, illuminating his office desk and chair...and its occupant. Dumont strained to make out the partially shadowed person who was sitting in his chair facing him.

"Ms. Schiffer?" Dumont asked, the surprise in his voice obvious. "Brandi Schiffer, is that you? How did you get in here?"

The chair she sat in was turned sideways to face where he stood at the side of the office. Dumont could see the woman was wearing a long light-colored overcoat, and had her legs crossed with her hands in the coat pockets.

"I know you set us up with the Gorgons the last time I was here."

Dumont raised an eyebrow, perturbed that she ignored his question, then took his cigarette case out of an inside jacket pocket. He methodically removed a cigarette and replaced the case. Walking around to the front of his desk, he lit the cigarette with a lighter he produced from another pocket, before settling into a chair facing his desk. He took a long drag then exhaled, blowing the smoke across the desk at his visitor. The smoke glowed in the moonlight that backlit the woman and now hid her features in shadow.

"Business is business. You're a spy, you know none of it is personal."

"As a human you betrayed your kind," his uninvited guest said. "And for what? What has it gotten you?"

Dumont blew another cloud of smoke across the desk. He tapped the ashes off the end of the cigarette into an ashtray on the edge of the desk nearest him, then sat back, crossing his legs and releasing a loud sigh.

"The choices we make are all in the interest of self-preservation. And I should say I'm not much of a gambling man. I tend to go with the odds that appear to be in my favor at the given moment. And the odds at the time warranted I work with Alexei Volkov and his organization. Are you a gambling person?"

The response Dumont received was no response at all. He rolled his eyes as he waved a hand in the air, dismissive.

"Americans," he scoffed. "You think you have it all figured out."

"On the contrary, I've learned a lot over the last several months."

Dumont narrowed his eyes as he tried to focus on the face staring at him from the shadow. "Care to share any of your newfound knowledge?"

"I've learned there's an entire world out there hidden from the eyes of most humans. That at any time the frail balance between us and the mythical creatures that run in that other world can shatter, forever changing everything we know and how we all survive. I've learned that the humans working with these monsters are monsters themselves, with no regard for life or their fellow man. And I've learned that those humans, like the creatures they are in bed with, need to be eliminated."

Dumont cocked his head to the side. He lifted his cigarette, holding it pinched between his first finger and thumb, and took another long drag from it. The smoke he exhaled swirled and danced around them. He leaned forward and exterminated the cigarette butt in the ashtray.

"Your oversimplified outlook will only lead to your undoing, Ms. Schiffer, or whoever it is you really are."

The bang from the Glock 19 was loud in the quiet of the office. The bullet burst through the desk and hit Dumont in his chest, just below his sternum. All his air escaped him and he groaned from the pain. He sat back in the chair as blood rapidly soaked through his shirt and suit jacket. Footsteps came around the desk, the click-clack of women's heels on the tile floor amplified through his ears as his body shuddered in agony. The woman stopped in front of him, and he was finally able to get a good look at her face, before it became obscured behind the barrel of her gun. The second to last thing he heard before the final bang of the gun was her voice.

"The name is Scarlett."

SCARLETT WILL RETURN

ACKNOWLEDGEMENTS

CODENAME: SCARLETT has been the most fun book I have written. You can tell I was heavily influenced by Ian Fleming's James Bond, and I can only hope that I did him some justice by creating an adventure that is both thrilling and compelling.

This is my third novel. Whereas the first, STARPHOENIX, was 14 years from concept to publication and my second, VAMPOCALYPSE, was five years from concept to publication, this only took three years, with less than a year of actual writing. I'm very proud to know that I've only become more efficient and stronger as a writer over the years. But I can't take sole credit for that growth, as I have had the privilege of working with an amazing group of people who have nurtured and supported me along the way.

First, a big thank you to my incredible publisher, Amanda Rotach Lamkin. The hard work, support, and words of wisdom you provide me routinely is invaluable. We've been together since my first novel, and I look forward to many fun and productive years to come. The same extends to everyone on the Line By Lion team. I'm so lucky to work with such an awesome and talented group of people.

Next is my personal editor, Rachel Roland. This is our second project working together, and I hope for a continued, successful partnership in the future. Others who deserve mention include Maria Redkozubova who proofed all my Russian dialogue and terminology, and Emily Horwitz who provided the amazing author photo used in this book. A huge thank you as well to all the real life people who volunteered to be characters in this book. I hope you find your fictional selves to be fun, even if you didn't all survive the story!

Thank you Emmy Powell and my remarkable son, Trystn Brown, for your support and work on the book trailer. And, of course, I can't thank my son without thanking my daughter Trinity who, along with my mother, are the strongest women I have ever personally known.

Lastly I want to mention that many liberties were taken when it comes to places and things that appear in this novel. While I did an incredible amount of research to get descriptions and facts correct, I had to fill in some gaps by using my imagination. So apologies in advance to those who may know better when it comes to Antwerp, Monte Carlo, Dubai, and Italy, as well as those in the Formula One racing community. I hope you all still find this adventure to be fun and worth the read.

To those who have supported my writing through the years, I cannot thank you enough. Your love keeps me going and, at times, keeps me sane.

CODENAME: SCARLETT
Original notes created January 9, 2018
Writing commenced March 2020 and ended February 2021

E.S.Brown

April 4, 2021

Vampocalypse

a novel by
E.S. Brown

CPSIA information can be obtained
at www.ICGtesting.com
Printed in the USA
BVHW091343210621
610125BV00014B/2942/J

9 781948 807159